PENGUIN BOOKS

GOOSEFOOT

Born in Donegal, Ireland, and educated at Galway University, Patrick McGinley now works in London in publishing. He is the author of *Bogmail*, also published by Penguin Books.

D1417076

PATRICK McGINLEY

GOOSEFOOT

PENGUIN BOOKS

To Patrick Heekin of Garaross,
for remembered laughter

Penguin Books Ltd, Harmondsworth,
Middlesex, England
Penguin Books, 40 West 23rd Street,
New York, New York 10010, U.S.A.
Penguin Books Australia Ltd, Ringwood,
Victoria, Australia
Penguin Books Canada Limited, 2801 John Street,
Markham, Ontario, Canada L3R 1B4
Penguin Books (N.Z.) Ltd, 182–190 Wairau Road,
Auckland 10, New Zealand

First published in the United States of America by
E. P. Dutton, Inc., 1982
First published in Canada by
Clarke, Irwin & Company Limited 1982
Published in Penguin Books 1983

LIBRARY OF CONGRESS CATALOGING IN PUBLICATION DATA
McGinley, Patrick, 1937–
    Goosefoot.
    Reprint. Originally published: New York: Dutton,
c1982.
    I. Title.
PR6063.A21787G6   1983   823'.914   83-8323
ISBN 0 14 00.6815 5

Printed in the United States of America by
George Banta Co., Inc., Harrisonburg, Virginia
Set in Times Roman

1

The postman took off his cap and wiped his forehead with the back of his pudgy hand. A hog's back of a hand, a civil servant's hand, smooth and hairless without a hint of bone.

"It's a warm day," he said.

"It's a long day," she replied. "And to think that it's only noon."

"Tomorrow will be longer."

He handed her a foolscap envelope from the Registrar of Cork University, threw his leg on his bicycle, and rode off with lazy wobbles while she read the printed letter in the shade of the oak in the lane. It was an old oak, crippled with arboreal rheumatism and choked with ivy that gave it the look of an evergreen in winter. The ivy bound the bole like fine whipcord tightening about a throat. She pulled at one of the cords but it gripped the bark with invisible tentacles that refused to desist from the stubborn work of strangulation.

As she expected, she got a first in her degree. The professor had told them that firsts were rare, and she had told herself that upper seconds were just a shade too common. No one, not even a genius, could be certain of a first, he said. And now that she had got it, she had to admit that she was pleased. It would mean nothing to her father and mother and two brothers, but it would make Uncle Lar smile and feel her biceps with his thumb. Her father emerged from a field of ripe barley, the tattered jacket on his shoulder half covering bright-red galluses.

"The post came," he said.

"Yes."

"Did he bring anything in the line of news?"

"No, not news."

"Did he bring anything at all?"

"Only a letter for me."

"A brown envelope. Never open a brown envelope till the day's work is done. It's always been my policy and so far I've never been mistaken."

"I'm going over to Uncle Lar's," she said.

"You spend your life at Lar's." He turned away.

Uncle Lar was in rolled-up shirt sleeves, changing a tractor wheel in the yard. Tall, trim, and wiry, he straightened slowly when he saw her and took the weight off his left leg, his bowleg, which he normally supported with a hazel stick. Lar without his bowleg would not be Lar. It gave him the air of a ship's captain, and it went well with his steady blue eyes and short white hair.

"You're just in time to give me a hand," he smiled. "As a man grows older, tractor wheels grow heavier."

They worked together for fifteen minutes while he regaled her with a story about a simpleton in the next townland who could never remember which way the treads of a tractor tire should face.

"I passed my exam," she told him when they finished.

"Good girl yourself." He took her hand and pressed her biceps with his thumb.

"I got first-class honors, which is more than I expected or deserved."

"So you're now a Bachelor of Agricultural Science. How many letters is that?"

"Six. B.Agr.Sc."

"I knew you had it in you. You're the first of the Teelings who left the land to learn about it, and that calls for a celebration. We'll all go to Roscrea on Sunday evening for a meal—you and me and your father and mother and Austin and Patsy. How's that?"

"Austin and Patsy won't come. They'd prefer a meal at home."

"I only want to please you, Patricia. Say what you want and I'll pay for it."

"Then I'll cook Sunday dinner here and we'll invite Desmond Deeny as well."

"The best ideas are the simplest," said Uncle Lar, guiding her into the house.

He was her only uncle, but in truth he was more like an ideal father, perhaps because he was a bachelor with no family of his own. In early manhood, he had been a sower of wild oats, drinking and gallivanting and making love to loose women. As he was the elder son, he expected to be left the farm, but one St. Patrick's night two neighbors carried him home from the pub and left him lying dead drunk in the middle of the floor. Her grandfather, an austere and sober man, was so dismayed at the sight of his son that he told him he had outstayed his welcome in the ancestral lodge, that he would never get a chance to squander his patrimony, that the land and house would go to his younger brother, who was now her father.

Lar never touched drink again. Shortly afterward he left for Australia and in fifteen years never once wrote home. Then one fine morning in the summer of 1950 he turned up in Killage, took a room in Phelan's Hotel, and said that he was looking round for a farm. As he had nothing else to do, he spent his time going to land auctions, fishing on the Delour, and listening to farming talk on market days. Within six months he had bought the farm next to her father's and enough machinery to make the best farmers in the parish green with envy.

Her uncle and father wasted no love on each other. They were opposites who could only reject what the other stood for. Her uncle had a better farm than her father, and a better way of working it. He had three tractors whereas her father had only two old horses. Her uncle's farm had a history of good husbandry whereas her father's was run-down from years of carelessness and neglect. Her uncle was the soul of sobriety and industry, with an effortless ability to improvise and find new uses for things that other men in their ignorance discarded. When the mirror in his bathroom broke, he took the wing mirror off an old van and suspended it on a piece of string for shaving. He had a genius that enabled him to give at least three useful lives to every object about the house. He would fill a gap in a hedge with an old bedstead or bicycle frame, and he would not do it out of meanness but because it complemented the pattern of life as he saw it. A seed fell on the earth and became a turnip, and the turnip made flesh and bone in a whitehead bullock. A bedstead bore the brunt of twenty years of tumbling and tossing, and when it could bear it no longer it stopped the whitehead bullock from breaking through a hedge into a field of young barley.

Her father on the other hand was a sour, disappointed man who spent too much money in pubs on market days and too much time in bed in the mornings. Without her mother, he would have gone bankrupt long ago. It was she who pinched and scraped while the family was young, and thinned fodder beet and built trams while her husband recovered from his hangovers. And it was she who, in spite of her husband's humorless objections, allowed Patricia to visit Uncle Lar at the weekends when she was only a schoolgirl of five or six.

Uncle Lar took to her at once. On market days he bought her special sweets called bull's-eyes and brandy-balls; at weekends he took her to Roscrea in his Ford Prefect and bought her fish and chips and vanilla ice cream; when she was ten he taught her to drive his light tractor and how to tie a fly for fishing on the Delour; and when she was thirteen he prevailed on her parents to let him pay for her education in the convent in Mountmellick. She disliked boarding school, but she did not blame Uncle Lar because he came to see her with a parcel of goodies once a week. Then, when she was seventeen, he asked her if she would like to go to university; and when she said yes, he told her that too many girls read languages and too few agricultural science. She had never been drawn to languages but she had excelled at physics and chemistry, so after she had thought about it she felt attracted to a subject which must surely be the preserve of men. Uncle Lar was delighted. He paid her fees and sent her a modest check which unfailingly arrived on the first Monday of every month. Uncle Lar had made her what she had become. He had molded her more surely than any of her teachers, and he had left her with a legacy more precious than land—an awareness of the existence of men like himself, so remote from the common run that a base or ignoble thought never enters their minds.

Her father and two brothers were reluctant to come to the dinner, but as usual her mother's will prevailed. Austin said he wasn't hungry; Patsy said he had to mend the stroke-haul; and her father said that Lar's dinner would be on the dry side, that he would sooner sup with the devil than a teetotal brother. Her mother reminded him of all Lar had done for his daughter and told them all squarely that she would never again lay a meal before anyone who reneged.

Lar presided at table like a baron in his baronial hall. He placed Patricia on his right and Desmond Deeny on his left and told the rest to sit where they liked. Then he carved the beef sirloin in his shirt sleeves, while her brothers and father made covert conversation at the other end of the table. The teetotaller surprised them. He provided a bottle of wine for Patricia and her mother and lashings of ale for the men, but he himself sipped a glass of the morning's milk. During the meal, he talked only to Patricia while her father and brothers behaved like silent vivisectors bent over the muddled remains of their handiwork.

Her mother, leaving most of the wine to Patricia, kept eyeing Lar like a hen with a sideways tilt of the head and expressed immediate and total agreement with everything he said. Lar, however, was not the man to acknowledge it. He made a string of harmless jokes and turned to Patricia as he laughed with a deliberate distension of his high stomach. Finally, he hooked a thumb in his galluses and with a thrust of the chin addressed the painting of Daniel O'Connell above her father's head.

"This is Patricia's day," he began. "The beef we've eaten was roasted by her, and the soup she made came from a recipe in an old newspaper I brought back from Australia. The apple crumble was the best I've had since my mother, God rest her, died. I mention this to remind us that Patricia was a good cook before she became a good scientist."

She had never heard Uncle Lar speak so seriously before. He stared ahead as if he were looking at the future, and with a heavy hand on one of hers he told them that though she was a woman she reminded him of nobody but himself as a young man. She was a Teeling. She had a mind of her own. And she would take life like a withe in her hands and bend it in the curve that best pleased her. Hadn't he done just that himself, and hadn't he said that she had taken after him.

"I said that this is Patricia's day," he continued. "But it's my day too, and I know she won't mind sharing it. I've known her since she was no higher than my knee. She began making tea for me when she was hardly old enough to hold a teapot, and as I watched her grow up I told myself over and over again, there's nothing in the world that that girl couldn't turn her hand to. She worked hard at school and she played hard when she came home in the evenings. She had the knack of never giving too much time to anything. She did everything with equal ease, as if in teaching her you were only reminding her of something she

6

had known before. When she was ten, I taught her to drive a tractor, and before she was twelve her hands were strong enough to milk a cow better than I could myself. Often as she came up the lane with the calves, I would say to myself that she was all the Teelings that ever lived rolled into one, and, God forgive me, I also said once or twice, it's a pity she isn't a boy. I take my folly back today because she has grown into a handsome young woman who could take and keep her place in any company in any civilized country. Her life is now before her. My only regret is that I haven't days to see her come into the fullness of it."

He removed his hand from hers and raised his glass of milk before the company.

"Now," he said, "I ask you to drink to her health and happiness, because happiness is what she gives to all of us. To Patricia, then!"

An indistinct murmur rose from the three silent men at the end of the table. Desmond Deeny echoed Uncle Lar, and her mother said, "Good health and good luck."

Patricia didn't know what to say. She turned to Uncle Lar, who was smiling at her, and she placed her hand over his splayed fingers on the table.

"I could never make a speech as good as Uncle Lar's," she laughed. "But I'd like to thank him for giving this dinner for me and for what he said about the cooking. And I'd like to thank him for educating me and for coming to see me in the convent in Mountmellick with parcels of food on days when he had better things to do. I can never repay him. All I can say is this: To Uncle Lar, may he stay strong and live long because he deserves to."

When they had drunk Uncle Lar's health, he looked at the painting of Daniel O'Connell once more.

"I'm an old man, or almost an old man," he said. "I'll be sixty-nine in September, and though I'm healthy, thank God, I need more rest than I used to. I have three men to do the work, but someone has to keep an eye on them because they're only human, and someone has to make sure that the right things are done at the right time. I long ago decided that I would leave my house and farm to you, Patricia, and now I have a proposal to make. I would like you to come to live with me and run the farm as if it were already your own. I'm still too active to sign over lock, stock, and barrel today, but until the right time comes I'll pay you a salary as good as any you'd get in any job you care to do. You'll be your own boss, coming and going as you please. You'll be doing work you know and like, and with a bit of luck what you learned at university may turn this into the best farm in the midlands. I'm not trying to interfere with any plans you've already made, Patricia, but I hope you'll take up the offer. If you do, you'll make an old man happy and you'll be doing yourself a good turn at the same time."

A stricture of silence gripped the air. Her father raised his head as if in wonder; her mother stared, willing her to reply; and Desmond Deeny half smiled his habitual smile of wistful innocence. Patricia's hand went to her throat, not to adjust her chiffon scarf but to tug at the whipcord she felt must surely be there. As the pleasure of surprise suffused their faces, she sensed her future as she had conceived it vanish into a swallow-hole at her feet. Her instinct was to flee, but she turned to Uncle Lar, to the blue that seemed to swim in the iridescent liquid of his eyes. His short white hair was thick all over, unlike her father's, which was thinning on the crown. His face was leaner than her father's and harder too, the face of a man who had lived cleanly, who had not let himself become bloated and raddled from too much drink or soft from lack of exercise and too much food. However, his years were tellingly expressed in the down-turned corners of his mouth, in the single line that scored each cheek, and in the knots of flesh that lay like the nodules of leguminous roots under the skin on both sides of his chin. It shocked her slightly to realize that it was the first time she had noticed them.

"It's good of you to think so highly of me, Uncle Lar. There's nothing I'd like better than help you run the farm, but I feel I'm not yet ready for the farming life. I've had five restrictive years in Mountmellick and another three in Cork, and now I'd like to spend a year or two in a place I've never lived in before. I was thinking of taking a job in Dublin. It's a real city, bigger than Cork, which is a city only to Corkmen. It is the kind of place, I hope, where I might wake up with new thoughts every day."

"Glory be to God, Patricia, but you're the strange girl," said her mother in dismay.

"I'm sorry, Uncle Lar."

"You must follow your nose, Particia, or you'll live forevermore with regrets," said her uncle. "If you have a hankering for the city, you must satisfy your lust. So we'll do without you for a year, but no longer. We want the girl we know. We don't want you picking up alien ways."

When they had eaten, she accompanied Desmond Deeny into the yard where he had parked his Land Rover. He was a young man, sinewy and tall like herself and confident in his belief that "The Forestry," at which he worked, was a great life. He had no land but he had a bungalow, and he hoped that one day she would share it with him. She liked Desmond. She liked the easy rhythm of his dancing, his lively, shining eyes, and his self-assured insistence that life was simpler than most people made out.

The dry June morning had turned to drizzle that wrapped them softly like a light cloak, making her wish for sunshine and a swim with Desmond in the Delour. The water in the deep pool would be cold and constricting, and the sun shining between the trees would warm her shoulders as she came out and cast running shadows on his glistening skin. She looked across the nearest field at Friesian calves swishing white-tipped tails and at Uncle Lar's tethered bull standing with his muzzle up, sniffing pleasure in the damp air.

"Lar is right," Desmond said. "If you go to the city, you'll never be the same again."

"He didn't say that."

'You're risking everything. If you go, you may never come back."

"I've spent the last three years with my nose in books. I feel like a calf with two heads, and I want to go to a place where I'll be alone for a little while. I want to put distance between myself and what I've come through."

"But think of the land, Patricia. Think of the land. How many young girls would give their right arm for the chance to jump at what you've been offered."

She knew that he loved her, that he meant well, but unbeknown to himself he was trying to fence her round like a farm. The arid restrictions of university life which he had not experienced lay like a paling between them. She remembered one of the lecturers, a shy bachelor who had taken a fancy to her and who cycled to college every morning in a rumpled raincoat and turned away whenever a woman threatened to look at him. With his back to her, he told her one day that she was too clever for the outside world, that her future must lie in the intellectual excitements of postgraduate study; and now as she looked at Desmond, she transformed an involuntary twitch into a laugh and told him that she wanted to go to a dance in Borris on Friday.

"I'll call for you at eight," he said, getting into the Land Rover. "I'll have to keep an eye on you from now on. When word gets round that you're a landed woman or nearly, the plot is bound to thicken."

Her uncle was alone in the house when she returned, her parents and brothers gone home.

"Let me do the washing up, Uncle Lar," she said.

"What kind of job do you hope to get in Dublin?" he asked too directly.

"I don't know."

"I knew you had something up your sleeve, and that's why I told you about the farm—to give you a sense of responsibility. You won't do anything rash when you know you have land behind you."

"What rash thing could I do?" she laughed.

"I'll leave that to you."

"In Dublin I'll be near Bray," she smiled. "I'll be able to nip out to Greystones to see if it's changed."

He laughed lightly, then allowed his features to freeze into a mask of serious concern.

"In Dublin you won't meet the right men. You won't meet farmers, you'll meet gurriers who never slipped in pigsh."

"But I can easily arrange for them to slip in pigsh."

"You're an attractive young woman with an appetite for change and excitement. Don't stay away too long."

He put a hand on her shoulder and, though she was as tall as he was, she felt like a little girl.

"I'm not a simpleton," he said. "The city isn't the only place of temptation. In the country there are men who might think more of the land than the landowner."

She spent the rest of the afternoon with her uncle and brought back his cows from the moor for milking. The drizzle had stopped and the evening air smelled of trees, grass, and wet clay. Though it was a Sunday evening with a beginning and an end, it stretched backward in time to merge with all the other Sunday evenings she had known in the country since she was a girl, Sundays of quiet, of minutes passing emptily, of longings now forgotten. The cows swished white tails, tore at the selvage of grass in the lane, or tried to mount one another in randy playfulness, while in a field of winter barley a neighbor was picking up doped crows and stuffing them into a sack. For a moment she paused to watch him but what she saw was the swirl of tide over black rocks. On the southwest coast you could stand on a cliff and, looking toward Florida or Spain, inhale the perfume of free-playing winds on the sea. But the midlands enveloped you like a womb. Here was a hidden Ireland, a darkly secretive landscape whose only hint of other worlds was in the sunset clouds on the horizon, reflections of far-off cities, Valparaiso or maybe Rome. She tapped the rump of the hindmost cow with a switch and watched them push forward suddenly with their heads up.

It was dusk when she got home. Her mother was sewing, her brothers watching television, and her father sleeping on the couch.

"Did Lar say anything after we left?" her mother asked.

"What could he say?"

"And you as flighty as a lark, turning your back on the best farm in the parish, tempting providence with your gallivanting up to Dublin."

Her mother was a strong, heavy woman in a wide skirt with gaping pockets, and she was wearing her brown beret because it was Sunday. Her black beret, which she wore on weekdays in and out of doors, was hanging on its peg by the window next to the peg for her father's hat. Her mother was a better farmer than her father. She could pitch bales with any man and thin a row of turnips while her slow-moving husband rummaged in his pockets for his tobacco knife. She was also the family banker. She kept the money in a biscuit tin in her bedroom, doling it out as she delivered a homily about the road to hell being paved with the coins that the thriftless spent on their way there. Her husband listened with longanimity and went straight to the pub. And when he had gone, she would say that she suffered him only for the sake of "the boys," and Patricia would think that in a house of men her mother was the most manly of them all. But, sadly, she paid the price of her manliness in a head which was as bald as an egg on top.

Though Patricia felt uneasy with her, she admired her flair for good husbandry. Without her mother's careful management, her father would not have kept his head above water when the children were young. But now, when her talents were no longer needed, she continued to exercise them to the detriment of her sons. Admittedly, Austin, the elder brother, who was self-reliant and remote, would probably survive her dominance; but Patsy, Patricia's twin brother, was sensitive and self-effacing, the kind of boy who needed light and space in which to spread his wings.

"I'd feel happier if Uncle Lar had said nothing about the farm. It hems me in, places me under an obligation."

"You're already under an obligation," said her mother. "You owe him your education and the style and airs that go with it."

"I was given what I never asked for."

"Well, if you can't think of yourself, think of Patsy there. Where will I get the money to buy him a farm when the time comes? If you had any thought for your family, you'd humor Lar while he's alive and do what you like with the land when he's dead. If you don't want it yourself, give it to Patsy, who's most in need of it. It's too good a farm to let out of the family."

"Why must you drag in my name?" Patsy demanded. "I don't want Patricia's land. Always plotting and planning, Mother—it's your greatest failing."

"But why have I got to plot and plan? Isn't it because your sister knows more science than sense. Running away to Dublin without a thought for—"

"I'm going just for a year. I told Uncle Lar I'd come back."

"You'll come back a different girl."

"Easier to go to town than leave it," her father said from the couch without opening his eyes. He rarely spoke in the house, but rumor had it that he was a witty and ingenious conversationalist in the pub.

"Go back to sleep, you," her mother told him.

"Easier to go to town than leave it," he repeated as he placed a newspaper over his eyes.

With a gesture of impatience, Patricia went out into the night. It was cool in the lane and shadowy under the trees. A lively wind was blowing from the west, crossing Connacht and the Shannon from the sea. She inhaled deeply, seeking the tang of seaweed and saltwater, but what she breathed was the scent of rank grass or maybe new silage. When she reached the gate, she stood on it and allowed it to swing closed with a clang. Desmond had gone to the airport to meet his sister, Desmond who saw life as though it were a May morning. Above her was a flying moon with a worn face and wild, unkempt, light-suffused clouds for hair. The fugitive face buried itself in the hair only to re-emerge in sorrow, hurrying, hurrying—hurrying without seeming to make overt progress.

2

Uncle Lar was a brick. When he heard that she had
landed a job as a science teacher in a secondary school in
Dublin, he bought her a secondhand car, a red Mini in good
condition, which gave her the feeling that all kinds of
impossible things were now in store for her. She left for
Dublin on August 24 so that she might have a chance to find
a flat before the start of term. It was a day of pure blue sky
and high clouds sailing, and she drove smoothly up the flat
Naas road, leaving the secrets of the midlands and the gold
of winter barley in the fields behind her. Aflutter with
excitement, she felt that all moving things, including the
heavy lorries with mysterious loads under green canvas,
were converging on the place of life and renewal which was
her destination. It was as if she'd been living in a cage and
had suddenly and unexpectedly been given the freedom of
earth and air and power over brute creation.

It was a feeling that remained with her during the following week, as she looked for accommodation and explored
the center of the city for sights, sounds, and smells that did
not remind her of Cork. However, with the first day of term
came the realization of anxiety. The day arrived with mild

sunshine and uncertain bird song in the back garden of the guest house which seemed as unreal as the uneaten rasher and hard-fried egg on her breakfast plate, heralding a surrealistic world from which all benchmarks had been obliterated.

The school consisted of a large red-brick house with two tall chimneys and a series of low prefabricated buildings set round a lawn which she soon came to know as the Quad. The red-brick house stood behind a concrete wall and high hedge, and the cheap prefabricated buildings behind that again, a world within a world, a world in which the only objects she recognized with a sense of comfort were two apple trees and four pear trees. As she passed through the heavy gate, she felt that she was saying goodbye to the sane world of mature men and women, and then the memory of the hated smell of gas in the chemistry lab in Cork caused her to forget everything but the queasiness in the pit of her stomach. A shout from one of the classrooms turned the geometrical Quad into a jungle clearing.

"Cannibals before a feast following a long hunger," someone laughed at her elbow, and suddenly she was surrounded by the other teachers full of ritual jests and ebullience soon to be quenched by the approach of the headmaster, who had signed himself in her letter of appointment K.I.D. Elsynge.

The morning dragged like a Ruskinian sentence punctuated by inexplicable bell ringing. The sun shone on the artificial-looking grass of the Quad; blackbirds came and perched on the backs of wooden seats; her pupils bent over their exercises too full of seaside holidays to take the pedantries of science seriously; and Mr. Elsynge crossed and recrossed the Quad like a man who knows that every teacher hides a shortcoming or two which a good headmaster will soon uncover.

At three in the afternoon he called the staff to his study, a small, overfurnished room with dark leather chairs that seemed to absorb what thin light came through the north-facing window. She took a seat at the end of the table while the other teachers sat on each side and the headmaster at the top. Her colleagues were all older than she, and already they had lost some of the ebullience with which they began the day. She had studied them in the staff room at lunchtime and decided that they were all teachers because of their reluctance to leave school. The Irish master, with his unruly hair and freshly freckled face, actually looked like an overgrown schoolboy, while the maths master, the oldest of them, had pale, otherworldly eyes that spoke of seclusion in a country far from the bustle of men. He ate his cucumber sandwich with obsessive care, patting his nether lip with his forefinger and licking crumbs from the palm of his hand, while explaining that he did not go to the seaside this year because he was growing six species of tropical grass in his greenhouse—six because it was his favorite rational number. They were all uncommonly polite and courteous. They told her what to do and what not to do, and she made suitable replies in the knowledge that her mind was a silk cloth at which they were tugging simultaneously from every corner.

She cast a glance at Elsynge, who looked, if anything, more schoolboyish than the others, the kind of schoolboy who might let off a stink bomb and get away with it. He was a lightly built sparrow of a man, red-faced and red-haired with a well-watered moustache that took the constant drip from his chapped nose. He now shuffled his notes as if searching for the joker in a pack of cards, and he told the staff that they could smoke if they wished, that he himself proposed to do so as soon as the extra strong mint he was sucking had melted. As it was the first day of term, he said, they were meeting for a brief discussion, but the "discussion" soon became a monologue which contained a word of headmasterly advice for each of them. To the English master he spoke of clause analysis and unattached participles; to the classics master of the inexplicable dread in which even the brightest pupils held the gerund and gerundive; to the maths master of the place of mental arithmetic in the age of the pocket calculator; to the Irish master of the trick of teaching city children a language of peasant vocabulary and agrarian imagery; and to Patricia of the importance of what he called "iso-tropes" in the housewife's daily round. The English master laughed self-indulgently at the word "tropes," and the headmaster, ignoring him, told her that at the end of term he would expect every schoolboy in her charge to know that in 22.4 liters of any gas at standard conditions—0°C and 760 millimeters pressure—there are 206,000 million million million molecules. She was about to tell him that he was grossly misinformed when the classics master put a furtive finger to his lips and winked at her from behind his other hand.

As soon as Mr. Elsynge had done, she was quick to escape from the musty smell of old leather. The pupils had gone home. Four sparrows were picking on the Quad and an open copy of Cicero's first oration against Catiline lay on a seat near a pear tree. She walked along the footpath by the Dodder, pausing under the railway bridge as a southbound train to Bray, Greystones, and Wicklow beyond hammered briefly overhead. It was a balmy afternoon, quiet and bright, and she felt a surge of happiness at the thought that the entire evening was her own.

"What do you think of God?" The exuberantly friendly voice came from behind. It was the English master, small and dapper with a head that looked too wide for his narrow shoulders. His pale cheeks bore little cicátrices of dry skin, and about his mouth she thought she discerned the vestiges of a childhood eczema.

"God?" she asked.

"Yes. K.I.D. Elsynge. It's rather a mouthful, so we call him God for short." His voice clicked drily as if his tongue were a metal rasp.

"From his conception of atomic numbers I would say that he is less than omniscient."

"He sees himself as a polymath and we all try to sustain

him in his illusion. We have agreed among ourselves never to contradict him on a matter of fact. I was pleased to see that you took his reference to "isotropes" on the chin. It showed esprit de corps as well as rare forbearance."

"It was merely that for a moment I felt he may have been right."

As she walked beside him, she felt uncomfortably tall. She looked down on his flat head, the tawny hair plastered as if to cover a bald patch, and yet he wasn't bald. In silence they reached Ballsbridge and paused amid the flow of southbound traffic.

"I always have a drink in McGuffin's after school," he said. "Would you care for one yourself?"

He was wearing a green tweed jacket with sharp shoulders, and, as he turned to look after a Dalkey bus, she could not help noticing his chest, narrow and shallow without the customary cushion of pectorals to support the shirt. He was a townee, she thought, and she had been raised among big-boned farmers. One thing was certain: there would be no pneumatic bliss with Mr. Foxley.

"What a good idea," she said aloud, imagining a cool pint of stout, well poured.

While she waited for her pint to be topped, he took a sip from his glass of lager and with serious deliberation enunciated his Theory of Clean and Dirty Drinks. Lager was clean and so was vodka, but stout, like whiskey, was dirty. There were excellent reasons why that was so, reasons he would explain at a more opportune time. Sufficient for the moment to say that he himself always drank lager or vodka. He was not a fanatic, however. He was not out to convert her. In short he was willing to drink and let drink. She listened to the dry rasp of his tongue with suppressed amusement and wondered how he could sound so funny and keep a straight face.

"You haven't taught before." He turned to her as the barman brought her pint.

"It was my first day."

"As the Irish master would say, it isn't every day that Magnus kills a bullock."

"Meaning?"

"Heaven knows. The man is Gaelic-mad. He even goes to Donegal for his holidays, and he never comes back without a notebook full of asinine proverbs. Last year it was 'good is the juice of a cow, alive or dead.' I wonder what gem of peasant culture he has unearthed for us this time."

"I expect we'll learn soon enough."

"Have you got the Dip. Ed.?" he asked.

"No, but I'm going to take evening lectures. I wouldn't have got the job otherwise."

"Where do you live?" He slipped in another question before the glass reached his puckered lips.

"I'm staying at a guest house in Northumberland Road while I look for a flat."

"Will you be sharing?"

"I can see I'll have to. I've been all over the place in the past week without once seeing anything I could both afford and bear to live in."

"We'll have to get you organized." He pulled an evening paper from his briefcase.

They pored over the advertisements for ten minutes, but they could find only one likely flat, one in Lazar's Park, a short walk from the school.

"Let me get you a clean drink for all your help," she said.

"You can get me a clean drink when you get your first check."

He bought her another pint and immediately reverted to his favorite topic, K.I.D. Elsynge.

"Keep out of his moustache for the first month and you won't go far wrong. It's the first month that tells. We've had three science teachers in as many years and they all fell at the first fence—they all tried to prove that they were scientists at the first staff meeting. Now, you came through today with flying colors, but tomorrow may not be as easy. He's an unhealthy specimen, and he's at his worst when he's got a cold. Normally he survives the Michaelmas term without a sniffle, but throughout the Hilary term his moustache is never dry. This is going to be a bad year. His moustache was dripping today and we're still three weeks from the autumn equinox."

"Who called him God?" she asked.

"It all arose from a misunderstanding. The last English master came into the staff room one day to find the other teachers talking about Elsynge, and he thought they were discussing the existence of God. They began calling him God after that until a crawthumping science master said that to avoid blasphemy they should call him Godling. The new name never took, though, and when the science master left, Godling became God. It all happened before my time, but the story is part of the folklore of the staff room. Every new teacher hears it and in due course imparts it to the next."

They parted outside the pub an hour later, but before he said goodbye he put his hand in his pocket and drew out two green and red balloons.

"Here, take this home and blow it up at leisure." He handed her the green one.

"Now, why should I do that?"

"Try it and see. It can be very relaxing after a grueling day."

"Are you going to blow yours up?"

"Oh, yes, when I get home."

She put the balloon in her handbag so as not to offend him and walked back to the guest house with the feeling that the city was as mysterious as the country. The advertisement said to ring after seven, so she rang at half-past six in the hope that she might be first. The phone rang for two minutes and, as she was about to put it down, she heard a weak "hello" from the other end. It was an unusual voice, quiet as a whisper, a mere exhalation above the muffled crackle of the line, and it said that she could call round in twenty minutes but not after forty as the owner of the whisper was going out. Half an hour later she paused before a red-brick and pebble-dash house in Lazar's Park, and a quiet wraith of a girl led her up the stairs to the second floor. The flat consisted of a living room facing south, a bedroom facing north, and a curtained-off kitchenette from which came the reek of fried steak and onions. She liked the living room best because the sparseness of the furniture gave an impression of light and space. The bedroom on the other hand was cramped and dark, dominated by an enormous double bed that looked like a too-high trampoline.

"That's the *grand lit,*" came the hesitant whisper. "As you can see, it's a cozy flat. The only drawback is the double bed. If you come, we'll have to share it, and it isn't everyone who likes sharing a bed. I myself wouldn't share with everyone, and not everyone would want to share with me."

"It's a tricky business but I'm willing to take a chance," said Patricia.

"First, we'll talk over coffee and then we'll both know better. I'm Monica Quigley."

"And I'm Patricia Teeling. I'm a science teacher, new to the town, just up from the country."

"Don't worry about that. I'm a culshie too."

Monica made coffee and sat on a faded sofa bearing pictures of a pink kingfisher in action. She was small and thin with yellowy skin and darkly darting eyes that kept returning to the ring on the second finger of her left hand. She had black, straight hair like an Indian, which appeared as a shadow on her upper lip and as a fine net on the white shins of her unstockinged legs. Everything about her was petite, and Patricia felt that she was the most delicately formed creature she had seen since the death of her pet rabbit when she was seven. Yet, in sitting upright on the edge of the sofa, she gave the impression of extreme alertness, of a hungry cat gathering strength for a spring.

They talked about the cost of living and letting live, about the jobs they did, and about what they both liked to do in the evenings, and perhaps because Patricia had just drunk two pints of stout they both found themselves laughing.

"Do you mind if I ask you a personal question?" Monica said.

"I'll tell you when I hear it." Patricia smiled.

"If you think it too personal, you needn't answer."

"What is it?"

"Are you experienced?"

"As a teacher?"

"No, as a woman."

"I've sat with men in the back rows of cinemas and dealt with wandering hands."

"I meant something more serious than hands." Monica revolved her ring as if she were trying to find the combination of a safe, and her eyes shone like dark beads on yellow silk.

"What do you mean?"

"Are you a virgin?"

"Are you?"

"Yes."

"I'm one too."

"You're not pretending?"

"Why should I pretend to something that most girls lose as easily as a paper handkerchief?"

"Would you call girls like that riff-raff?"

"No, but I would say that they think life simpler than it is."

"If one of them came a cropper, would you enjoy a sense of *schadenfreude?*"

"Who is he when he's at home?"

"Would you glory in the bad news?"

"I might in a curious way wish it had happened to me."

"You're not a puritan, then?"

"Now, you are being personal."

"I ask only because I like risqué talk but not risky behavior."

"Now can I ask you a personal question?" Patricia smiled.

"I'm from Ballyhaunis. There's no such thing as a personal question in Ballyhaunis."

"Why did you bring up virginity?"

"Because the last girl who shared this flat with me, Sarah-Jill, lost hers while she was here and lost what little dignity she had with it. Don't think I'm a prude, because I'm not. It was just that she tried to make me feel inadequate. Sharing a bed is a personal thing. The sheets of a shared bed give off two smells, not one. I woke up one morning to find that the second smell was that of stale semen."

"How did you know if you're a virgin?"

"I've read all Henry Miller. He calls it jism, which, I think, is a distracting word. It makes me think of joss sticks."

"Joss sticks are sweet-smelling," said Patricia. "They also grow shorter as they burn."

"If you want to share this flat with me, you're welcome." Monica rolled laughing, liquid eyes.

"I can't help feeling that we're two of a kind," Patricia laughed.

"Before you say that, I'd like to ask you a final question. What name do you give the male sexual appendage?"

"Do you really need to know?"

"Sooner or later the conversation is bound to come round to it, and I believe in establishing the nomenclature in advance."

"Being a virgin, I haven't called it anything since I was a girl and played with my two brothers in the hayloft."

"What did you call it then?"

"A lad most times, but sometimes a micky."

"We're too mature now to use childish language," said

Monica. "Sarah-Jill told me that her boyfriend, who was from Donegal, called it the Diúlach but she herself called it a cock, and that, I think, is vulgar."

"It's what men themselves call it, and they should know."

"No, Patricia, we'll have to find something less obvious in case we talk about it on buses or trains. Penis is too medical and flute has musical connotations that might suggest aberration. The Honorable Member for Cockshire is too English and—"

"I know," said Patricia. "We'll call it the *membrum virile* and then, if necessary, we can talk about it in the company of men since so few of them know Latin."

"Brilliant," said Monica. "We'll call it simply the *membrum* because it might be unscholarly to imply that all *membra* are *virile*. I now see that you and I are going to get on well together."

"I'd like to move in tomorrow evening if it's all right with you."

"I'll now take you downstairs to meet the landlord, Mr. Mullally. He's very old, very deaf, and absolutely daft about horses. Since Mrs. Mullally died last year all he does is study form. When she was alive, he used to cook and wash for her, and she would sit all day in the armchair and tell him how much better she could do everything herself if only he would cure her arthritis."

Mr. Mullally was in his armchair surrounded by the racing pages of *The Irish Times, The Daily Telegraph,* and *The Daily Express*. He was tall and fragile with a bony head on which four long strands of hair ran backward like twin rail tracks. His ears and fingernails were also long, his loose cardigan was moth-eaten, and his wet lower lip drooped over a chin which had long since receded into his neck.

"This is Patricia Teeling," Monica shouted. "She'll be sharing the flat with me from tomorrow."

"Sir Launfal will win the 3:15 at Doncaster tomorrow, mark my words. He'll win by a short head from Trilby."

"Can I get you anything from the shops tomorrow?" Monica asked.

"The last time I rode was with Larry Olivier in *Henry V*. I was only an extra, but he said I could handle a horse."

"We must leave you." Monica lingered by the door.

" 'He which hath no stomach to this fight,
  Let him depart; his passport shall be made,
  And crowns for convoy put into his purse.' "

"Goodbye," said Patricia uneasily.

"What you girls need is a little touch of Larry in the night." Mr. Mullally gave a cackle of a laugh which turned into a phlegm-laden splutter.

"I've never seen a man so old," Patricia said outside the door. "He looks as if he were made from papier-mâché."

"He's a good landlord. He never hears a thing."

As they came out of the dark passage into the hallway, Patricia glimpsed a man's backside vanishing up the stairs.

"If you listen now, you'll hear the crash of cutlery," said Monica. "He's an Englishman by the name of Baggotty and he beats his wife if he doesn't like his dinner."

3

The morning was clear and windless as she walked the short distance between Lazar's Park and the school. The sun came through the tracery of dirt in the top corners of the windows onto the heads of the juniors as she told them about atmospheric pressure and how to construct a simple manometer. She opened a window to let in the crispness of the morning, noting that God, enjoying one of his many free periods, was walking in the Quad with his forefinger in a black notebook. She watched him approach the lab with a handkerchief to his moustache but before he reached the door he veered and vanished from view. Explaining why a manometer is a more sensitive instrument than a Bourdon gauge, she walked to the back of the class to find him sitting outside under the window like a red-brown stag with up-turned nose, already assessing her performance in her second week.

"In the last few years the manometer has been superseded by the electrical pressure sensor," she said curtly, snapping the window closed.

At lunchtime Robert Foxley drew her attention to God's white socks.

"They're pure wool, knitted by his wife," he said. "She's afraid he'll catch his death spying under windows during classes. I noticed he was paying not a little attention to the science lab this morning."

They both went into the staff room, where their colleagues were smoking like chimneys, out of the sight of the pupils, who were no doubt smoking in the lavatories.

"God is sporting his woolen socks rather early this term," said the history master. "Last year he didn't don them till after Michaelmas."

"He must be planning a change in the weather," said the classics master. "His socks are a barometer, an aneroid barometer in the sense that they are dry, not wet."

"Aneroid meaning 'not wet,' " said the Irish master, who had a passion for conversational annotation.

"We are aware of that," the classics master reproved.

"Do you mean that his feet don't sweat?" the Irish master inquired.

"Like all students of Irish literature you have an unerring nose for the obvious," the classics master replied.

"He should not have donned his woolen socks so early," the Irish master pursued. "As they say in the Gaeltacht, do not make or break a custom."

The classics master turned to Patricia.

"A word from the wise." He took her arm. "I saw you close your window this morning while God was eavesdropping. A tactical error, my dear. Better to let him hear, to let him hear you make a deliberate mistake. He will then take you aside to put you right and, having proved that the headmaster knows more than the master, he will leave you in peace for the rest of the term. Your problem is not a simple one because he knows even less science than Latin. Perhaps you could leave a misspelled word on the blackboard—"

"*Isotopes* for *isotropes*," laughed Foxley.

"Brilliant," said the classics master. "He will then tell

you that the correct form is *isotropes,* you with tongue in cheek will agree, and headmasterly honor will be satisfied."

After classes Robert Foxley took her to McGuffin's to celebrate with a drink and a multicolored balloon. She had come to like his sober demeanor and grave intonation, rare in a man of twenty-five and rarer in a man who was not lacking in humor. She also liked him for refusing to allow her to buy him a drink. He was old-fashioned and reserved, unlike those modern whippersnappers who expect the girls they take out to buy drink for drink. She was reluctant to impose on him, however; so when he asked her if she would like another pint, she said that she must go, that she had some chores to do before dinner. He then gave her a pear-shaped balloon, reserving for himself a long-shaped one, which he blew up until it was as big as a marrow. For a moment he held it out vertically in front of her, then pricked it with a pin from his lapel and said, *"Sic transit gloria mundi."*

"Why did you do that?" the barman asked.

"I've got plenty more at home," said Foxley.

She walked back to Lazar's Park with a feeling of dreamful unreality brought on by the drink and the unexpected bursting of the balloon. On the hallway table was a letter from her mother, which made her think of the dairy, the farmyard, and the balance which hung from a beam in the barn. As she smiled at the "S.A.G." on the back of the envelope, a disheveled young woman opened the door. She was laden with shopping, three parcels in one hand and two carrier bags in the other; and as she put them down, her large mirrorlike spectacles slid to the tip of her curt-looking nose. She looked vaguely graceless, perhaps harassed, and she reminded Patricia of a backward boy to whom she had given an imposition that morning.

"You live upstairs?" the woman asked. "I'm Gladys Baggotty, I live in the first-floor flat."

She smiled uncertainly at the stained glass of the hall

window, which cast a green triangle on the pallor of her cheek. Patricia took a backward step as if to avoid an eye that could see only incipient necrosis.

"I'm Patricia Teeling. How do you do?"

"I'm exhausted, if you must know. I've been shopping in Grafton Street—it's so expensive—and my feet and back are killing me. The first thing I'm going to do is make a nice cup of coffee. Perhaps you'd like one too?"

Her thin, damp hair barely covered her ears. Little beads of sweat had formed on her upper lip. She was fleshless and fragile, the kind of woman who would have fainted regularly had she lived in the nineteenth century.

"I mustn't. I should be getting the dinner," Patricia said.

"Oh, come on. I've got a Bewley's brack. I never come home from Grafton Street without one."

Patricia followed the thin, flat shoes, calfless legs, and narrow bottom up the stairs. The young woman seemed a strange, otherworldly woman, a woman you could easily imagine being beaten after dinner every evening and accepting it as part of the inexorable scheme of things.

The flat was full of creaky furniture and a smell of mice that was sharpest by the kitchen door, and the dark green walls were hung with tiny modern paintings of indeterminate horsemen, ancient warriors perhaps returning in defeat from battle. The warriors were shadowy silhouettes, and the sky behind them, a burning yellow, made windows of sunlight in the gloom of the walls and seemed to extinguish what little brightness came through the net curtains of the real window.

Mrs. Baggotty vanished into the kitchen, from which soon came the whine of an electric coffee grinder. Patricia sat on a frayed sofa with patched cushions and stared at one of the warrior horsemen, who seemed to be wearing a high-heeled shoe, and she found herself thinking that people fail to fulfill themselves in many ways. Mrs. Baggotty came back with the coffee and brack and sat on the other frayed sofa. It was lovely coffee, strong and hot; it could have been made only by a woman who appreciated good things and knew how to make them. In a word, Mrs. Baggotty wasn't as helpless as she looked. Without spectacles, her face had a certain secret beauty that made her green eye shadow the natural concomitant of her porcelain-pale cheeks. Patricia had seen that face before. She had seen it in a painting, but she could not say when or where. She found herself warming to Mrs. Baggotty; she felt half-ashamed of the wish for withdrawal she experienced when she first looked at her in the hallway.

Mrs. Baggotty was not a conversationalist. She drank her coffee with absent-minded enjoyment, while Patricia made small talk about the fine weather, the price of vegetables, and Mr. Mullally. Yet Patricia did not feel uneasy in her company. Her silences were thoughtful, not embarrassed, and they made Patricia wonder about the nature of the man who could choose such a rare creature for a wife and then, if Monica was to be believed, ill-treat her. As Patricia put down her empty cup, Mrs. Baggotty suddenly remembered to say something.

"We could have had so much," she mused. "If only Bernard were a different man. While he was a Fleet Street journalist, we were relatively well off. But the day he got the idea that he was an artist and gave up journalism to write put an end to all that. Now we never know where we are. He's hopeless with money, and the worry of being without it keeps him from working. Some writers don't need money, but Bernard needs more of it than many a banker. When he's broke and unhappy what he writes is no good; and when I tell him so he says I'm being disloyal."

She placed the cups and saucers on a tray as if she had never uttered a word, and Patricia thought that she would not speak again for perhaps another half-hour. She smiled sweetly, however, as Patricia rose to go.

Patricia was pleased to be alone again, sitting by the window of the living room, which Monica called the turret room because it was at the top of the house and seemed to overhang the street. The red-roofed houses on the other side looked only an arm's length away and the narrow gateways between the hedges seemed far below. It was all an optical illusion, she told herself. The street was at least fourteen feet wide, and she was only three stories up. She closed her eyes, grateful for the silence of the street and flat. Then the phone rang in the hallway, and as she went to the landing Mrs. Baggotty called up the stairs. Monica had rung to say that she would be working late at the bank and that she did not want dinner. Alone again, Patricia sat by the window and opened her mother's letter:

Dear Patricia,
The weather is cruel bad for September. How is it in Dublin? It's just as well most of the harvest is in—today you wouldn't put out your dog. Austin and Patsy went to Nora McCormack's wedding. The breakfast was in Phelan's and Old McCormack fainted in the middle of his speech and had to be anointed. At forty-five she's lucky to get a man. It was her last chance. Des Foley left her ten years ago for Kitty Galvin, and when Kitty finally ditched him he went back to Nora cap in hand. As my grandmother used to say, "When all fruit fails, you're welcome, haws." Barley straw is going 70p a bale. Tom Burke was fined in court last week for switching an ear-tag, and at the last mart bullocks were only going 69p a pound. I hope you're looking after yourself and eating enough. Don't eat too many sweet things, and don't forget to write to Lar. Your second cousin Hugh is over from Australia. He's staying with Lar, but he's off again in two weeks. Remember to come home next weekend to see him. He's a Teeling through and through, and Lar mightn't like it if you made little of him. I hope you're saying your prayers at night and watching yourself on strange men.

Cheerio and God Bless,
from Mammy

Fighting back unaccountable tears, she folded the letter and turned again to the window. A bald-headed man passed underneath, not a man but a circular patch of naked scalp and a high tuft of hair on top like a hogbacked island with a thicket of quicken trees. As a girl she swam in the cold, clean water of the Delour, and in November she picked hazelnuts while Uncle Lar told her about the blackberry sprite who contaminated blackberries at the coming of winter. During the dry summer five years ago Uncle Lar filled a drum with water from the electric pump overnight. The water came through a plastic pipe and the first trickle made music in the empty drum. She stood in the dusk with Lar listening to the sweetness of the sound, and the following morning they went to Dooley's Cross and drew water with a rope and bucket from thirty feet down. Yesterday in desperation she told the class a riddle. "If a tinker had 13,600 patches on the seat of his trousers, what time would it be?" And when no one answered, she said: "Time for a new pair!" The incredulous guffaw from the class concealed the approach of God.

"You have time for riddles, Miss Teeling," he observed.

"Mnemonics, Mr. Elsynge."

"A riddle is a riddle is a riddle, Miss Teeling."

"I'm trying to get them to remember the density of metals—13,600 is the density of mercury in kilograms per cubic meter."

"Riddles are a distraction. I can say to you now, both categorically and apodictically, that they will remember the riddle and forget the density. The business of the teacher is to teach, not entertain. For entertainment we turn to our politicians."

It was strange to think that Uncle Lar and Elsynge lived on the same planet, that Dublin and the countryside from which she came were only a two-hour drive apart. In embracing both she was a cracked mirror. She was not one woman but several, and there would be no repose and therefore no integrity until she had become someone else.

She grilled two chump chops, tomatoes, and mushrooms, and ate on yesterday's newspaper because a properly laid table with a tablecloth would have been a lie, betokening a permanency she could not imagine. When she had washed up, she sat down to write to her mother but no words came to mend her broken world. She closed the pad and opened the book that Monica had been reading, a translation of *Silva Gadelica* by Standish O'Grady, realizing as she did so that she could not bear the solitude of the flat any longer, that she could overcome her sense of unease only by going out.

After a quick bath she powdered herself back and front before the full-length mirror in the bedroom. Pirouetting with arms above her head, she looked over her shoulder at the reflection of her buttocks, firm and muscular like Satan's in a Fuseli painting she had once seen in a book on a coffee table in Cork. Her legs were long, her bottom drooping, her waist high, with shoulders too narrow for her hips. Her breasts, because of her height and size, looked small, and she told herself that on a girl like Monica they would look more than generous. She was proud of her breasts. Their beauty did not consist in their size but in their shape. They began just beneath her collarbone, rising and falling as she breathed, fully rounded and so close together that she could have put an unsupported rose in her cleft. Because of her breasts she liked low-cut dresses, and because of a low-cut dress perhaps she had won a spot prize at a students' dance for what the poster described as Mammary Pulchritude.

Her face was soft, almost childish, oddly out of keeping with her sturdy frame. It was round and plump with a retroussé nose and pouting lips, so she tended to smile easily in the hope that her perfect teeth would light up a face that lacked the clear-cut, classical features she so admired in the pictures of women she saw in color supplements. Her glory she considered to be her lustrous black hair, which she wore short like a boy's. Once she had let it grow long in the hope that it would make her more womanly, but it only made her feel like a figure from Celtic mythology, great-bladdered Emer or warlike Maeve tossing tousled locks before the surge of battle.

Altogether, she felt, it was the kind of body that a youthful farmer, though not a youthful poet, might dream of. Her faults were those a farmer might appreciate, height and strength and sturdy legs, and an ample bottom more suited to the wearing of loose dresses than tight trousers. She had six dresses, two white, two cream, and two the colour of fine claret. Because of her height she wore low-heeled shoes, and in these she walked with easy strides like a well-muscled countryman going out to walk a wheat field on a clear June morning. She pulled a face, allowing her full lips to pout, did another pirouette, and laughed at the thought of going out for the evening alone.

When she had dressed, she dabbed two or three tissues with eau de cologne, checked the money in her handbag, and turned the key in the door. The evening was livelier than the morning with the smell of garden fires rising on faint breezes between the houses. Uncle Lar would be doing his rounds in the yard, a bucket in his right hand and a stick in his left, the trousers tighter on his bowleg than on the other. She parked in St. Stephen's Green and found a pub off Grafton Street where she could read her evening paper in peace.

She liked Dublin pubs. She liked sitting on a high stool at the counter, watching busy barmen pouring creamy stout, conversing affably with customers without neglecting their craft. On the marble slab she placed her newspaper and the green tin in which she kept her tobacco, cigarette paper, matches, and loose change. Since coming to Dublin she had taken to rolling her own, not to be eccentric but to have more money to spend on stout. Before her was a row of pints waiting to be topped, all of them poured to exactly the same level, about four-fifths of the way up the glass. When the pint was first poured, it was a uniform creamy brown. Then the brown began falling in gentle waves to create the black while at the same time tiny bubbles rose to make a creamy collar on top. She could watch this simple phenomenon forever, not only because of the wonder of the goodness both rising and falling but because it reminded her of an hourglass and time passing pleasantly. Finally, when the black had separated from the white, the vigilant barman would put the tumbler under the tap until a thick, creamy top rose in a perfect convex over the rim. The separate black and white represented a world in which evil and good cohabited, in which the delights of evil are best tasted through the mollification of the good, as the black must be drank through the white.

She drank four pints and smoked five cigarettes while she read the advertisements in the paper and checked locations on the street map she carried in her handbag. She had decided to go to a dance in a hotel on the north side of town where she would be borne on a surging tide, thrown to and fro as in a battle without rhyme or reason. The drink, the smoke, and the music would fill the cavities within and conventional phrases would whirl her backward and forward in time as if life itself was a never-ending danse macabre.

"Planning an attack or a retreat?" A young man sat down beside her. But she was in no mood for male badinage, so she swallowed the remainder of her pint and left him rummaging for what comfort he could find in his pockets. In the ballroom of the hotel she sat under a red light and lit one of the cigarettes she had already rolled in the pub for the occasion. She preferred sitting to standing because most of the other women reached only to her shoulder. She looked round, counting the men who were six feet or over. Only four, and one had a squint. That made three, and she could not count the timpanist who was too busy with his brushes.

A man in Donegal tweed who did not look in the least like a Donegal man hovered like a trout considering a lure, and then she faced him on the floor, registering at a glance the broken veins, the matted hair, and the verdigris of his sharp-toothed smile. She wondered if her own teeth also shone green in the revolving lights as he told her that he was a translator of the English classics into Irish, that he proposed not to let her out of his sight because she was the only woman in the hall with the shin to match a man of his physique. She tried to escape twice from the current of his unworldly conversation but he held her until she told him that she was bursting for a pee. She had to wait her turn in the ladies, which gave her an opportunity to rethink strategy and to puzzle over the more obscure of the graffiti. Listening to the rush of her stout-swollen water against the bowl, she decided to be firm with him, to tell him that she would not allow him to occupy her evening with talk of the intransigence of language, of the impossibility of translation, of the waywardness of English and of Irish going to pieces under the strain.

The stout had worked its magic. She glowed with well-being and self-confidence. She was proud of her height, strength, and capacious bladder, and she told herself that in her heart she could not really blame the translator for taking a fancy to her. But she wanted at the same time to be free of him, to talk to a score of limber men, high fielders who would delight in her healthy body and in their delight transmute the base metal of dance-floor conversation into gold. She made a confident return to the music only to find the translator shouldering his way like an earth-mover in her direction. A light-fingered tap on the shoulder made her turn.

"Voulez-vous danser, s'il vous plaît?" And gratefully she faced the stranger and said, "Oui, merci."

They were already dancing before the earth-mover came within reach. She looked at the man before her, tall and fair-skinned, confident but remote. He was certainly not a translator, but judging by his accent it was possible that he might require the services of one.

"Did you come to dance or to think?" she inquired to puncture his cocoon of abstraction.

"I often come to dance but tonight I've come to think. I find that the barrage of noise and the helpless drift of the dancing clarify my thoughts. The resolution rarely comes to me on the floor, but if I'm lucky it comes on the way home."

His accent was not quite French but he paused for breath in the oddest places as if living linguistically from hand to mouth.

"What do you do besides dancing and thinking?"

"I'm an osteopath, an Austrian osteopath, rare in Dublin."

"I'm a vet, a lady vet, rarer I should say."

"What a shame! You're too healthy to need my services and I'm too human to need yours."

She laughed as the music ended and out of the corner of her eye spied the disgruntled translator skulking behind a pillar.

"Can I buy you a drink?" asked the Austrian osteopath.

"I'd love a drink," she said with relief.

As there was no draft, she surprised him by asking for two bottles of stout in a pint jug. The translator, who had followed them, took a seat opposite and gazed across at her over the rim of his tumbler. She turned to the osteopath, finding comfort in the sane objectivity of his abstraction.

"I've been pursued by a translator all evening. I did everything to discourage him but I cannot shake him off."

"What does he translate?"

"He's at present Irishing *The Canterbury Tales,* and he cannot understand why his publisher, who is a businessman, wants them in modern rather than medieval Irish."

"A fanatic," said the Austrian osteopath. "This island is full of them. If he ever founds a republic, only citizens who have read Chaucer in medieval Irish will be given the vote. But why pick on you? If you don't mind my saying so, I'm sure he could have found metal almost as attractive."

"He's a perfectionist," she laughed. "He says that 'almost' will not do. Besides, he likes physique. He told me that he never looks twice at a woman under five foot ten."

"Though I'm neither a perfectionist nor a fanatic, I concur entirely in his judgment. In short, I wish to see you home."

She looked at the disconsolate translator and then at the Austrian osteopath, who seemed to view her from an altitude that was Alpine in its rarefaction.

"I'm a lone ranger. I come dancing on my own and I go home on my own."

"Why do you wish to be alone?"

"Because I wish to be myself."

"I think I know why. It's because you're waiting. When I asked you to dance, you turned to me and I read the look in your eye. It said, 'Are you the one who is to come, or do I look for another?' "

"I think there was less in my look than met your eye."

"You're a romantic, mademoiselle. Your heart and soul are pure. In Austria we have a saying which is not for romantics: Everything does not come to him who waits."

"I don't understand you, but if you want to do me a favor, you might walk with me to the door. That way the translator will hardly follow."

"Are you sure you won't let me drive you home?"

"I drive myself."

"What about a drink during the week?"

"I'm a solitary drinker too, but thank you, nevertheless."

Monica was reading in the *grand lit,* propped against a pillow, looking at least forty because of the hairnet that reduced her skull to the size of a grapefruit.

"Did you go dancing?" she asked as Patricia undressed.

"I went for a drink." Patricia tried not to lie.

"With a man?"

"No, with a girl I knew in Mountmellick." She found she had to lie to end the desperate catechism.

"Men are coarser than girls," said Monica. "All they can think of is *cur isteach.* If only all men were like Connla in *Silva Gadelica,* all women would be married. He had a fragrant apple that no amount of eating would diminish and the girl he loved said that 'our delight, both of us, is to continue in looking at and in perpetual contemplation of one another; above and beyond which we pass not, to commit impurity or fleshly sin whatsoever.' When I think of Connla and then go to a dance to find some red-faced gurrier trying to relieve himself against my leg, I feel I could die of defilement."

Patricia turned off the light and stretched between the sheets with her back to Monica. The sheets, which had just been washed, smelled of bleach. They were Monica's sheets, rough to the touch with seams in unexpected places. Monica put her back against Patricia's and pulled the covers under her chin.

"When you think of men, what do you see?" she asked.

"I see their faces," said Patricia. "Some smooth and soft, some hard and lean. I like the lean ones best."

"You're very pure, Patricia. When I was sixteen, I used to imagine men's faces, but when I began following rugby I could only think of their thighs because you can't see their faces in a scrum. I kept seeing men's legs till I was nineteen, and then quite suddenly I found myself thinking about their necks. You can tell a man's character by his neck. An inquisitive man will have a long neck, and a man who looks the world in the face an erect neck. A self-indulgent man will have a flabby neck, and a greedy man will have closh."

"What's that?"

"A swollen neck. I saw a man with closh in D'Olier Street last Saturday, and he had two women with him, one on each arm. But worst of all are the men with no necks, with heads that sit on their shoulders."

"What do they suffer from?"

"Oh, Patricia, men are so coarse, and the coarsest have necks like tree trunks. When I see the circumference of some men's necks, I think sex is the art of the impossible."

Patricia was drifting into sleep when Monica rubbed her verrucous heel against her calf.

"These are precious days, Patricia, but soon they'll be gone forever. Soon we'll both meet men and we'll marry and lose our virginity. We're like two ships in dock taking on supplies, waiting for the captain to come aboard. One morning he'll come up the gangway whistling, and before we can say 'I do,' we'll be out on the open sea answering to his touch on the helm. We'll sail the oceans of the world under our separate captains, and we'll never lie back to back in bed again."

"Will you go to sleep now, Monica?"

Just then there was a sound of breaking crockery from downstairs, as if a plate had fallen in the sink.

"He's just come in, the beast. He's beating her again," said Monica.

4

A piercing hoot erupted through the witty syncopations of the blackbirds in the Quad and with slow beats the Bray train, seven minutes late, clanked between the stone walls behind the school. Undismayed, the blackbirds came in again like soloists giving a passage of bluff heartiness from a longer work in progress. She wrote on the blackboard:

The volume of a given mass of gas at constant pressure is directly proportional to the absolute temperature. In other words V/T remains a constant value.

She turned to the class to find Julian Warner flicking a ball of chewed blotting paper at Paul Wilkinson.

"What is the name of the gas law I've just explained to you?" She glided toward him.

"Boyle's, Miss." He raised his freckled face.

"Charles's, Miss," said Paul, eager to avenge the blotting paper.

Julian hid his face in his hand and put out his tongue at the textbook on his desk. Standing behind him, she got hold of the short hairs on the back of his neck and tugged at the loose flesh.

"Now, write down Charles's Law and waste no more of your time."

The blackbirds made a musical joke. She looked up to see God's moustache moving up and down in a chomping action outside the window. The glazed door opened, and one of the blackbirds executed a turn on the solo flute with all the poise and elegance of the French baroque.

"A word for your private ear, Miss Teeling." The headmaster smiled with inturned teeth.

She followed him outside and faced him with one hand on the closed door. His moustache was thick in the middle and wispy at both ends. At least a centimeter too long, it must surely get in the way of his morning porridge. With a watery smile he took off his spectacles and swung them withershins in his right hand, looking like a naughty boy who resented being unhealthy and small, and who bore a grudge against his mother for making his turned-up trousers at least four centimeters too short.

"You've read my Staff Directives, Miss Teeling?"

"Yes, Mr. Elsynge."

"Can you recall Directive Eleven?"

"Not offhand."

"It's the Charles's Law of the Staff Directives. By that I mean that it is as fundamental to the running of the school as Charles's Law is to the behavior of gases. It says quite simply that a teacher must never touch a pupil in either anger or affection. I just saw you touch Julian Warner."

"But in neither anger nor affection. I touched him in a moment of absent-mindedness."

"You touched him, Miss Teeling. A palpable touch, I say quite apodictically though I wasn't in the classroom at the time. You see, we do not agree with corporal punishment at St. Columba's. We believe that all punishment should be psychological. The errant boy must be made aware of the enormity of his behavior. He must be made to feel the shame of his transgression rather than the weight of the teacher's hand."

43

"But I didn't punish him."

"You pulled his hair. Hair-pulling today becomes clouting tomorrow. We live, Miss Teeling, in an age of escalation. Remember what happened in Vietnam."

She held her right hand in her left to maintain her self-control. She could have taken hold of him by the shoulders and pressed him down till his knees gave way beneath him, but she reminded herself to keep her sense of proportion. What she should really do was to debag him in the Quad and raffle his trousers for charity in the staff room. She looked up from the toecaps of his shoes and spoke with quiet deliberation.

"You are making a mountain of a molehill, Mr. Elsynge."

"I never bandy words with my teachers. Memorize my Staff Directives." He turned his back on her. She watched him hurry toward the house, leaning forward with one hand in his trousers pocket. His jacket had a vent at the sides, and with each springing step the flap bounced off his narrow bottom.

If I ever marry, she told herself, my husband will have only one vent in his jacket. I can't stand the sight of men with two.

In the staff room they turned as she entered.

"A contretemps?" inquired the classics master.

"He asked me to quote Directive Eleven."

"In the staff room we call it Decretal Eleven," said the Irish master.

"Thou shalt not touch a boy in either anger or affection," quoted Robert Foxley.

"I pulled a boy's hair and he accused me of resorting to corporal punishment. I told him he was making a mountain of a molehill—"

"A distinct faux pas," said the classics master. "He will now pursue you for the rest of term. Mark my words, from now on you will do nothing right."

"Don't mind him," said the maths master, putting a

rheumatic arm round her shoulders. "He's a toilet-paper tiger, a man of mildewed straw. I taught with him in Marino twenty years ago and then he was the laughingstock of the whole school. The pupils thought him mad and the other teachers thought him an ass. He was the butt of every joke until Mrs. Elsynge, who was then Miss Marion Dobbins, whispered the word 'headmaster' in his ear. He was like clay in her hands. She knitted him woolen socks, gave him soup between periods, and told him to grow a moustache. Within a year she had married him and within three she had made him headmaster. But she'll make a pope of him before she makes a man of him."

"Don't worry," said Foxley after classes. "To help you forget, I'll cook you dinner."

The invitation pleased her. She did not wish to become obsessed with Elsynge, yet he seemed to grip her consciousness like a leech, sapping her strength and self-confidence with every day that passed. She drove out to Donnybrook at six and found Foxley in the kitchen in a white pullover and tennis shorts and shoes.

"Have you been playing tennis?" she inquired.

"No, but I felt like a game."

"I'm afraid I don't play."

"That doesn't matter. I only put on this gear to feel the part. I find that if you go through the motions, the psychological effect is as if you had actually done what you intended. For that reason I often wear pads watching cricket on television. Do you think that odd?"

She looked at his legs with their fuzz of reddish hair and wondered if they would please Monica. His neck was nondescript, neither long nor short, neither flabby nor lean, but at least he wasn't suffering from closh.

"Why should I think it odd? It would only be odd if you scored a century in your living room."

"You have the most incisive mind I know. I suppose it comes from being a scientist, from having been exposed to modes of reasoning denied to us humanitarians. But now you must excuse me while I change into something less comfortable."

He put her sitting by the window in the living room and gave her a mug and a pint bottle of stout. He was the most considerate of hosts. He even allowed her to pour her own drink, thereby showing the tact of a man who realizes that the way of a girl with her stout is as great a mystery as the way of an eagle in the air.

The flat gave an impression of delicate airiness, reminding her of the guest of summer, the temple-haunting martlet, and of choices deliberately made. The predominant color was white broken by shelves of books which seemed arranged by binding, not subject. It was not the flat of an impoverished schoolmaster. She had heard in the staff room that Foxley had private means, so she drank her stout and rolled a cigarette with the feeling that she might roll one here again.

The dinner—potato and leek soup, trout with almonds, and pears in red wine—was simple and good. In fact it was so good that she could have eaten twice as much. Foxley, not being a trencherman himself, obviously could not conceive of the capacity of a trencherwoman. When they had finished the hock, he gave her brandy and coffee, put on a record of lute music by Weiss, and sat beside her with an arm round her shoulders.

"After dinner is the best time of the day. The man who is not content after dinner needs a new cook," he confided.

"What do you normally do after dinner."

"As little as possible. That way the evening seems longer, the morning and the classroom further away."

He poured her another brandy and felt her pulse with the seriousness of a medical student.

"I've got a favor to ask you," he announced. "I'd be very grateful if you'd let me rub your tummy."

"Whatever for?" she laughed, aware that in her tipsiness she could have misheard him.

"It's very soothing. When I was a small boy I suffered terribly from wind, so my mother used to put me lying on my back on the bed and rub my tummy for hours on end."

"My mother rubbed my back."

"The tummy is more sensitive, more erogenous. I had, as you may imagine, a very happy childhood."

"But why do you want to rub mine? I would have thought that on the contrary you would be looking out for someone to rub your own."

"I like you, Patricia. I just want you to see how nice it is."

"Do you ask every girl you meet if you can rub her tummy?"

"You are the first. Lie down on your back and I'll show you."

"I don't feel like it this evening. Perhaps another time."

"You're a special kind of girl. You must have lots of men friends."

"Not really."

"I know because I can speak to you as I would to a man. And yet it's twice as exciting."

"It's because I'm so tall. Men think I'm one of themselves."

"Do you ever wear trousers?"

"No, they make me look even taller. My legs, you see, are too long for my back."

"You look lovely in skirts, especially when you stoop. I saw you stoop today to pick up a pencil in the Quad, and I noticed how God looked guiltily away. Even the Deity is circumscribed by lust. I'll bet that—"

"Oh, don't let's talk about him. Remember, I came here to forget."

"If I rubbed your tummy, all trace of the day's irritations would dissolve."

"Thank you very much, Robert, but I'm quite comfortable as I am."

"I'm not very good with women. I always say the wrong thing."

"You're doing very well."

"If we're ever to become more than friends, I must do better."

"Did you love your mother?" she asked.

"I was lucky. She died before I was ten, before I had time to outgrow her. Many men live to find their mothers a nuisance. So many mothers live to become a nuisance. A mother who dies before that happens is with you always. Now, you'll make a good mother, Patricia. When you walked in the gate on the first day of term, I said to myself, 'Now, she's a born mother.' Do you think it unnatural in a man to desire a son from the womb of a particular girl, to think of that before he thinks of the act that must precede it."

"It isn't unnatural, but it's unusual."

Foxley's innocence was a source of recurring pleasure. So many men got their way with women by boring the knickers off them. Most of them had only one subject—themselves. Their conversation was a message of desperate urgency, that they themselves were top-flight, top-drawer, or quite simply and incontrovertibly tops. If they took you for a drive, it was to prove that they could change gear more smoothly than you. If they took you to a restaurant, it was to demonstrate that they could distinguish between a collop and a scollop. And if they took you to the theater, it was to explain the more obvious points of the play during the interval. Foxley also talked about himself, but he talked about himself with unassuming amusement. He was generous without showing it, he was as helpful as an unworldly man can be, and he made no demands that could not be treated lightly. Yet, sadly, he was not real to her in the way of Desmond Deeny and Uncle Lar. He was not a man with height and breadth and depth, a man you could walk round and view from the front, the sides, and the rear. Perhaps that was not his fault but that of the place of sand in which she had found him.

"I would like you to have a memento of this evening," he

said as she left. "I would like to give you this recording of Weiss's suite in G minor for the lute."

"But I have no way of playing it."

"No record player!"

"Possessions are encumbrances. I have very few possessions."

"Never mind. Take it and keep it. One day you will play it and wonder where you heard it before."

The following day, during a free period she went for a walk by the Dodder. Halfway between the railway bridge and Ballsbridge eleven ducks were paddling lazily to maintain their position against the current, and as one of them upended she saw before her the bed of the Delour, a kaleidoscope she could watch from morning to night, especially in the brightness of the days of summer. She would sit with Desmond Deeny under a tree and wait for the shadows of the branches to cross the pool. In the center, where the water flowed fastest, smoothly worn stones glanced in the sun while nearer the bank the water slid gently over mossy rocks, twisting in little eddies so that she could not tell the direction of the current. And the afternoon sun would play on the surface of the water, casting reflections like gold coins on the gravel of the bed. The Delour, which cut her uncle's farm in two, was a living presence. Here was a secluded pool in which she and Desmond swam; here a fast-flowing reach where water frothed among boulders; and there a shallow where minnows chased shadows and the shadows overtook them in crazy impossibility.

"Days like these are a lifetime, but like a lifetime they're too short," said Desmond. "Sometimes they seem long because we're waiting for life to begin. It will begin when we get married."

As another duck upended, she wondered how it could feed in such a cloaca and escape poisoning. The Dodder was a stream that cut its way through a rubbish dump, through car tires, bicycle wheels, plastic dustbins, old mattresses, disused vacuum cleaners with white hoses, and skeletons of chairs from which the upholstery had been ripped away. Every day after school she walked along this stretch to McGuffin's with Robert Foxley. Perhaps if she had chanced to swim with him in the Delour, she would see him as a different man.

After shopping she went back to the flat to put a joint of beef in the oven. When she came to make the Yorkshire pudding and found that she was out of flour, she nipped downstairs to borrow a cupful from Gladys Baggotty. She knocked on the dark green door and waited for something to crash inside. The door opened and before her stood the Austrian osteopath in a torn shirt and paint-bespattered trousers.

"So you've changed your mind," he smiled. "But how did you discover where I live?"

"I haven't changed my mind. I live in the flat upstairs, and I've come down to borrow a cup of flour from your wife."

"She's out for the day, but come in and I'll see what I can do."

The flat was in chaos. Over the carpet lay a torn dust-cloth on which stood a stepladder and a gallon can of white emulsion. The keen smell of fresh paint had extinguished the smell of mice by the kitchen door, but Patricia advanced warily as if she expected the floorboards to give way beneath her. The warriors were no longer on the walls. Gladys seemed far away.

"What a coincidence!" He turned to her. "I travel into town to a dance only to meet the girl next door."

"Are you really an Austrian osteopath?"

"No, that's my fantasy persona, strictly for the dance floor. During the day I'm a disillusioned Englishman. I was once a journalist, but now I'm a writer."

"Why not an English osteopath, then?"

"I tried all that but it didn't work," he smiled. "I've even tried being French, but I found that I could never live up to girls' expectations. They know next to nothing about Austrians, and naturally they're curious. Are you really a vet?"

"No, I'm a science teacher, but I do know about cattle. I didn't mislead you as much as you misled me."

"Now, where does Gladys keep the flour?" he wondered.

"Try the kitchen. I imagine you'll find it in a tin marked Flour."

"Will you come out for a drink with me one evening?"

"What would your wife say?"

"If you can keep a secret, she isn't to know."

"I have no secrets. They make for guilt feelings. I prefer to be an open book."

"There would be no harm in it. It would only be for what you Irish call 'the crack.'"

"Thanks for the flour. I'll let you have it back."

"You'll always find me in on Wednesdays. It's the day Gladys visits her friend."

"Goodbye," she said and closed the door.

5

The city was a cold desert on a dark night. She walked between red-brick houses, past black iron railings, elegant street lamps, and doorways with semicircular fanlights; but, when she looked for her reflection in them, all she could see were the images of childhood, motionless and unchanged—green winter wheat with patches of faded yellow, a tree reflected in a pool of water under a moiré sky, gold cornfields on a misty morning with blackthorns like ghosts in the distance, a muddy pond like an evil eye in a meadow, driving rain like a thousand skivers on an unplowed field. She had come to the city with a thirst for experience, but so far her experience had been one of reservations. She longed to respond to the embrace of life as a· child responds to the embrace of its mother. She wished to go into each new day as a swimmer dives off a rock into the sea, but instead each morning brought a fascicle of questionings. If she knew the nature of the experience she craved, she might be able to find it, but all she could say at the end of each day was that she remained inchoate and incomplete. She was a well of cool spring water at which no traveler had stooped to drink.

September stole into October, the days shorter and crisper, the tap water in the bathroom colder in the morning. Already she had decided that she must leave St. Columba's at the end of the school year. She did not care much for the pupils and their smart-aleck city jokes and she detested the headmaster with his schedules and syllabuses and staff directives. She felt that he had it in for her, and she looked forward to December, when the weather would be too cold for him to sit outside on the benches under the lab windows.

There were compensations, however. Foxley always took her for a drink in McGuffin's after school. He was good company most of the time but he found it difficult to conceal from her his tiresome belief that he should be making love to her. Sadly, he could not get it into his head that it was possible for a woman to enjoy the company of a man without wishing to go to bed with him. She told him as much once or twice, but whenever they found themselves alone together the lifting of her skirt was never far from his thoughts. Perhaps she would not have minded if he truly desired her; she could not help feeling that it was an act he put on for her benefit rather than his own. He begged to see her every evening of the week but she rationed him to Tuesdays because she felt guilty about all the money he spent on her without a commensurate return. On Monday, Wednesday, and Thursday evenings she went to the H.Dip. lectures at the university; on Friday evenings she went drinking and dancing on her own; on Saturday evenings she went dancing with Monica; and on Sunday evenings she wrote letters and washed her hair.

She and Monica lived a life of placid austerity. They had neither radio nor television in the flat, and for relaxation they played cards or read books from the library. Monica earned more than Patricia but she never spent a penny foolishly, apart from what she spent on dancing. She was an indefatigable self-improver. She read books on banking, commercial law, and accountancy for pleasure, and to broaden her mind for Mr. Right, who was never far from her thoughts, she read history, biography, moral philosophy, and the review pages of *The Sunday Times*. Like some cats, she was crepuscular in her habits. She went for walks at dusk, just as people were turning on the lights in their houses and before they drew the curtains. Then she would criticize the decor of each front room and tell Patricia that the true pleasure of life could be enjoyed only in a house of one's own. She herself was saving for a house, and she had also laid by a little nest egg against the day when the ardor of Mr. Right would make necessary the purchase of a trousseau.

Saturday evening was the acme of her week. She spoke of nothing else from Wednesday onward, and she ironed her dancing dress at least twice and polished her dancing shoes at least five times in anticipation of the great event. As Patricia was tall and Monica small, they decided that it might encourage male ribaldry if they were seen together in the dance hall, so they always went their separate ways for the first two hours and met at eleven for a drink and a brief review of strategy. After spending the evening being pursued by men of different sizes—Monica by small, ox-eyed men with pointed shoes and Patricia by red-faced high fielders with heavy shoulders—they enjoyed a sense of sisterhood in the bar.

"Have you made a connection yet?" Monica would ask.

"I've made several, but I'm afraid they may be faulty," Patricia would laugh.

"I've got two on the boil but they lack neck," Monica said one evening. "They are the types who can only think of a court against a wall or in the back of a van. The wrong men come to dances. The serious ones stay at home."

"What is a serious man?" Patricia asked.

"He is a man who takes himself seriously. He prefers gin and tonic to stout and he doesn't waste his money on other men in pubs. He takes his girlfriend out three times a week—to the best restaurants and to see plays and films that get reviewed in *The Sunday Times*."

"Must he have a particular kind of job?"

"He is likely to be handling other men's money, but there may be exceptions. He'll probably work in banking, insurance, accountancy, or real estate."

"We've come to the wrong place, then," Patricia laughed.

"We've got to come here till we meet someone who will take us to dinner dances in the Shelbourne."

Patricia found it difficult to believe that a fragile creature like Monica could entertain such monstrous beliefs about men. She had a sallow complexion with a small, tight mouth, thin lips, and little lipstick-stained teeth that looked false but were really her own. To look at, she was the kind of girl about whom it might be said by an unwary man that butter wouldn't melt in her mouth.

"What's your verdict on tonight?" Patricia asked.

"We'd be as well off at home in the *grand lit*. It might make better sense to have a drink on Saturday nights in one of the better hotels. They're usually full of men."

"Married men," Patricia said, "men with more experience than hope. They might take us for high-class courtesans."

"It's a knotty problem," said Monica as they got their coats.

She had become even more suspicious of men since meeting a student of philosophy at a dance a few Saturdays before. The following Tuesday he took her to a film and sat in the dark beside her, keeping her well plied with chocolates and marshmallows. At length he took her hand and began caressing her wrist with his fingers. An inexperienced Platonist, she thought as he put her hand in his trousers pocket.

"You can imagine my horror," she told Patricia later, "when I found that there was no lining in the pocket. To be explicit, he wished me to masturbate his already tumescent *membrum.*"

"And what did you do?" Patricia asked.

"I got up and left him. I should have known when he said he was a philosopher that he wasn't a serious man."

"He may have been serious about Schopenhauer. I suppose he just happened to be wearing his cinema trousers."

"You mean you've heard of that sort of thing before?"

"Quite simply, he was a *cinéaste* with a passion for *cinéma-vérité.* I'm surprised at you, Monica. To be over twenty and not to have heard of cinema trousers could only happen to a girl in Ireland."

They discussed *cinéma-vérité* and cinema trousers at length in the *grand lit,* but Monica would not see reason. The very thought of them made her shiver, made her shiver as if all the perfumes of Arabia would not sweeten her little hand.

Patricia saw Mr. Baggotty from time to time on the stairs and he always nodded and said, "I'm still waiting for your answer." She tried to give both himself and his wife a wide berth, but Gladys would see her coming home from school and open the dark green door as she came up the stairs.

"A cup of coffee, Patricia? I've got the kettle on the boil."

Then they would sit with cup and saucer, Gladys thoughtfully and Patricia talkatively; and in the silences between conversation Patricia would wish for the older woman to reveal something of the strange ambivalence she sensed in her. Gladys never said much at a time, but gradually over some weeks she told Patricia of her loveless childhood, how both her parents died before she was six, and how she was brought up on a farm by a brute of an uncle who tried to rape her on her sixteenth birthday. She was an only child and she never made a friend till Bernard made her laugh at the office Christmas party. She was a typist and he was a journalist, and she married him because he told her that she had a Pre-Raphaelite complexion and that he always wanted to marry a woman who looked like a picture by Dante Gabriel Rossetti. At that time she did not know that he spent words as recklessly as he spent money.

"But you love him?" Patricia said.

"Of course I love him. Beside him other men are so commonplace, headpieces filled with clichés, with all the individuality of stock-bricks."

"You must be happy then."

"I'm as happy as I have a right to be—most of the time. But it's difficult to be happy if you have to save for a new dress in pennies, not pounds. If only Bernard didn't gamble . . . But he's very good to me, you know. Always brings me home a bottle of vodka when he gets a check, and then I spoil him for a week, cook him his favorite supper—mussel soup, poached sole, and chocolate soufflé . . . The funny thing is that in the five years I've known him he's never once called me 'darling.' And when I asked him why, he just said that certain words are so abused that they've lost all meaning, that people who care about language should give up using them. He's different from other men, you see, and that makes him hard to live with. He's unhappy when he's not writing, and when he's writing he wants to be alone. But sometimes when he wakes up in the middle of the night he can put the bad days from my mind until the postman brings more bills in the morning."

At other times Gladys was more pessimistic. and then she would reveal a deeply misanthropic streak. "Marriage is a feather bed for men and a bed of nails for women," she would say. "Men are of two kinds, those who want a mother and those who want a skivvy. Both are insensitive. They know nothing of women's suffering."

Patricia's mother wrote every week with news of the beet and potato harvest and above all of Uncle Lar and her cousin Hugh. In every letter she would quote some witty remark supposedly made by Patricia's elder brother, Austin, but Patricia well knew that the remarks were made by her twin brother, Patsy, who came only second in her mother's esteem. Austin, like her mother, was a miser. He neither drank nor smoked, and whenever there was kissing on the television he left the room. It was pathetic that her mother had to put Patsy's jokes into his mouth.

At the end of October Patricia drove home and stopped in Naas on the way. It was lovely to be among country folk again, to hear the midland intonation making poetry of midland preoccupations. In the pub she sat opposite two farmers who looked as if they themselves were being fattened for market. They were wearing collarless shirts which protruded like tires between their skimpy waistcoats and ample trousers, and their battered hats looked as if they had made a bed for a litter of piglets.

"You've never seen dirtier cattle," one of them said to the other.

"But wasn't he always famous for dirty cattle? He sold fourteen Friesian bullocks last February and every fuckin' baste of them had a hundred pounds of matted dung on his flanks. I heard it said for a fact that they killed out at only fifty-six pounds a hundredweight."

"Too mean to buy bedding."

"Too lazy to shake himself."

"Some men don't wipe their own arses. You can't expect them to wipe a bullock's."

It was so different from the talk in the staff-room, the arch discussions about the existence of God and Foxley saying that no one could really be sure, "that a large quercus hung over the whole issue." Or again Foxley saying that he'd seen God chastising a boy in the Quad, "absolutely leguminous with rage." All that literary flippancy seemed clever in the first week of September, but now as she listened to two farmers talking about dung she realized that she had come again among her own people.

Her mother was pleased to see her, and her father in a moment of verbal profligacy said, "Welcome home." Uncle Lar smiled happily, felt both her biceps, and introduced her to Hugh. She was somewhat surprised at his unexpected appearance. He was broad and stocky, unlike any Teeling she had ever seen, and because of the width of his back and shoulders he looked shorter than he was. He was the very picture of physical strength. His neck reminded her of a bull's and his stumpy fingers made her wonder if he could bend a length of bull-wire in one hand. It was his head, though, that made her look twice at him. It was basically a cube that had been rounded or perhaps slightly worn at the edges—a condition which, according to Desmond Deeny, may have flattered him because "it gave his head the appearance of having been used." She smiled at the thought of Desmond's jealousy and took in Hugh's hair, short and close, no more than half a centimeter high on the crown. Her mother said that he looked like a wire brush on top, but Uncle Lar said that it was the haircut of a man who meant business, that it reminded him of a haircut he himself once had in Alice Springs.

Desmond Deeny told her that Hugh was unnatural. He went dancing every Saturday and always came home on his own. Then, unexpectedly, he went out with Desmond's sister and tried to do something to her that no other man had done before.

"What was it?" she asked, brightening with interest.

"I can't tell you. It's too dirty. A girl like you wouldn't believe that such a thing could happen between a man and a woman."

She looked at Desmond, at his open, unlined face and eyes that always danced, with or without reason, and she wondered if goodness must necessarily come out of simplicity.

"I don't know anything about Hugh," she said. "But I'm sure Uncle Lar will take his measure."

"Lar likes him. I saw them together at the mart last week. Patricia, I think you should come home."

"Why?"

"The city and the country repel each other like oil and water. And like God and Mammon, they can't be served at the same time by the same person."

"I'm not committed to the city. On the contrary, I'm pleased to be back."

"And I'm afraid that something may go badly wrong."

"It's I who should be afraid, not you. Didn't you once say that life is simpler than most people realize?"

"But it's also more perverse. It's perverse in its simplicity."

The following day was Saturday. She got up early and went over to Uncle Lar's to cook his breakfast, but she was disappointed to find that he and Hugh had already eaten. They spent the morning lifting potatoes in the field by the road while she cleaned and polished and cooked dinner. She was looking forward to a conversation with her uncle, but at table he and Hugh talked mainly about mustering cattle in the outback, and she listened and smiled whenever they laughed.

"Have you got long holidays?" she asked Hugh.

"As long as I want to take."

"He's as free as a brumby," Uncle Lar laughed. "But even a brumby will meet his breaker."

After dinner she walked with them across the fields, muffled against the stiletto stabs of the wind. The fields of stubble looked bleached and sodden. The already threadbare hedges would be denuded by mid-November. A squeal from the ditch made Lar cock his ear. Pushing back the brambles, Hugh stooped and pulled out a rabbit by the neck. The rabbit, wriggling in his hand, released a jet of piss down the front of his anorak. Hugh raised his arm and gave the animal a sudden chop on the back of the neck.

"Why did you do it?" Patricia demanded.

"He caught his hind leg in a snare. It was nearly severed. I could only put him out of pain."

"It was the sensible thing to do," said her uncle.

The killing of the rabbit troubled her. She would have

preferred if her uncle had killed it, and as she walked home alone, she could think only of Hugh. He was an alien presence in her uncle's house, but he was an undeniable presence. His blocklike skull cast a shadow across the kitchen like a stone menhir darkening a moor, and she reacted to him as she might to a menhir. She wanted to walk round him, look him up and down, touch him here and there, and feel his rough surface with her hand.

Driving back to Dublin on Sunday afternoon, she could hear the intermittent buzz of conversation in her ears, the voices of Lar and Hugh and gunshots of inexplicable laughter. The country had a disquieting effect on her; it made the city and the school seem irrelevant. The city to which she was returning was inhuman in its indifference. It was a place of decaying brickwork and stinking waterways, a river that rose and fell with the tainted tide, and two canals of rotting lock gates and floating debris. It was a place of mindless despoliation where no building was sacred except the GPO, and she was returning to a school in a corner of that wasteland, to a headmaster who expected her to correct over two hundred exercises a week, and who would choke and splutter when he discovered that she had not corrected a hundred. He would look sideways over his cheap spectacles, thrust a hand into his trousers pocket as if he were ascertaining whether his left testicle was really more pendulous than his right, and say with the chill of winter, "As you know, Miss Teeling, this will never do . . ." And she would refrain from laying violent hands on him and later go for a walk toward Ringsend, where the gulls cried and the smell of coal sharpened the air.

Monica was out when she got back. Her nylon undies lay on the bedroom floor like the forgotten exuviae of some tropical reptile that had slithered into the dark beneath the *grand lit,* while in the unflushed bowl in the bathroom was a trace of menstrual blood. Patricia had thought of having a bath, but when she heard Uncle Lar and Hugh imitating the call of the whipbird in her mind's ear, she knew that she could not stay in the flat another minute, that she must go out and drink four pints and smoke six cigarettes before going to a dance.

On Saturday morning she went into Dublin to buy a book for Robert Foxley's birthday. As she was trying to save, she thought she might buy him a secondhand copy of something unusual, so she went to Greene's, first pausing outside to see what was new, then climbing the wide stairs, the closely packed shelves leading her upward to the first floor.

"We meet again." A forefinger tapped her shoulder.

It was Bernard Baggotty, so fine-featured and fair-haired that he could have been one of the men about whom Pope Gregory the Great said *Non Angli sed angeli.*

"Are you in a hurry?" he asked when they had exchanged a word or two. "Come for a drink. There is something I want to say to you."

"I don't think I should."

"Then come for a turn in the Green."

As they walked from Merrion Square to St. Stephen's Green, Bernard chatted amusingly about the mild weather. The morning had the enveloping softness of April rather than the harsh stricture of November, and he apparently was not the only one who thought so. A young man and a girl were kissing against a tree, but Patricia told him that ten-thirty in the morning was too early for kissing, that kisses, like port, tasted better after dinner. Suddenly she felt the poetry of the country in the city. The sun sliced sharply through bare branches, giving her a feeling of airy cleanliness and reminding her of the warmth of the summer when she went about in a cotton dress and no knickers.

In the pond the ducks were paddling lazily, some upending as they fed, some snoozing in the sun, their heads turned back, their beaks tucked under their wings. Now and again one of them would open an eye and paddle briefly to change course. Two more ducks came in over the trees and made a wide wake with their feet as they landed. They were followed by three seagulls that landed so lightly that they barely scored the water. They were more restless than the ducks, though. They seemed to be looking for something, and when they didn't find it they rose again and planed away smoothly over the trees.

"I don't like gulls," Patricia said.

"They're no friends of young ducklings," Bernard replied. "Last spring I used to feed the ducks on the canal in the morning. One duck had a clutch of four and I watched them disappear one by one. I had no idea what happened to them until an old man I met on Leeson Street Bridge told me that they had been carried off by the seagulls."

They paused on the bridge to watch middle-aged men feeding the water fowl from crumpled paper bags. She was pleased that he was an observer of nature, that he talked seriously about serious things and more lightly about subjects that could be illuminated by a joke. He looked about forty. His hair was thin on top, growing in fuzzy tufts that made his head look like a field of grazing in which cattle had left tussocks of couch grass uneaten. His high forehead, like an exposed upland, gave him the look of a man who had withstood wind and rain and spiritual torment; and the bone of the skull beneath the transparent skin made her see the burning of midnight oil and the cold comfort of wisdom, however hard won. She reminded herself that she was too impressionable, that he was a man who possibly beat his wife, but all she could remember was the morning she had seen him in the hallway with rain clinging in bright droplets to his hair as if it were young corn after a heavy dew.

"I'm reminded of an experience I had in Dorset as a boy," he said. "I was walking along a river outside a town when I saw seven big sewer rats setting on one. The outcast fought back as he retreated, and when he found himself on the riverbank he turned and jumped in. The others gathered on a big stone at the edge and watched him swim for the opposite bank. He was going like the clappers, so that he could not have seen the ladylike swan and her three cygnets until he was within two feet of her. He dived to avoid her, but she made a sudden dart with her neck and flicked him like a coin in the air. He fell on his back and she picked him up in her neb and tossed him contemptuously while the cygnets clung in a cluster behind her. The rat came down again but this time he did not swim. The water folded over him, and then he floated on the surface for a moment until the current pulled him under. I looked at the placid swan and then at the stone on the bank but the seven sewer rats had gone. I think of that incident nearly every day."

"It's the story of a born loser," said Patricia.

"It's the history of mankind."

"Have you written about it?"

"No, I'm condemned to write only about things that don't impinge on me. The things that matter to me as a man I can't face as a writer."

"Maybe you will," she said, and she felt that she meant it.

He was obviously a respecter of words, those fine instruments of imprecision without which there can be no intellectual fossicking. Unlike Foxley, he would never say that so-and-so was "as irrational as a surd" or that "he talked a load of old collyrium," and therefore he was closer to the living language and to life itself. Besides, he had been born and brought up in cities; he was a man who might find his way round a labyrinth in the dark.

"Will you have that drink now?" he asked.

"I think I might," she replied.

He took her to The Inkwell in a cul-de-sac off Grafton Street, a secretively grotty pub divided into two bars by a smoke-blackened partition that glistened with greasy finger marks. They ordered pints of stout and sat in the front bar listening to the barman discussing form with much nodding and winking. The freshness of the morning had invaded the pub. Glorious sunlight spilled through two tall windows onto the theater posters on one of the walls. A boy came in with more posters and two draymen began unloading barrels outside the door.

"There is nothing more delightful than to sit in a pub in

the middle of the morning, drinking a pint and listening to the thud of empty barrels on the pavement," she said.

"The thud of full ones is sweeter."

"Is that why you use the front bar, so that you can hear?"

"People sit here who wish to see. They sit behind the partition if they wish to talk. The back bar, you see, is the home of darkness, mist, and literary conversation, a kind of Irish Niflheim."

"Let's go in, then."

It was dark behind the partition. There were no windows, only a single electric light about which the cigarette smoke swirled like mist over Uncle Lar's moor.

"On a good—or, if you wish, an indifferent—evening you will find more poets per square foot of floor space in this bar than in any other in Dublin. Sadly, most are bad poets. Gresham's Law, you know. They have driven out, or perhaps killed, the good."

"Why do you go to dances if you're a married man?" she suddenly asked without meaning to.

"Because I'm looking for something."

"Something called sex?"

"Not necessarily. I go to enter into other lives. I have a feeling that the relish of life has departed, but I glimpsed it for a second when you told me you were a vet."

"I'm sorry to disappoint you. But if you're interested, I have a degree in agricultural science."

"I can sense a glass wall between myself and everything I do," he said as if he had not heard her. "I know there's a wind blowing, but I cannot feel it on my face. My indifference—it's more like paralysis—may be the effect of approaching middle age. But what it means is that I have lost my sense of ecstasy. A beach pebble is now a piece of granite or limestone whereas ten years ago it was an object of wonderment, a piece of the universe."

"All you're saying is that you're no longer a child, that you have put away childish things."

"That's the end of a writer, to have put away childish things. Except ye . . . become as little children . . ."

"If what you say is true, you retained your sense of wonder longer than most. There are boys in my junior class who have lost it already—"

"And you are helping them to lose more of it with every received idea you put before them. Every baby is born a poet, but first parents and then teachers make him see the world in prose. Over a year ago I went to an exhibition at my nephew's school, and the first thing that struck me about the verses and pictures on the walls was the difference between the precocious children and the plodders. The precocious children painted sub-adult pictures and wrote sub-adult verse, while the plodders wrote and painted from their own experience. That's what I want to be—a plodder. You see, a child soon aborts his sense of the poetic, the precocious at four, the plodders perhaps at ten. In the spiritual life of a child, the parent and the teacher are no more or less than abortifacients."

"You think I'm on the side of the devil, then?" she asked.

"You can't help it, but I think you could help me. I move too much among literary people. I need to talk to someone with the gift of first-hand experience. All I wish for is to meet you for a drink and a conversation now and again."

"We'll see," she said, taken aback by his casual egotism.

"I'm going out for a paper now. I'll be back in a second."

"Why a paper when, as you've been saying, you have me?" she smiled.

"I want to see what's running at Doncaster."

"Another Mullally?"

"There are two things in life I take seriously—horses and literature. They are both equally problematical, equally difficult to judge."

Alone for a moment, she looked at the other customers. They did not look in the least like poets. In the way they leaned confidentially toward one another they looked like ex-rugby players about to form a conversational scrum. Opposite her were two students from Trinity to judge by their scarves, sickly and thin with nervous hands that kept clutching at their tumblers without lifting them.

"I say, she's got a most arresting frontispiece." One of them looked across at her.

"I wouldn't mind having a look at her endpapers," said the other.

"I'd give half my scholarship to get my nose in her prelims." And they both laughed so loudly that the confidential conversationalists withdrew their heads from the scrum and looked up wondering if they themselves had been overheard.

"Are the men who use this pub straight?" she asked Bernard when he came back.

"It didn't take you long to catch on. Don't be shocked if I tell you that I call this place The Bender and Stoker."

"Why the bender and why the stoker?"

"I'll tell you when we meet next week."

"I don't think we should."

"Why?"

"Your wife gives me coffee. I'd feel a right bitch."

"But there's no harm in it. It's only for the conversation."

"My flat mate thinks you beat your wife whenever she overcooks the dinner." She decided to challenge him.

"Well?" he laughed.

"Well, do you?" she smiled.

"I don't believe in corporal punishment."

"A witty answer, but wit is not the best conveyor of truth. There are more half-truths per page in *The Oxford Dictionary of Quotations* than in any other book except *Das Kapital*."

"Do you think I beat my wife?"

"No." She could not bring herself to say yes.

"Then, that's all that matters. Now will you agree to meet me?"

"On one condition. That we both drive here and back in our own cars. That way it will be as if we'd met by accident."

"If you insist."

"I'll see you here on Sunday evening, then."

"On Sunday at eight." He followed her into the street.

6

She began meeting Bernard on Sunday evenings. They usually met in The Inkwell, talked for two hours over two pints, and then drove home in their separate cars. At first she thought of their evenings as sober little rituals in which she tried to drink stout as slowly as Bernard, but soon she found herself looking forward to them. The truth was that she was lonely in the city. She did not like the native Dubliners because of what they had done to Dublin, and she failed to respond to countrymen in Dublin because of what Dublin had done to them. Most of them tried to emulate the Dubliners in cockiness. They put on self-conscious airs like heavy overcoats, and they talked too loudly as if loud talk could conceal the fact that they still had one foot in their ancestral bogs.

Like Foxley, Bernard was different. To be with him was to escape from both country and city, from both culshie and gurrier. And for the most part he was undemanding. Though she never gave him anything she could not have given a casual acquaintance in a casual conversation, at the end he always said that he would like to meet her again. It was as if she had become his confessor, as if all he craved was her unbiased ear.

Though he talked mainly about himself, she would not have called him introverted or egocentric. He was light-hearted and amusing, by no means the dour, self-absorbed manic-depressive that Gladys so often described to her over coffee. In London he had been a successful journalist on a national daily, and when the troubles broke out in Northern Ireland he was sent to Belfast, where he met and married Gladys. He remained in Belfast for two years, and when he was named "Journalist of the Year" for reporting a war he did not understand he decided that it was time to do something else. After the horrors of the North, he could not face the flippancies of Fleet Street, so he came south to Dublin to try, in his own words, "to earn a living as a real writer in a tax haven for pulp merchants."

Being "a real writer" wasn't easy, but he kept body and soul together on book reviews, articles for Sunday newspapers, short stories, and occasional plays for radio and television. The financial uncertainties of a life of literary foraging were never far from his thoughts. He could not forget the well-paid job he had forsaken, nor conceal from himself the disquieting intimation that at forty he still had to find his voice. His problem was that as a journalist he had known comparative riches. He had acquired a taste for expense account living, and now he could not help feeling bitter at being paid less than the price of a good dinner at an expensive restaurant for a short story that took a week to plan and write. He had an uncomfortably ambivalent attitude toward money. While affecting to despise it, he lusted after the comforts it could command. Nothing he could now afford was quite good enough, and he had a disturbing suspicion that the stories and articles from which his meager income derived were not quite good enough either. He was a twice-haunted man; he was haunted by a past he could only despise and by a present in which he had failed to immerse himself to the point of self-forgetfulness. Once after winning forty pounds on a horse he took her to a restaurant off the quays to buy her dinner. They began with smoked mackerel, which was delicious, but the less than tender *bistecca alla pizzaiola* which followed threw him into a fit of self-accusatory depression. "If only we had gone to another restaurant!" he agonized. "But I decided to spend only thirty pounds on the meal and put the other ten pounds on another horse." She told him that the meal would pass muster, that his conversation made up for the *bistecca,* but no words of hers could dispel his awareness that he had eaten better meals as an overpaid journalist.

Although she longed to smooth the tortured wayward-ness of his thoughts, she herself felt guilty at seeing him in secret while continuing to listen to his wife's whining over coffee. She tried to assert her independence by paying for her own drinks, but in doing so she only managed to sharpen her awareness of her debt to Robert Foxley, who bought her drinks every day after school without ever receiving as much as a balloon in return. As a gesture of recompense, she decided to invite him home to dinner one evening. Monica was thrilled at the prospect of helping to cook for a man of private means who was himself a capable cook and something of a gourmet. She questioned Patricia about how long she had known him and told her that she was so secretive about him that their relationship must be very serious. As they lay on their backs in the *grand lit,* Monica returned to the subject.

"Do you dream about him at night?" she inquired.

"Now and again."

"Have you ever made love to him in a dream?"

"Not as far as I know. He is not that sort of man."

"Have you ever made love to any man in a dream?"

"Why do you wish to know?" Patricia parried.

"I'd like to know if a woman can dream of something she has never experienced."

"Of course she can. Many dreams begin where experience ends."

"It isn't true of my dreams about men."

"Perhaps sex doesn't count for you as wish fulfilment."

"Have you ever lain with a man in your dreams?" Monica decided to be direct.

"No, not lain, but I have run with men, which is the same thing."

"My dreams are not true to life."

"But isn't that what we mean by a dream?"

"Let me tell you what I mean," Monica said. "I'm walking naked over a stretch of moorland, up to my knees in heather, when I see a big dark man like a bird flying in from the sea. I turn inland and begin to run, but my feet sink in the moss and the heather grips my thighs. The cold shadow of the man-bird falls on me. I run faster to get away but his shadow keeps covering me no matter how I veer. The heather tugs at my legs. I fall flat on my face, and his thigh feathers tickle my bottom. Suddenly his shadow lifts off my back, the sun is warm on my shoulders, and I begin to come in a great empty space with nothing to hang on to, like a church bell vibrating after it is rung."

"Every young woman has dreams like that."

"Tell me yours, then," said Monica.

"I'm running last in a relay race with three men."

"Oh, how kinky."

"I'm waiting for the third man to reach me with the silver baton in his hand. He's wearing loose white shorts and I can see the outline of his megaliths flopping about inside them. Then, as he comes up to me, I begin to run, holding my hand like that for the baton. It seems like an age, he takes such a time to reach me. My running becomes more reckless, my legs uncontrollable, but suddenly the baton is in my hand, and against my will I begin to come. It's a long, long coming, lasting all the way down the straight with the flags waving and the crowds cheering me on, and then I feel the cold tape on my breasts, it's all over, and I wake up all floppy and out of breath with my heart pounding inside me."

"It's better than my dream," said Monica. "It's more triumphant. I like the bit about the crowds cheering. It reminds me of Fairyhouse, the Grand National, and the last furlong. But it's not true to life."

"There is more truth in the chastity of dreams than in the hiss and steam of copulation."

"Maybe we'll never get married, then."

"I think we shall. At least I shall. Dreams are as necessary as food for the journey of life, but marriage is necessary as a preparation for death."

"Because married women die many times before their death?"

"No, because marriage begins by quickening the flesh and ends in mortifying both flesh and spirit."

"Oh, Patricia, I'm so pleased." Monica hugged her.

"You mustn't touch me. I dislike being touched by another woman."

"I'm so pleased," Monica repeated. "Don't you see that your dream means that you're still a virgin, that you haven't fallen like Sarah-Jill. You can bring Robert Foxley here any time and I'll help you cook for him."

Robert Foxley came on a Friday evening with three balloons: one for Patricia, one for Monica, and one for himself. Monica was suspicious of the balloons, but she was delighted when he pronounced her chocolate soufflé a distinct success, in fact a perfect ramulus. Her excitement had hardly diminished the following day. She squeezed Patricia's hand several times during the morning and said:

"My, my, but you're the close one. Knowing him since last September and never saying a word to a soul! I've never seen a better-matched pair. You'll be married before Lammas, wait and see."

Patricia went home at Christmas, pleased to escape from the city, the school, and Baggotty and Foxley. In the seven weeks since October the countryside had been transformed. The hedges and ditches were bare, the wet fields forlorn without cattle. In the lane the trees froze stiff in the

cold, all dark against the sky except the garroted oak with
its cloak of evergreen ivy. In the house the wind filled the
kitchen with a shiver whenever anyone opened the door,
and they all made a circle round the fire except her father,
who slept on his back on the couch. In church she knelt
beside her mother on Christmas Eve while the choir sang
carols in semidarkness. At the Gloria all the lights came on,
brightening her memories of other Christmases, of things
once familiar but now strange, of unconsidered kindnesses,
of ceremonies of innocence forever drowned.

She never went to Mass in Dublin because she could not
bring herself to worship with strangers. Now she was
among friends and neighbors, but the thought that she was
really a stranger in disguise made her weep silently into her
scarf. Her life was a colander of spouting water. She had so
much to give, so much bodily warmth and comfort, so
much intelligent support and sympathy, yet all she knew
was indifference and waste.

On Christmas morning she went to her uncle's to cook
his Christmas dinner.

"We'll eat Australian," he said, taking three enormous T-
bone steaks from the fridge.

"You'll have the best of both hemispheres, Patricia,"
said Hugh. "You'll have steak with us today and cold
turkey at home tomorrow."

She grilled the steaks and fried some onions and tomatoes on the gas cooker while the parsnips and potatoes
cooked on the range. Lar opened a bottle of claret for her
and Hugh and began telling her about Christmas in the
Northern Territory before the war. Since Hugh's arrival he
talked a lot about Australia. She listened because she
wished to know about his past, but she regretted that it was
a form of reminiscence in which she could not share.

Hugh sat opposite her with his back to the window,
blocking the grey light that filtered through the condensation on the panes. He and her uncle had more in common

than her mother thought. They were both serious and self-sufficient, with a sense of humor that showed only among friends. Hugh, however, lacked her uncle's sensitivity. He looked vaguely unmade, or perhaps not quite finished, but when he sat down and placed his broad hands on his knees he imparted a sense of immobilized strength that made her wish to sit beside him.

On the morning of Boxing Day Desmond Deeny came round to take her for a walk in the woods. Outside all was bright and blue with a sharp sun and no cloud, and the north wind so icy that it burned her cheeks and pinched the lobes of her ears. They made their way between the trees, scuffing oak and chestnut leaves with their wellingtons, jumping over wet patches, and flinging broken sticks in the air. The trees were close and interwoven, naked but for the oaks which still retained some withered leaves on their lower branches. Desmond, picking one of them, said that it was like paper, put her standing against the trunk, and kissed her on the mouth, his nose cold against her cheek. Then he thrust both his hands down inside her knickers and began kneading her buttocks as if they were lumps of dough.

"Your bum is freezing," he said.

"And so is your snout."

"A cold bum is a sign of a warm heart."

"I think we should keep walking," she said. "It's not very erotic weather."

"Have you many friends in Dublin?" he asked after a while.

"I share a flat with a girl from Ballyhaunis."

"Do you know any men?"

"I know the men who teach at my school."

"Patricia, I can't help feeling that you're unhappy."

"Who is happy?"

"I would be happy if I knew you were."

"Happiness is a gift from heaven. You are born with it as

you are born with blue eyes or red hair. It cannot be bought—"

"But it can be foolishly thrown away. Many people make themselves unhappy by seeking things they were not made to find or things that are not there to be found. What do you want, Patricia?"

"I want to be myself."

"But you are yourself."

"My true self, the seeking self, is never where I am. When I'm in the city, it's in the country; and when I'm in the country, it's in the city."

"I wish I could help you, Patricia."

"If we can't help ourselves, how can we help other people?"

She was almost glad when the holiday was over, though the thought of school was like a douche of icy water. The douche became a reality on the first day back when Elsynge took her aside and told her that he had been looking at the science exercises over Christmas.

"Do you ever actually read them?" he asked.

"Of course I read them and correct them too." She threw up her head with a spirited show of shock.

"You never correct misspellings."

"I'm the science, not the English teacher."

"May I remind you of Directive 18B: 'All teachers are English teachers. All teachers will be required to enlarge the pupils' vocabularies and above all to correct misspellings.' There is also Directive 14: 'All teachers will give a minimum of two written exercises in their subject every week, bearing in mind that writing not only reinforces memory but also makes the ideal of scholarship—the exact man.' Have you given two written exercises a week, Miss Teeling?"

"Yes, as far as I know."

"There were sixteen weeks in the Michaelmas term. You gave exactly seventeen exercises."

"It was all I had time for."

"Then you should have told me, Miss Teeling. Directive 26 says: 'Any departure from the Staff Directives, be it witting or unwitting, must be reported to the Headmaster forthwith.' Good day, Miss Teeling. And remember, do not bear a grudge, because your Headmaster never does."

She resolved to keep her temper, to see the school year out without laying a finger on Elsynge. After a drink with Foxley in McGuffin's, she went home in tolerable good humor and began preparing dinner for herself and Monica. At five-thirty the telephone rang in the hall and Bernard's voice came through, gentle and clear with a hint of uncertainty.

"Sorry about ringing you, but it's the only way I can reach you since you won't talk to me in the house. A bachelor friend of mine who owns a house in Booterstown is going to the country this weekend. He has given me the key so that I may do some writing in solitude and feed his beloved cats when I have done. Now, I wondered if you would spend Sunday with me in Booterstown, not the evening but the whole day."

"Why the whole day?"

"I want to talk to you at great length. All over Christmas I looked forward to your return."

She was flattered to think that her company meant so much to him, so she made a note of the address and told him to expect her about eleven-thirty on Sunday morning.

He had been writing in the living room before she arrived, sitting in shirt sleeves before a portable typewriter with a sheaf of typed pages on the table. It was a large, high-ceilinged room with apricot walls, vaguely surrealist paintings, and an enormous cheese plant that obscured the french windows. There was no carpet on the floor, and the varnished boards creaked infuriatingly under her low heels.

"I want this day to be perfect," he said. "I want us to talk and be ourselves without possibility of interruption.

But first I must finish what I'm doing. I shan't be long. I've only got to do the last paragraph."

She moved closer to him, slightly shocked at the atmosphere of male homosexuality in the room.

"What are you writing?"

"A weightless short story for *The New Yorker*."

"Weightless as opposed to weighty? You mean not authoritative, not the product of serious thought?"

"No, I mean lacking in mass. All *New Yorker* stories are weightless. They float like gossamer in the air. For a moment you think you see them. You snatch at them and they are gone."

"Have you ever sold a story to *The New Yorker* before?"

"No, but an American I met last night told me that you could live in comfort on three *New Yorker* stories a year. Think of it, a mere twelve thousand words."

"What's the catch? The rejection slips?"

"Now leave me in peace, can't you see I'm writing?"

She wandered into the bright and clinical kitchen, an operating theater with a fridge that contained only a bottle of milk.

"Don't bother to cook lunch," he said when she came back. "We'll have bread and cheese and a bottle of wine."

"But there is no bread and cheese let alone wine. I'd better go out and get some."

They ate at the deal table in the kitchen, enclosed by white walls hung with an array of bronze pots and six unnerving carving knives.

"Why does he need so many scalpels?" she asked.

"Interesting that you should notice. I think the quiddity of this kitchen is to be found in them. Now, if I were describing this kitchen—"

"Have you finished your story?"

"No, I got stuck on the last sentence. If only I could believe in the validity of experience. Am I, I ask myself, a blank screen on which the Great Projectionist is casting fantasies which are not my own."

"You flatter yourself. The Great Projectionist has more to do than pester you with problems of ontology."

"This morning I asked myself, 'What is today? Why is it different from yesterday or the day before?' While you were on holiday, I dug the garden, thinking I'd never seen such a day. I leaned on my fork and counted the things that made it different—the purity of the sky, the keenness of the air, robins hopping and blackbirds searching for worms, a pair of incorruptible knickers on the clothesline in the next garden and a woman with a butch bottom stooping beneath them, the blister on my palm, and the smell of twigs burning—yet these things, either singly or together, failed to express the essence of the day. I went up to the bathroom for a pee and a better view. The garden was not the same. There were more birds because I had gone and the seedbeds seemed more tidy because I was farther away. The shadow of the fence made a more obvious pattern on the grass and the stooping woman was smaller, her bottom less overwhelming. I was filled with an intimation of the impossibility of writing about anything, of communicating anything. I knew that if I went to my typewriter that minute, I should capture an entirely different day, or perhaps a thousand days—one for everyone who read my description."

"The goose that laid the golden egg didn't do so by looking up her crotch," Patricia said.

"I wouldn't be myself if I laid without watching."

"Is that why you brought me here, to tell me about writing?"

"No, I asked you here to help me conduct an experiment."

"What kind of experiment?"

"A pseudoscientific experiment of first degree standard."

"Say no more. When do we begin?"

"Not yet. I must first make an obscene telephone call."

"Is that necessary?"

"Not necessary, but unfortunately desirable."

"Desirable for whom?"

"For the recipient, of course."

In disbelief she watched him put his hankerchief over the mouthpiece and dial a number he obviously knew. Impatiently, he tapped a foot, and then suddenly he was speaking in the overprecise tones of the Austrian osteopath.

"You've never seen me, darling, but I follow you to the shops nearly every day, walking with measured step behind you as you wheel home your groceries in a pram. I note your crystal-glass ankles, your Grecian bum as your crimson knickers blush through the magnolia of your skirt. Like an acolyte, I raise your chasuble and have you, not over a barrel, but your pram. And not because I wish to fill it with anything less inert than lamb's liver but because I love the lilt of your instep, the silk-softness of your footfalls, and the erotic wrinklings of your crotchless panties. Why crotchless, you may, in your innocence, ask. But if they weren't crotchless, how could I have you over a pram while you're waiting for the traffic lights to change? Be sure to go shopping tomorrow at 3:42 P.M. I shall shadow you with naked foot and puncture you twice *in petto* before the R.D.S. clock croaks four. But look where I come, the flow of cream-colored blood marbling the glorious crimson of your bum . . ."

Horrified, she tugged the phone from his hand and put it down.

"How can you frighten some innocent girl with your disgusting ravings?"

"But that's my wife. If a man can't make an obscene phone call to his wife, I don't know what the world is coming to."

"Did she know it was you?"

"Of course not. She thought it was the Austrian osteopath."

"But you're the Austrian osteopath."

"Last August Gladys started getting obscene telephone calls from a man who described himself as an Austrian osteopath. At first she was afraid and asked me to listen in, but gradually she began to look forward to them and finally she wouldn't let me listen in at all. Just before Christmas the phone calls stopped. Gladys got depressed. She wouldn't let me answer the phone; she thought that every time it rang it was for her. I couldn't let her eat her heart out over some knicker fetishist with a continental accent, so to cheer her up I began ringing her myself. Now I'm in a fix. I can't just stop, and though I'm a writer I'm running out of things to say about her bum."

"I think it's disgusting. You're treating her like a rat in a laboratory experiment."

"For all I know she may be in an experiment, but I can tell you I'm not the scientist. She's obsessed with growing old, with losing what she describes as her 'looks.' She stands before the bedroom mirror, studying the bluish tinge of her thighs. Last week she told me they were the thighs of a plucked chicken, but yesterday she asked me to run my fingers over the coarse goose flesh and tell her twice that it was smooth. I'd tell her anything out of pity, to shore up what's left of her self-esteem, but when she threatens me with a bread knife—"

"Why are you telling me all this?"

"Because I want to forget it. But now it's time for our little experiment."

"I'm not conducting any experiment after that phone call."

"You're irrational for a scientist."

"And you're insensitive."

"We'll go for a walk then and watch the sun go down."

"Behind chimney pots?"

"All right. We'll go down to the sea and look at where the sun will come up tomorrow."

It was cold by the sea, the water flat and grey, the clouds in the east tinged with dirty crimson. Wrapped against the wind, she walked at his side while his pipe glowed like Uncle Lar's. Yet he would never achieve the solidity of

Uncle Lar. She would never sit beside him on a cold day under a hedge and find warmth in his tobacco smoke crossing her face like blue silk. The Bray train clanked above them and she asked him to take her back.

"Come here and sit beside me," he said when he had lit the gas fire.

"I don't think it would be a good idea. I came on condition that you wouldn't touch me."

"But I'm not going to touch you, you suspicious creature."

"And what are you going to do?"

"I'd like your help with my experiment. I don't know if I've ever mentioned it, but I'm a very keen dowser."

"You look for water with a hazel rod?"

"Among other things. I sometimes look for metal, for example."

"Wouldn't a metal detector be more efficient?"

"More efficient perhaps, but not such fun."

"And what do I do while you're dowsing?"

"I shall ask you to hide a coin—a tenpenny piece—in your underclothes, and with the help of my dowsing rod I'll try to find it."

"Well, I must say you're a trier—and original too."

"I'm being perfectly serious." He spoke solemnly with offended dignity.

"Was this why you invited me here?"

"Not entirely. Motives are never so simple. Will you play the game?"

"What happens if you find the coin?"

"I shall be pleased."

"And if you don't find it?"

"I shall be disappointed."

"I don't have to hide it in my underclothes. Much simpler to put it in my pocket, for example."

"That would hardly be in keeping with the spirit of the experiment."

"And what is the spirit of the experiment?"

"To increase the fund of human pleasure rather than knowledge." He drew a coin from his pocket and tossed it.

"Heads, I find. Tails, I fail. Ah-ha, it's heads, an omen of success," he laughed. "Now, you hide that coin somewhere in your underclothes while I'm out of the room, and call me when you're ready."

When he came back, he pulled a hazel dowsing rod from his hold-all and put her lying on her back on the sofa. Then he bent over her like a doctor, holding the rod in both hands, moving it up and down over her breasts and stomach and between her legs.

"I'm disappointed that you don't recite a little incantation," she joked.

He paid no heed, but with half-closed eyes lingered over the hollow of her groin.

"I give up," he said impatiently. "There's too much electricity in the air, or perhaps in your underclothes. I'm getting an indication of water all right, but that's obviously from your bladder."

"Don't worry," she laughed. "I played a little trick on you. The coin is under the vase on the mantelpiece."

"Now what was the point of that?" he demanded humorlessly.

"All right. If you leave the room again, I'll hide it in my clothes this time."

"Not in your clothes, remember. In your underclothes."

When he came back again, she was lying on the sofa, smiling with conscious superiority. He bent over her again with half-closed eyes, deep in concentration.

"I've found it!" he almost shouted, excited as a schoolboy. "It's there below your navel." He pointed with the rod.

"I don't know how you did it, but you're right."

"Well, let's see it, then."

"If you leave the room for a moment—"

"What if you've played another trick on me? How am I

to know you've got it in your knickers unless I see you recover it?"

"You'll simply have to take my word for it, even though it may not be as scientific as you would wish."

"Why?"

"You don't really expect me to fish a coin from my underclothes before your eyes, do you?"

"I don't see why not. I'm not a prurient adolescent. I'm a jaded married man who has seen a pair of knickers before."

"That's got nothing to do with it. I'm going to the loo," she said, getting to her feet.

In a flash he had put one hand round her waist and lifted her skirt with the other. She tried to push him away but his hand was already inside her knickers.

"Eureka! I've struck silver."

"Let me go, let me go," she shouted.

She tried to swing away from him with all the strength of her body. He lost his balance and fell on top of her on the sofa, stroking her pubic hair and belly with his hand. He was kissing her on the neck and cheek, seeking her mouth, smothering her with the urgency of his tobacco breath. She pushed hard with one hand against the back of the sofa and fell on top of him on the floor.

"Oh, fuck!" he yelled. "You've bitten me."

"You deserved it, you brute, after promising not to touch me." She stood over him as he patted his ear lobe with his hand.

"You're as strong as an ox." He gave her back the handkerchief in which she had wrapped the coin.

"It's just as well."

"Pax," he laughed, holding out his hand. "First we'll have a drink, and then I'll cook you dinner."

"I'm not spending another minute here with you," she said, going to the door.

"Please, Patricia, don't ruin the whole day. If you don't want to stay here, we'll go to a pub and eat out. Be reasonable. Can't you see that it was unpremeditated. My enthusiasm for the mantic art simply got the better of me."

"Where are we going to eat?" she asked, conscious of the mollifying effect of his offer but aware of her determination not to pay for dinner.

"We'll go into town. I know a little place called the Flounder where they do lovely sole."

"I hope you can afford it because I spent all my money on lunch."

After she bathed his ear in hot water and painted it with iodine, they drove into town in their separate cars. They had two or three drinks in The Inkwell and listened to two middle-aged poets discoursing on something called biomass and the simplest method of weighing a live elephant in the bush. At nine o'clock, when the poets in their obsession with elephants began a heated discussion about the weight of a pink elephant's molars, she said to Bernard that she'd heard enough nonsense for one evening, that it was now well past dinnertime.

"I'm afraid I'm short of money, Patricia. All I have is a fiver. I hope a plate of fish and chips will do."

She could not help laughing, it seemed so much in character. He was always short of money except at the bookmaker's. He always had a pint when she was buying and a half when it was his own round, and yet he wasn't mean. It was just that he would go without food and drink in order to have a pound to put on a horse.

They sat at a Formica-topped table with two teenagers who drowned their chips in vinegar, dotted their fish with gouts of tomato sauce, and ate as if they were standing on a street corner chewing gum. At last they left, and then Bernard reached across the table to touch her hand.

"No, Bernard, if we are to continue seeing each other, you mustn't touch me."

"I can't stand this any longer. I want you to marry me and have done with it. It's the only solution."

"Don't be ridiculous. Why should you want to marry me?"

"Because you are more real to me than any other person I've ever met. I have a theory that we all fall in love with the person who seems most real to us, the person we can think of in the same way that we think of ourselves. Am I real to you?"

"How can you expect to be real if you make obscene phone calls to your wife and search for coins with a dowsing rod in my undies? For all I know, you may be real in another place at another time, but I can assure you that you're not real to me here in Dublin on this cold January night. Anyhow, why do you bring up marriage when you're married already?"

"Only in name. Gladys is tired of me. She'd be happier with a bank manager who'd buy her mink coats and take her on Mediterranean cruises. She's obsessed with money, Grafton Street, and eating out. We can't go on much longer. With or without you, we'll break up."

"Do what you like, but leave me out of it."

"Gladys and I will get an English divorce, and you and I will be free to marry."

"But I don't want to marry you."

"We'll talk about it more calmly when we meet next week."

"We won't be meeting next week. I think tonight has proved that we can't be friends without causing havoc and upheaval."

"You take life far too seriously."

"No, I don't. And to prove it, I'll end by asking you an unserious question."

"About the Austrian osteopath? I think I can see it coming."

"No, about the knickers on the clothesline in the garden. Why were they incorruptible?"

"Because they were sea-green."

"You should be compiling crosswords, not short stories, you old fraud."

They said goodbye outside the fish-and-chip shop, and she drove home in a fog that came up through the floor of the car and gripped her ankles with icy fingers. The world was a place of darkness and cold, and you needed all the love and companionship you could find to light a fire that would glow in the night and warm your freezing hands. Baggotty, Foxley, and Monica—those were the three that had helped to keep her fire alight, and now there were only two. Bernard heaped more brands on the fire than the others, but if he increased the light or the heat he took the good out of it by scoffing at what he had done. He had an eerie effect on her, as if he were more of a ghost than a man, as if he belonged to a world between two lights, where neither day nor night ever reigned supreme. During her waking hours he was shadowy and insubstantial, but at night he nudged her in dreams that in the morning left a vestige of unease, reminding her of a clump of rushes on her uncle's farm with a hollow in the center where a wild hare had lain.

She wiped a tear from the corner of her eye and tried to think of Foxley. He was above all a harmless man, gentle in manner and amusing to talk to, the kind of man who would ask permission to rub your tummy rather than take you by force with the aid of a dowsing rod. Perhaps she had been unfair in neglecting him. Perhaps a man who bought her so many drinks deserved more of her attention than he'd been getting lately.

When she got home, Monica was sitting on the *grand lit*, blow-drying her wispy hair.

"Do you ever feel afraid of what a man might do to you?" she asked Patricia when they were both in bed.

"No, why should I?"

"Men are so strong."

"But I'm even stronger."

"You're lucky in Robert. He's lightly built, delicate, and not too heavy."

"I agree he's lightly built but I'm as innocent of his weight as you are."

"I often think of the weight of men in the middle of the night. Some of them are so big, they'd wreck a lightly built girl."

"To think of men like that is a sin against Hope, a sin that will not be forgiven lightly," Patricia teased.

"It's all right for you. You can look after yourself, but I'm as light as a coracle. Last summer I saw a coracle on the sea at Killiney and it was bobbing like a cork on the water. There was a shirtless man in it, and he was rising and falling like a jockey in a steeplechase."

"You see things no one else sees. I'm sure I never saw a coracle at Killiney."

"Does your chin ever get raw from going out with men?"

"Not my chin, but my nerves."

"It's my chin that gets raw. Most men, even those that shave morning and evening, have rough skin, and they can't kiss without chafing. I often put Oil of Ulay on my chin before going out with them, but it's still no good. Of course, you're lucky. Robert has such lovely skin."

"I can see you've been thinking about him."

"I can't help thinking about his balloons, they're so original."

"You think about him more than I do."

"You're not serious about him, then?"

"He takes me out for drinks and he keeps me amused. That's all."

"He rang me today and asked me out one evening."

"Well, are you going?"

"Do you think I should?"

"It's entirely up to you, not for me to say."

"It's only to the theater, to see a play by Ibsen I'd never heard of."

"It will be a dull evening," Patricia predicted. "Ibsen is far too serious."

"But I like serious plays. You can hear every word the actors say because there's no laughing."

"You've made up your mind, so?"

"I didn't say yes but I didn't say no either. I wanted to ask you first because our friendship is more important to me than Robert."

"If that's the case, I think you should go," said Patricia.

7

The following morning the staff room shook with laughter. She was greeted with smiles as she entered, and the classics master told her to relax, that the Deity had gone down with flu.

"I predicted this last Friday," said the Irish master as if he himself had been the vector of the very bug that had laid the Deity low. "His moustache was dripping like the eaves of a Donegal cottage in December and Mrs. Elsynge brought him two linen handkerchiefs with his leek soup at eleven."

"How long will he be under the weather?" Patricia wondered.

"This is an annual visitation," said Robert Foxley. "He never recovers before the spring equinox. Feel free to touch your pupils however and wherever you please."

At lunchtime Mrs. Elsynge came into the staff room and said that Mr. Elsynge had been delirious in the night, that the doctor was puzzled, and that she herself had told her husband that he must give up his elocution classes. From the window Patricia watched her go back to the house with her gown billowing and her grey hair standing like a stook in the wind. If she had not been bowlegged, she would have resembled a rampant cart horse. As it was, she walked as if she bore an enormous grapefruit between her thighs which she was at pains not to drop like a turd in the Quad.

"She walks in beauty like the night," said the maths master, who liked to think from time to time that there was more to life than dodecahedrons.

"Not like the night but with gluteal eloquence," said Foxley. "As a Christian I envy her because she is alone in wishing her husband a speedy recovery."

All day Patricia enjoyed the luxury of teaching without having to worry about Elsynge. She felt so untrammeled that in the last period she gave the pupils an exercise to keep them quiet and took her ease at the back of the class. She imagined him with a hot-water bottle to his back and a coal-tar burner under his nose while he coughed and spluttered and muttered directives in his well-deserved delirium. She did not wish him irrevocable harm, however. She did not pray for his death. She merely hoped that his flu would leave him weak and disheartened, in need of a long convalescence, preferably in the southern hemisphere where the tsetse fly might bite him, but not too painfully, bestowing on him a mild form of sleeping sickness from which he would recover after the end of the summer term, after she had left St. Columba's forever.

At four she walked out the gate with Foxley and faced him confidently in the road, but he smiled as if he knew more of life than she and said that he would see her tomorrow. It was the first time since September that they had not gone for a drink after school. Somewhat saddened, she walked home, trying not to apportion blame. She had thought of Robert as a lasting friend. She had enjoyed his company without wishing to pant beneath him on the nearest divan, she had laughed dutifully when he said that God had gone down with schooliosis, and whenever he asked her to blow up one of his balloons she did so without batting an eyelid. She had seen him as a brother, but evidently he had not seen her as a sister. Like most modern men, he could not conceive of a relationship with a woman who did not flatter his insecure ego in sexual surrender. Was there, she wondered, a man so manly, so contemptuous of the common expectation, that he would as lief have the ease of conversation as the kerfuffle of copulation?

She hurried home, remembering that Gladys Baggotty had invited her to coffee with a hint that she had something to tell her, perhaps something light-hearted for a change. A whispered hint about the sexual obsessions of the Austrian osteopath? She picked up a letter from her mother in the hallway and knocked on the dark green door. When it did not open, she knocked again and listened.

"Anyone home?" she shouted, wondering if Gladys might have fallen asleep on the less frayed of the sofas, which was her favorite.

The door opened slowly and Bernard stood stoopingly before her.

"Is Gladys in?" she asked.

"Yes, come in."

He looked drawn and pale and he turned up the palms of his hands in a doubtful gesture of invitation.

"Sit down," he said, lighting a cigarette.

"I didn't know you smoked cigarettes."

"I only smoke them between catastrophes."

"Will you tell her I'm here?" she said, aware of the constraint that lay like fog between them. But perhaps it was merely the gloom of the flat, the heavy secondhand furniture, the green-painted walls, and the net curtains which should have been white but were yellow for want of a wash.

"Where is Gladys?" she asked when he did not answer.

"A terrible thing has happened. Gladys has been murdered." He put both hands to his face.

"Murdered?"

"I came home fifteen minutes ago to find her lying on the bed—but don't make me think about it."

92

"Have you rung the police?"

"No."

"Where is she?"

"In the bedroom, but you mustn't look. I looked and I don't want ever to look again."

"I'm going to ring the police." She got to her feet.

"No, don't, Patricia. It isn't that simple." He crossed the room and stood between her and the door.

"You said it was murder, didn't you?"

"Yes, and at the moment the evidence points to me. Whoever did it came in without having to force a window or a door, and he left without touching a thing. The motive could not have been robbery. The murderer probably knew her, he may even have had a key. So I am the prime suspect as any reader of detective fiction will tell you."

"But what earthly motive could you have had?"

"Perhaps I wished to end a burdensome marriage. Perhaps I wished to get married again."

He stood before her, pale, serious, and unshaven, an Angle rather than an angel.

"You say it must have been someone she knew . . . have you any idea who?"

"Oh, yes, the man who was always ringing her up to talk about the fragrance of her knickers."

"But that was you!" she said, not realizing the import of her words until she heard them.

"You see what I mean. I knew I was in the hot seat as soon as I saw her dead."

"Don't be ridiculous."

"I forgot to tell you. After I spoke to her from Booterstown on Sunday, he rang her with a mysterious request. He wanted to meet her to do a certain thing."

"What thing?"

"She wouldn't tell me—or at least she wouldn't tell me the whole story. All she would say is that he wanted her to cook him a meal, to make him a very special omelette. Like you, I can only guess what it was."

"And your guess is?"

"That it was to be a knicker omelette."

"How absurd!"

"She said herself that the meal was a beautiful and at the same time a comical thing."

"Are you telling the truth or are you making fun of me?"

"It's too serious for fun. He could have met Gladys. She could have invited him back to the flat to cook the omelette and—you know the rest."

"How did she die?"

"She was stabbed in the left breast with the bread knife."

"Another coincidence. You told me she threatened to stab you with the bread knife."

"As you say, another coincidence."

"I want to see her."

"No, you mustn't, it's too horrible." He stood at bay with his back to the bedroom door.

"Now, sit down, Bernard, and I'll ring the police."

"No, no, I want to think before I act. And I want you to go up to your room as if you hadn't seen me today. When you're questioned, say you know nothing. Do you understand?"

"I don't see the point of cloaking anything. I have nothing to hide. Have you?"

"We live in ambiguities, in a world in which everything is seen at once by a good eye and an evil eye, in which the most innocent action takes on the shadow of the dark. Until the police have finished their sport, I shall not be concerned with the truth but with clearing myself of all suspicion. No, don't say a word. I know what I'm doing. And another thing, you mustn't say that we've been seeing each other on the quiet. For all you know, I'm just the chap in the flat downstairs."

"I'll tell the police everything I know, which is next to nothing. And I'll tell them we used to meet for a drink—if they ask. To conceal it would be to imply guilt. And I'm not guilty."

"But can't you see the implication of what you say?"

"What is that?"

"That *I* am guilty."

"Nonsense, Bernard."

"Then, why didn't you say, 'We're not guilty'?"

She went up to the flat and sat by the window, looking down into the street, waiting for the police to arrive. She waited an hour but nothing happened. It was five o'clock; Monica would soon be home. She prepared some vegetables to accompany what was left of the Sunday joint, but at six Monica rang to say that she was going out with Robert, that she would not be home for dinner. Patricia ate alone, and still no police arrived. She wondered if she should go down to see Bernard again to try to make him see sense, and then she thought that the best way to forget was to go out for a drink and perhaps to a dance.

She walked to town to save petrol and to give herself time to think. A fog hung over the canal, the sodium lights were daubs of yellow on dirty canvas, and the buses ran noiselessly as if the fog had carpeted the road. She drank four pints before the thin gloom drifted from before her eyes, and then she heard music and saw sleepwalkers moving in a dance. It was an evening of small men, the tallest reached only to her ear. She stood close to him because she wished for a man who would buy her the odd drink in the evenings between now and the end of the school year, but he showed her his back and the man who faced her was so strong and silent that the only women he would question would be the women in his dreams. Again she stood near the tallest man, but she was tapped on the wrist by a light-footed teenager with an oily quiff who sheltered beneath her breasts and thrust his right leg between her knees as they glided up the floor. No word passed between them, no nod or wink, only the insistence of the erection in his trouser leg and then the feeble beat of the glans against her inner thigh as he disembogued, the cheeks of his upturned face suffused with brightening red, his eyelids heavy with the consciousness of lust too easily satisfied. She disengaged herself and without a word left him standing in the middle of the floor. She hurried to the cloakroom, fighting back tears, her mind empty of all but the memory of Robert Foxley in McGuffin's "going to the bog to disembogue."

Two panda cars were parked in the road when she got home, but there was no sign of the police in the hall or on the stairs. She made herself a cup of instant coffee, picked up one of Monica's books, and waited. The knock, when it came, was soft rather than peremptory, and the man who took off his hat to her seemed broader than the door.

"I'm Detective Inspector Farrelly."

He unbuttoned his navy blue mackintosh, reminding her of the man with closh whom Monica said she saw in D'Olier Street. His wide face was round like the lid of a skillet pot and his wider neck sprang like a tree trunk from his too tight collar. For a moment she hesitated, wishing that Monica were home, but then he smiled at her with his cleft chin and she invited him in. Sitting opposite her with the cup of coffee she offered him, he smiled again, the well-spaced teeth of his prominent lower jaw concealing the upper row. Quietly and slowly, he told her that Mrs. Baggotty downstairs had been found murdered, that he was interviewing all the occupants of the house, and that he would like to know if she knew the deceased.

"I knew her only the way you know neighbors in the city," Patricia said after registering appropriate shock and disbelief. "We met from time to time on the stairs and sometimes she would invite me in for coffee."

"Did she have lots of friends?"

"She had at least one friend whom she visited on Wednesdays."

"A woman friend?"

"Yes."

"Was she talkative?"

"She listened more often than she talked, but now and again she would stretch her legs over coffee and reminisce about shopping."

"Did she ever talk about her husband?"

"Only to say that he was once a well-off journalist who turned himself into a poorly paid writer."

"Do you know Mr. Baggotty?"

"Not very well. We sometimes talk in the hallway, and once or twice he took me to a pub for a drink."

"What did he talk about?"

"His writing mostly. Which is why I know so little about him."

"What does his writing say about him?"

"It's too confused to say much. I understand the words but not the paragraphs."

"A cryptographer. No good to a policeman," he smiled.

He made notes as she spoke, moving his heavy, closely shaven jaw as if his writing depended on it and smiling disarmingly at the end of each question. He reminded her of a man she had once seen in an advertisement for razor blades, and she could not help feeling that he was a good man, kind to his wife and understanding with his colleagues.

"Where are you from?" He picked up his mack from the sofa.

"I'm from Laois."

"Ah, farming country. I'm from farming country myself, a short way south of Naas. Gardening in the Dublin suburbs is no substitute."

As he laughed, she imagined his face rising over a hedge like a full moon, and she thought that country people should never leave the country.

"Do you live here alone?" He opened the door.

"I share with another girl. She's out now but she'll be back soon."

"I'll see her in the morning."

When Monica returned, she sat calmly on the edge of the bed and said:

"I knew it all along. I knew it would end in murder. All that shouting and breaking of crockery couldn't end in anything else."

"But we don't know who murdered her," Patricia protested. "For all we know it could have been some madman."

"Never believe it. It was Mr. Baggotty."

"I'll leave that to the police."

"What did you tell them?"

"All I know, which is very little. I'm glad I didn't know more. I don't want to go to court and have my name in the evening papers."

"You're right," said Monica. "It's one thing to know, but in court it's another to convince the jury that you know. Barristers twist words out of shape and reason. They ask you questions with answers that tell more about you than the culprit they're defending."

The following afternoon two women from the road stopped Patricia as she came home from school.

"You poor girl!" said the first. "You must be frightened out of your wits."

"It's a shock," said Patricia.

"But you took it calm," the second woman marvelled.

"And to think you shared a house with her," the first seemed truly amazed.

"Just fancy that!" The second woman smacked her lips.

"I didn't know her very well." Patricia tried to escape.

"Oh, she was a queer one, God have mercy on her." The first plucked Patricia's sleeve. "Dressed common and shopped in Grafton Street."

"Nothing but the best for some." Her friend nudged Patricia's elbow.

"She never looked healthy," the first explained.

"She was a quiet person," Patricia told them. "I never heard her say a harsh word about anyone."

"Himself's the cold fish." The first raised a snob's profile to the breeze.

"Is he English?" asked the second.

"Yes," said Patricia.

"It tells," said the first. "Walks about like there was a bad smell under his nose."

"He spoke to me once," said the second. "And the next day he just looked far away over my head."

"The *Independent* said he had a play on television," the first confided.

"It's an ill wind . . ." her friend said. "Now he'll have more to write about—not wishing harm on any poor soul, you understand."

"God between us and the devil." The first woman looked prayerful and Patricia left them in the road.

Early in the evening a man in a donkey jacket knocked on the door. He spoke to her with a girlish lisp and puckered his lips as if he were hoping for a kiss. He had not come about kissing, however. He was a journalist from one of the Sunday papers and all he craved was ten minutes of her valuable leisure time. Did she know the deceased? Did she have any theories about the murder? Had she been interviewed by the police? Did she know how the murderer gained entry? Was she afraid he might come back? He had tried to get in touch with Mr. Baggotty but he seemed to be incommunicado, poor man. When Patricia told him that she had nothing to say, he offered to write her a check for one hundred pounds there and then if she gave him a description of the inside of Baggotty's flat. And when he told her that the police were being suspiciously secretive and that the public had a right to know, she threatened to ring Detective Inspector Farrelly if he didn't hop it that very minute.

They buried Gladys on a wet Wednesday at eleven

o'clock in the morning. Less than a score of mourners came to the funeral, most of them men who knew Bernard. Gladys, it seemed, had no friends apart from Patricia and two or three women in the road. Bernard sat behind the coffin, staring wildly at the officiating priest, a bald roly-poly of a man with foxlike eyes and a voice that rose with each biblical reference to a blood-curdling yelp. He told them that Death tried to rival Procrastination as the thief of time, but that Death was only a would-be thief, doomed forever to disappointment. "Christ being raised from the dead dieth no more," he yelped. "Death hath no more dominion over him. Death is now but a shadow of his former self. Because of the Resurrection, this most cunning of thieves can steal only trash. He can filch the decaying body, but the glorious spirit runs like water through his fingers."

"Lies, lies, lies." Bernard rose from his seat.

"Death hath no more dominion over her," yelped the priest.

"Dead, dead." Bernard strode down the aisle. "She's dead as a trussed turkey," he called from the door.

The priest continued his address with a pious reference to the ravages of grief, and Bernard did not reappear until the coffin was being placed in the hearse to be taken to the cemetery.

"He's an atheist," Monica said on the way home.

"He was overwrought," Patricia said quietly.

"Now he owes God two deaths, not one," Monica pronounced, but Patricia did not answer.

At the inquest Bernard was the first to give evidence. He said that he had spent the early afternoon in the National Library, that he returned to the flat at four and found his wife naked on the bed, covered in blood with a bread knife through her breast. He must have rushed from the room, probably to ring the police, because the next thing he remembered was waking up on the floor of the lounge at seven. He had fainted and could not remember clearly. He felt distressed for no apparent reason, and it was eight o'clock before he rediscovered the body and rang the police. He told about an anonymous telephone caller who upset his wife the previous Sunday, and how she would not tell him what he said, only that it was obscene.

He spoke slowly and so convincingly that Patricia almost found herself believing every word. She had to remind herself that she had spoken to him at four, which meant that he had four hours alone with the body before he rang the police, four hours in which he might have expunged finger-prints or done whatever murderers do when they tamper with the evidence. Yet she could not believe that he was guilty. When she looked at the suffering in his face, her heart so cried out against the thought that she felt defiled for having entertained it.

Monica's voice trembled like her hands as she gave evidence. She stared at the floor, revolving the ring on her finger, and said that she knew nothing of Mr. and Mrs. Baggotty except that they'd had the most unearthly rows. Patricia said that she'd had coffee with Mrs. Baggotty from time to time but that she never mentioned obscene tele-phone calls or indeed anything else that might shed light on her death. Bernard sat with his head bent but he looked straight at her when the coroner asked if she had heard rows in the other flat.

"I can't say I have," she replied.

"Did you hear anything?"

"Noises, mainly late at night."

"What kind of noises?"

"They were too vague to describe. They may have been voices. I often thought that they could have come from the radio."

She did not know why she said it. All she knew was that she could not say anything that might make life more difficult for Bernard Baggotty. On the way home Monica was silent, but no sooner had they closed the door of the flat behind them than she accused Patricia of contradicting her evidence.

"But I didn't contradict your evidence," Patricia told her. "I just wasn't as confident as you."

"But you never contradicted me when I used to say that they were throwing crockery at each other."

"That was because I thought you were joking."

"You make me feel guilty," Monica said. "As if I had something against Mr. Baggotty."

"What could you have against Mr. Baggotty?"

"That's right. I've never spoken to him except to say good morning or good evening, and he never spoke to me except to say 'Good day to you.' "

A week later, as she returned from school, Bernard opened the door of the flat and asked her in. He looked pale and preoccupied, his hair uncombed, his shoes unlaced, and a stare in his eyes as if he were trying to make out someone else in the distance behind her.

"I want to talk to you," he said. "I don't seem to have talked to anyone except the police for the past fortnight. They have interviewed me over and over, a different man each time asking the same tiresome questions but in a different order."

"You've got to help them if they're to catch the murderer."

"You're being ironic, of course."

"I don't see what's ironic about it."

"Can't you see that they think I'm the murderer?"

"Why didn't you tell the truth at the inquest. It would have been simpler."

"Why didn't *you* tell the truth?" he asked.

"How could I without contradicting you?"

"I know what I'm doing. They spent nearly a day in the flat, going over it with a fine-tooth comb. I knew they were determined to get me. I wasn't going to hand them a ready-made case against myself on a plate. Whether or not I spent four hours in a faint is neither here nor there when my freedom, such as it is, is at stake."

"But don't you want them to catch the murderer? Without wishing it, you may be hindering them by concealing the truth."

"But I haven't concealed the real truth, the only truth that matters—if it's the real truth they're after. The murderer is the anonymous telephone caller, and on that subject I've told them every jot and tittle I know."

"You told them that he rifled every room and stole nothing."

"That was to lend my story the telling tint of verisimilitude, to make them realize that they are looking for a madman."

"I don't understand you."

"I think I'm walking round in a ring. What I'd like is to take you to the Bender and Stoker and forget the whole gory business, but I'm convinced that it's better to lie low for a couple of weeks. I went out to the shops today and discovered I was being followed."

"Ridiculous."

"Not ridiculous. For the moment we mustn't be seen together. It might vitiate the value of your evidence at the inquest. The carefully built house of cards might collapse."

"What are you talking about?"

"Don't desert me, Patricia. I need you now more than ever."

She climbed the stairs to the flat and lit the gas fire though the afternoon was mild.

What would have happened, she asked herself, if I'd told Detective Inspector Farrelly and the coroner all I know—the last conversation I had with Bernard and the obscene telephone call to his wife?

She got up and went to the window, knowing in her heart that she had asked the question too late.

8

Throughout the sharp-edged days of February, good humor flowered in the staff room. Mrs. Elsynge reported that Mr. Elsynge had contracted pneumonia, which Patricia considered to be a fair substitute for sleeping sickness. Robert Foxley inquired if it were broncho-pneumonia or brumby-pneumonia, and Mrs. Elsynge replied that fortunately it was common pneumonia but that that was bad enough. Her husband had a temperature of a hundred and three and was coughing up what the doctor called "rusty sputum." The Irish master said that he was sorry to hear it, but that they had a word for "rusty sputum" in Donegal that did not sound quite as fatal as the English, and when Mrs. Elsynge had gone to give God his soup the classics master took the Irish master to task for offering unnecessary consolation to the enemy. Then the French master told them laughingly that they were all mortal, that coddin' was catchin', and that there were a few rare spirits, such as himself, for whom La Rochefoucauld did not speak when he said that we all have enough strength to bear the misfortunes of others.

One afternoon toward the end of the month Patricia went

to the supermarket to buy a piece of bacon which she planned to cook with marrowfat peas and cabbage for dinner. As both she and Monica were country girls, they ate bacon and cabbage once a month in case they should forget the flavor of the soil; and as neither of them was immune from the crepitatory effects of cabbage and peas, they never went out with men on these evenings but remained indoors, washing and cleaning and writing home to their mothers. As she climbed the stairs with the bacon in her string bag, the telephone rang behind her in the hallway.

"I should like to speak to Miss Teeling." The excessively cultured voice fell oddly on her ear.

"I'm Miss Teeling," she replied, wondering if she'd heard the voice on television at Robert Foxley's.

"I have something to tell you about yourself, something you may never have realized. The universe is your box of toys. You dabble your fingers in the day-fall. You are gold-dusty with tumbling—a good word—amidst the stars. You make bright mischief with the moon. The meteors nuzzle their noses in your hand. You tease into growling the kenneled thunder and laugh at the shaking of its fiery chain. You dance in and out of the gates of heaven: its floor is littered with your broken fancies. You run wild over the fields of ether. You are my secret paramour, and not even he who chases the rolling world can take you away from me. With a kiss for every breath you draw till you hear again from me, I give you goodbye."

"Hello!" Her voice broke from her. "Who is it?" But the man at the other end had put down the phone.

Breathless, she went up the stairs. If it was Bernard having a joke, it was a joke in bad taste. And if it was someone else . . .? She knocked at Bernard's door but there was no reply. If he was out, he could have rung from a telephone box but she could have sworn that she heard neither pips nor the sound of coins falling. To keep her mind from racing until it was time to cook dinner she washed her hair and dried it with Monica's blow-drier. Already she felt calmer, and she was reminding herself that hair-washing always had a relaxing effect on her when someone knocked at the door.

"Are you Miss Teeling or Miss Quigley?" The tall man drew closer and raised his heels off the floor.

"I'm Miss Teeling. Who are you?"

"I'm Detective Inspector McMyler, a colleague of Mr. Farrelly, whom you've met." He raised a soft hat with a kid-gloved hand. "I thought I might call to have a word with you, if it is not inconvenient."

"Come in," she said with an unexpected glow of warmth, the kind of warmth she might have felt on meeting a familiar face in a place of strangers.

He looked knowledgeably round the living room, first at the ceiling, then at the carpet, windows, and gas fire, as if he had seen them all before and was trying to remember if they had changed. He was as tall as she was, narrow-shouldered and slightly stooped with a face that looked thin under the bruised brim of his hat. He was wearing a heavy, dark overcoat, possibly a Crombie, which his slight body did not quite fill, and from his shoulder hung a blue canvas bag which he unslung and placed on the floor beside the chair she offered him. Then he took off his gloves but not his hat and straightened the tails of his overcoat beneath him as he sat down in case he should crease them. A careful man, she thought, but above all a dry man, dry in the sense that he lacked moisture. He would never sweat, no matter how great the exertion. In the warmest summer his skin would feel rough, perhaps even imbricated, to the touch because it would lack the lubrication of skin that secreted sebaceous substances. He could not have come at a better moment; it was as if she had been expecting him. And now she sat opposite him, noting his unpolished shoes like large whetstones and telling herself that she understood him, that he was a sad man, disillusioned and self-critical, a man who had paddled with criminals in the waters of crime, who knew the indignities of compromise, who looked at death without flinching—in short, an effective policeman.

"You've probably guessed why I've come." He smiled. "It's about a few loose threads that have been worrying Mr. Farrelly and myself since the inquest. I've read the reports of the evidence and I thought that a word in your ear might not be amiss. A very messy business, and a business that is by no means over. The inquest solved nothing, and we, the police, have insufficient evidence to proceed."

"I told all I know to Inspector Farrelly and the coroner. I'm afraid there's nothing else I can add," she said, sensing that Bernard might not have been exaggerating, that he might still be under suspicion, and at the same time aware of her disappointment at Inspector McMyler's conversation. She had been expecting something more eccentric, perhaps even original.

"There's always something else," he said. "A stray thought, a momentary insight, a forgotten phrase that suddenly springs to mind. I thought I might have a word with you to see if you saw or heard more than you're aware of. You shared a house with Mrs. Baggotty, which in itself is the beginning of imaginings, however vague, of speculations that may or may not bear fruit."

"I have no idea what you mean. I know nothing of Mrs. Baggotty, or next to nothing."

"But in knowing what you call nothing you may know everything. We can't bear to know people as imperfectly as we invariably do, which is why we invent whole lives and histories for our friends without realizing it. We can't help it. In our separate ways we are all would-be novelists. Otherwise real novelists would have no readers."

"I must be unusually incurious. I never thought of Mrs. Baggotty except to remember when she invited me to coffee."

"But you must have given some thought to the kind of person she was. If someone had told you that she had gone to Greenland for her holiday, would you have been surprised? Would you have said that Majorca or Salthill would have suited her better?"

"It would have been a matter of total indifference to me."

"But not the kind of indifference you might feel about the ignominious defeat of the Italian army by the Austrians at Custoza in 1866."

"What a coincidence!" Patricia laughed. "I was reading about Custoza only yesterday, and I must tell you that my indifference to the result of that particular battle is less than total. Military success came too easily to Piedmont in the early years of the risorgimento. Custoza was a necessary douche of cold water."

Detective Inspector McMyler took off his hat and laughed too. Without his hat he was extraordinarily handsome. His thick straight hair reached back from the faint halo left on his forehead by his hatband, and his aquiline nose gave him a look of wise experience, unusual in a man in his early thirties. He turned his head and she saw that, though his hair was black, his sideburns were brown. She wondered if he dyed his hair black or his sideburns brown, and she thought the latter because there would be less hair to dye. She felt certain of that because she took him for a thrifty man, but a man who nevertheless looked after himself well.

"You are a student of history?" He rubbed his hands and placed them over his hat like a bishop ordaining a priest or a magician who feared that the bird inside it might fly away.

"No, merely a reader of historical novels."

"Are you a romantic? So many romantics have an unexamined fascination with the past."

He patted his hat with sensitive fingers, gentling it, encouraging it to remain quietly in its place. It was a well-worn corduroy hat, dented at the side and faintly agrarian, the kind of hat a midland farmer might wear to market but not to church.

"I'm a teacher of science. I tell my pupils that they live in a world that can be measured and understood."

"You *are* a romantic, then. I think that romantics are to be treated more warily than classicists. A romantic might conceivably condone a murder, for example, provided the murderer was sufficiently eccentric or flamboyant, but a classicist would never condone a murder he had not committed himself."

"What is the difference between a classicist and a romantic in terms of detection?" she asked to put him off the scent.

"They are both best seen in terms of photography. A classicist will reduce by at least one-third because he likes to be in control of his material. A romantic on the other hand blows everything up larger than life, while a few rare spirits see everything S/S."

"What's that?"

"Same size. They are the men who are neither classicists nor romantics, the men who solve the most ticklish cases."

"Are you an S/S man?"

"I am a modest man and therefore I must not say . . . but we were speaking of Mrs. Baggotty. It is now time to speak of her husband. Did you know him before the murder?"

"Only slightly. We used to say good morning on the stairs, and once or twice he took me out for a drink."

"What did he talk about?"

"Like all the men I've ever met, he talked about himself." She was conscious of bending the truth, but Detective Inspector McMyler did not encourage truth.

"What do you seek in a man, Miss Teeling? Self-forgetfulness?"

"Sincerity."

"You seek a lot. Did you find it in Mr. Baggotty?"

"I didn't seek it in Mr. Baggotty."

"What did you seek in him?" he smiled.

"Deliverance from the fraudulence of men who spend more words than they've earned."

"Do you despise all Irishmen, Miss Teeling?"

"No."

"Did you find that in the spending of words Mr. Baggotty is the linguistic equivalent of a monetarist?"

"I found in him the gift of words on the snaffle of Anglo-Saxon husbandry."

"What would you call his greatest gift?"

"Innocence. He has a degree of innocence of which no Irishman can conceive."

"Innocence, Miss Teeling, is an odd word for a reader of history to apply to an Englishman."

"If it offends you, I'll call it purity of spirit, a rare commodity in this island of confused nocturnal alarms."

"You admire Mr. Baggotty, then?" he encouraged her.

"I don't admire him, but I'm grateful for his lack of material success. In a city of semiliterate gombeen men drunk on Common Market wine—they can tell it isn't Guinness because of the color—it is little short of reassuring."

"Do you dislike all men?" McMyler looked positively pleased.

"Only gombeen men."

"Mr. Baggotty has the advantage of not even knowing the meaning of the word." He smiled as if he had got her king and queen in a fork at chess.

"Mr. Baggotty is too absorbed in his own recondite fictions to care."

"Did his wife ever mention him?"

"Only to say that he was a poor manager of money and a poorer judge of bloodstock."

"Did she say that his literary ambitions were beyond his means of achievement?" he asked.

"No."

"The most significant thing about Mr. Baggotty is not his passion for slow horses but his lack of literary judgment. He is a journalist and therefore affects a knowledge of men's affairs that is not his. Writers, artists, composers, and politicians, all pass beneath his gaze and are found wanting. Tolstoy is too didactic, Shakespeare too tolerant, Wordsworth too humorless, Mozart too effeminate, and Margaret Thatcher too mannish. The only man in his pantheon who is above criticism is Sir Winston Churchill, whom he once referred to as St. Winston, and whom he describes at all times as an unparalleled stylist, a politician who could write better English than Thomas Hardy or D. H. Lawrence. Can a man of such wayward literary judgment be trusted, I ask myself."

"You seem to know him better than I do."

"He is easily observed, he talks too much in pubs."

"Surely he is not to be condemned for having only one hero?"

"All I shall say is: Beware of him."

"Do you think he's a romantic?" she laughed.

"I fear so. He sees more in the world than there is. Romantics in the twentieth century are isolated and lonely. They seek their own kind with unscrupulous single-mindedness. When they meet, nothing must stand in the way of their conjoining; they must grapple soul to soul with hoops of steel. If you are not careful, Mr. Baggotty will grapple you. He must be curious about you. He may even feel that you possess some devilish knowledge that is not to his advantage. He may think that a hoop of steel is not enough, that only the thrust of steel will do. In short, your life may be in danger."

"I was going to tell you . . . I had an anonymous phone call before you came."

"Obscene?"

"No, literary. But distressing, nevertheless."

"Did it show poor literary judgment?"

"No, it showed intimate acquaintance with celestial bodies."

"An astronomer or an astrologer perhaps. Did you recognize the voice?"

"It was dark and syrupy and self-consciously cultured."

"Like Mr. Baggotty's?"

"No, it was the voice of a very superior newsreader, or perhaps the voice of a lector in a cathedral reading Isaiah or St. Paul."

"How fascinating. But we must not let fascination obscure the danger. You see, Mrs. Baggotty—according to Mr. Baggotty, that is—received anonymous phone calls before her death. I'm not trying to alarm you. I'm asking you to be on your guard and to remember that I shall not be far away. Now and again you may see me in the distance. All it means is that I'm looking after you."

He got up and stood before her.

"I must go now but I shall still be with you."

He placed one hand on top of his hat, thrust the other beneath it, and drew out a little red notebook.

"These are extracts from the *Upanishads*." He took her elbow. "I should like you to read them."

"What are the *Upanishads*?"

"Ancient Hindu scriptures, a treasure-trove of wisdom. Will you have them?"

"I'm afraid I'm not religious."

"It was only a thought, but if you ever need them, I shall have them at the ready for you."

"You're a very unusual detective, not at all like Inspector Farrelly."

"Farrelly is a classicist. His whole concern is with the shape of the vessel into which the liquid of life is poured. He pursues his cases by reducing the facts to the simplest proportions. I pursue mine by seeking in them the Vedic verities, by making the facts into something more resplendent, more universal, than they are. It may encourage you to know that though our methods differ, we unfailingly get our man."

He released her arm and put his hat on his head with the *Upanishads* inside it. He was standing close to her by the door with his hand on the latch, and as he turned to her, her knees trembled and she held her legs together to contain the damp fire between them. She blamed it all on the scent of sweet basil from his breath. She wanted him to take her there and then, to press her into the sofa without taking off his whetstones or his hat.

"Where does that trapdoor lead to?" He pointed upward.

"To the loft. Why do you ask?"

"It's unusual. Trapdoors are normally on the landing, that's all."

"I thought the same when Mr. Mullally, the landlord, had a man in to relag the pipes a few weeks ago."

She wanted him to come closer, to touch her even on the elbow.

"I'm pleased you mentioned it. I shall keep a weather eye open for a relagger with the enunciation of a lector reading Isaiah or St. Paul."

For a moment he leaned closer to her, smiling. She did not want him to go. She wanted to ask him if he chewed sweet basil as some countrymen chew tobacco, but before she could speak, he had said "Not a word to Mr. Baggotty" and was gone.

She went to the window to watch him go out the gate. An unusual policeman, she told herself, a man who obviously believed that to solve mysteries you must yourself be a mystery. He appeared below her on the garden path, the blue shoulder bag under his left arm and the corduroy hat sitting sideways over his left ear. Then she noticed that there was something strange about his walk. Each time he put his right foot forward it described a little arc in the air, which made his progress down the road vaguely reminiscent of a bird's. She held her breath, unable to credit the force of her feelings, unable to believe that a stranger could have such an effect on her without even being aware of it. To recover her sense of self-sufficiency, she had a cold bath and a change of knickers. The cold bath, she knew, would have had the approval of the nuns in Mountmellick. However, she did not mortify the flesh for reasons of religion but to make her body, which had become an alien machine, once again her own.

She was pleased to be able to cook to take her mind off McMyler. She put the bacon in a saucepan with an onion and covered it with water, and while waiting for it to boil she chopped the cabbage and wrote to Uncle Lar. She changed the water on the bacon twice, and when it was almost cooked she smeared it with honey and put it in the oven for the last half-hour. She was about to sit down to write to her mother when a knock came to the door.

"Not McMyler again." She caught her breath, but this time it was only Bernard.

"Will you come out for a drink this evening?" He looked grave and disheveled as if he had got up after six months of serious illness.

"It's a bad evening for me," she said, remembering the cabbage and peas. "I planned to stay in to do a few odd chores. Besides, I thought we were going to ignore each other for a while."

"The need for that seems to have passed. For the first time in three weeks I wasn't followed today. Come on, be a sport. I badly need an evening out."

She had been expecting him to come to her and she had already made up her mind to say yes. The last three weeks were a vacant waste ground. She had gone drinking and dancing on her own, but she could not bring herself to talk to any other man. She wondered, however, if he could be taking her out to celebrate having got away with it, but it was a thought more worthy of Monica than of herself, she decided.

"I'll come down for you at half-past eight," she said.

"No, eight. And I'll come up for you." He touched her hand.

They drove to The Inkwell in her car, silent between occasional sentences. After the first two pints, however, Bernard began telling her how he had spent the day.

"All day I've been walking, going nowhere and coming back from nowhere. In the morning I walked to Drumcondra and then along the canal to Phoenix Park. I couldn't bear to go racing, so I walked through Chapelizod and Ballyfermot to the Grand Canal and followed a young woman into Grafton Street."

"Did you speak to her?"

"No, but I sat opposite her in the Wicklow while she had a vodka and bitter lemon. She wasn't good-looking but she had a good figure and she was wearing a pair of tight blue velvet trousers with the nap worn around the rear cleft. I couldn't help noticing it because I walked behind her for an hour."

"Is that why you walked behind her?"

"I think I expected her to lead me to something."

"Will you be seeing her again?"

"How can I? I don't know where she lives."

"You're just a dirty old man," she laughed to cheer him up. "All that business of the worn nap is highly suspicious, a typical male fantasy."

He looked at her seriously, refusing to smile.

"I think you're wrong. I think I followed her because I expected her in some unimaginable way to lead me to Gladys."

"Who are those two? I never noticed them here before," she said to change the subject.

"They're two poets from the country. I met them here yesterday lunchtime. They're the two most Irish poets I've ever met."

"What's the difference between an Irish and an English poet?" she teased him.

"Irish poets are stronger." He looked at her as if she should have known.

"You mean that English poets use weaker rhymes?"

"No, I mean physically stronger. English poets are thinner and more languid, and when they shake your hand they leave you with the impression that they are wiping their fingers. But these Irish poets—look at those two—are strong as cart horses. One of them clasped my hand at lunchtime and nearly pulped it."

She went downstairs to the ladies to break wind after the peas and cabbage, and when she came back she said:

"I'd like to meet a country poet. Let's go over and talk to them."

"Like the Leaning Tower of Pisa, they are best observed from a distance."

"Come on, Bernard. You know how much I like big men."

Bernard introduced her, saying that she was Patricia Teeling, a scientist who collected strong poets, but that unfortunately he had forgotten the names of the poets.

"Never mind," said one of them. "I'm Tom-Tom O'Malley and my friend here is Sean De Barra."

They looked like twins, tall and broad with red, freckled cheeks, thick necks, and shiny ear lobes that stuck out like little balloons asking to be pricked for devilment. They looked different when they smiled, however. Tom-Tom had beautifully even teeth while his friend had sharp, pointed teeth with uneven spaces between, which, Bernard told her later, had earned him the nickname Bow-Saw De Barra.

"One thing I'm sure of, I haven't met you before," said Tom-Tom O'Malley. "If I had, I'd remember you. So many girls these days are like books you've read as a boy. You know that when you open the first page, you'll remember the ending."

The poets stood one on each side of her and laughed as much as they talked. They were rough and ready, not too literary, more like farmers who had once met scholars, and they drank their pints as if each one was the first and put their arms round her and whispered warmly in her ear. The bar was a sea of faces, the cigarette smoke swirled above their heads, and the swell of conversation rocked her like a small boat on a choppy lough. She had never enjoyed herself so much in the company of men, the only irritant being the shadow of Bernard's brooding disapproval. She knew he disliked the poets, that he wanted to have her to himself, but she wasn't going to let him ruin her evening with boyish jealousies.

Bernard drove home because he had drunk less than she, and he invited her in for a cup of coffee. He seemed in a hurry, certainly not his usual slow-moving self. He gulped down his coffee, kissed her quickly on the sofa, and thrust a determined hand up her skirt.

"No, Bernard. Why must you be so tiresome?"

"Now what's wrong?"

"There's nothing wrong with me."

"Is it because of your religion?"

"I have no religion."

"If it were religion that was holding you back, I'd understand. But this is ridiculous."

"It isn't time."

"Be sure to tell me when it is," he laughed sarcastically.

"There are men who need to be told, I'm sure."

"Do you think me insensitive?"

"No."

"Do you think me a fool."

"No."

"Then why do you withhold yourself? You gave more to those two rustic rhymesters this evening than you gave to me. If you don't want to bare your body, the least you can do is to bare your soul."

"You're always after something you can't have."

"All I'm asking for is personal truth. I came to Ireland to escape from the defilement of English social fantasy, from the spurning of personal truth for the tawdry myths of class and tribe, but you Irish are just as hypocritical—and with less reason."

"You're the writer. It's you who should be laying bare your soul. Look round you tomorrow evening in the pub. The hungry sheep look up, and are not fed."

"Never mind the sheep. Who will feed the shepherd?

Anyhow, the sheep are not hungry but smug to repletion. If I bared my soul before them, they'd scoff at me for my lack of good taste. It is I, the writer, not they, who thirsts for truth. But I'll have the truth from you. There is so much personal falsehood in the world that one bare soul could save us all from the fate of Sodom and Gomorrah."

While he was still talking, he pushed her down on the sofa and lay like a missionary on top of her, going through the motions of violent sexual intercourse. She thought that it would be a good moment to break wind, but she lay becalmed beneath him while he pressed his *membrum* further into her groin with each exaggerated thrust.

"I'm not going to let you use me as a wanking machine, Bernard. If you don't stop this tomfoolery this minute, I'll get a half-nelson on you that not even Lady Hamilton would break."

There was a loud knocking at the door and he jumped up as if the sergeant of death were on the threshold.

"You needn't tell me. Inspector Farrelly has lost his notebook and must take every statement again. You get it, Patricia. As well be hanged for a sheep as a lamb."

She got to her feet, adjusted her skirt, and touched her untidy hair. It was dark in the hallway and she had to look twice before she recognized the poets.

"The cream of the top of the evening to you," said Tom-Tom O'Malley.

"We are looking for lute music," said Sean De Barra.

"Lute music?"

"We were invited out to Ballsbridge to sink a jar and listen to lute music by a vicious composer called Weiss, but now we can't find the house and Tom-Tom says he's lost the address."

"So you came here instead?"

"What a coincidence," said Tom-Tom. "We meet you in the pub, we say goodbye, we see a street door open, and we come up and find you here."

118

"But have you got any lute music?" asked De Barra.

"As it happens, I have a suite by Weiss."

"Another coincidence," said Tom-Tom O'Malley.

"Come in," she said, opening the door wide.

"What's this?" Bernard asked suspiciously from behind.

"They've come—"

"For the lascivious pleasing of a lute," said Tom-Tom.

"But we have no lute," said Bernard, horrified.

"We have a record of a lute," said Patricia. "If you don't mind, I'll nip upstairs and fetch it."

The poets sat on the less frayed of the sofas and she went upstairs for Robert Foxley's record while De Barra told Bernard of the unbelievable coincidence by which they had arrived. They were talking about ostriches when she came back, and Bernard was sitting skeptically on the edge of his chair, already wondering when they would leave.

"We're trying to raise the money to start an ostrich farm in the Wicklow hills," said De Barra.

"Will the ostriches like the hills?" Bernard asked.

"I believe they prefer the flat," said Tom-Tom. "But we can prepare the way for them by exalting every valley."

"And by making the crooked straight and the rough places plain," said De Barra.

"This is an agricultural country," said Tom-Tom, "but it's an inefficient agricultural country—all because the bullock is an inefficient converter of fodder. What we need is an animal that will convert a hundred grams of fodder into a hundred grams of meat. The nearest to that ideal is the capybara, but I can't see your conservative midland farmer eating boiled capybara instead of boiled bacon with his cabbage. The next best is the chicken, but its eggs are too small for making omelettes for large families or in large hotels. That's where the ostrich scores. By cracking only one of its eggs, you can make a dozen omelettes. Think of the revolution in the kitchens of the Shelbourne."

"Think of the boon to the conservationist," said De

Barra. "The ostrich doesn't poach the soil as seriously as a cow or bullock."

"And think of the drumsticks," said Tom-Tom. "For once copywriters will be able to call something king-size without stretching the truth."

"But best of all is that no part of the ostrich is wasted," said De Barra. "You can sell the feathers for a fortune. You can even sell the skin."

"Do you want to listen to the lute?" Patricia asked.

The poets lit their pipes and they all listened without a word.

"It isn't as pleasing as I expected," said Tom-Tom when the record ended.

"Nor as lascivious," said De Barra. "The Bard raised false hopes."

"Now that the rather elaborate prologue is over, perhaps we could come to the purpose of your visit," said Bernard.

"But our visit has no purpose," said Tom-Tom.

"I know you're English and that therefore you expect social intercourse to have an object, but what we told you is true. You are no more surprised by this meeting than we are," said De Barra.

"Tell the truth. You followed us here in the car," Barnard said.

"But why should we follow you? We are poets, we set the pace."

"You're both new to The Inkwell. I suppose you hit upon it by coincidence as well."

"No, not by coincidence. All roads lead to the Mount Helicon of Dublin."

"I have been patient. I have listened to your vaporous chit-chat about ostriches. Don't think I can't spot an allegory when I see one."

"There are men who couldn't spot one on the banks of the Nile," said De Barra.

"I can see we're intruding," said Tom-Tom. "To make up for it, we'll come out with a bottle one evening when the weather is more sociable."

"There is no need to make amends," said Bernard.

"We know there's no need," said De Barra. "It is merely an ancient bardic custom."

"Would you care for a cup of coffee?" Patricia tried to be agreeable.

"Not now," said Tom-Tom as they both got up to go.

"You could have been more civil," she said when they had left.

"Why did they come to talk about ostriches? Tell me that."

"How should I know?"

"What does the ostrich suggest to you?"

"A strong digestion coupled with a capacity for self-delusion."

"To me an ostrich suggests naked thighs running. But you may be right . . . 'I'll make thee eat iron like an ostrich, and swallow my sword like a great pin, ere thou and I part.' We'll simply have to wait and see."

"What are you talking about, Bernard?"

"Ostriches."

"I don't share your view of the poets."

"Before calling them poets, we should first hear their poetry."

"Perhaps we shall."

"I'll bet it doesn't rhyme."

"But surely it doesn't have to."

"I know it doesn't have to," he said witheringly. "But I also know that it is easier to fake free verse than rhyming couplets. Real poets are equally adept in both. I think we must demand to hear some travelers' samples."

"I hope we meet them again."

"They're ginger."

"As opposed to sage?"

121

"They're queer."

"But they had their arms round me all evening."

"They were using you to make each other jealous."

"You have a very small mind, Bernard. I can see why you write prose."

When she went upstairs, Monica was reading in bed, a grey cardigan draped over her thin shoulders.

"Those peas were sulfurous." She looked up from her book. "After you left, Robert called unexpectedly and I had to suggest that we go for a walk. On the way he complained bitterly of the cold, but what could I do?"

"I went to a pub and kept going to the ladies for light relief."

"I wish men weren't such romantics," said Monica. "All this ridiculous posturing would then be quite unnecessary.

"I'm worried about Robert," Monica continued when they were both stretched side by side in the dark. "I'm afraid I'll lose him."

"Why?"

"He's very highly sexed. He keeps wanting to rub my tummy and put his hand up my drawers, which would all be very enjoyable if we were married."

"Perhaps he's merely testing you, amusing himself in sallies of reconnaissance without promise of serious engagement."

"That's what worries me. Virginity is a coin you can only spend once."

"I often think that as a coin it's overvalued. It certainly depreciates exponentially with age."

"How can you say such a thing, Patricia. Surely you're not weakening already."

"What keeps my maidenhead still intacta is the fear that with it will go an incomparable world of dreams, that the silver of experience will drive out the gold of imagination. What we need is a system of bimetallism in which both would be legal tender."

"Bimetallism won't help me. Tonight Robert asked me to take what he calls his macropenis in my hand."

"And did you oblige him?"

"I said I might if he swaddled it in cling-wrap first. I was afraid it would be like handling a stick of dynamite, not knowing when it would detonate."

"Isn't that life," said Patricia. "We make each move in semidarkness with an imperfect knowledge of the position of our opponent's pieces."

"And who is our opponent?"

"At the moment yours is Robert Foxley."

"He has put me in a spot. When I don't let him have what he wants, he says I'm a prude; and when I let him have everything except the final favors, he says that my morality is purely prudential. Is there an answer to that?"

"No, your morality *is* prudential."

"I wonder what he'd say if I surrendered the final favors."

"It would depend on whether he liked them or not. If he found them moreish, he might say that you were a born philosopher; but if he found them disappointing, he might call you a trollop."

"His conversation is another worry. When he says I'm being 'over-siliceous' or that something I say is 'absolutely calcareous,' I can only laugh and pretend to understand. I often wish he spoke French or Italian instead. Then at least I could take evening classes—"

"Don't worry," Patricia said. "He'll grow out of it. In the meantime tell him that you find his jokes 'filarious.' Like all men, he doesn't crave to be understood so much as to be thought well of."

"What would I do without you, Patricia? You're such an experienced manager of men."

Before they fell asleep, Monica said that she was determined to retain her grip on Robert's imagination, that she was convinced that men were lost by the woman's failure to enliven their dreams.

123

"You can starve a man of sexual intercourse," she said, "but you'll starve him of auto-eroticism at your peril."

"Nonsense," said Patricia. "The proverb knows best. The way to a man's heart is still through his stomach. If you're wise, you'll invite him to dinner."

9

Monica spent the next two evenings wondering about the various dinners she could give Robert, but as she was no more confident of her cooking than of her conversation she decided in the end to confine herself to the entrée and let Patricia make the hors d'oeuvre and dessert. That way they would share the honors if the evening were a success, and the blame if it were a disaster.

"There's no need to worry," said Patricia. "He enjoyed himself the last time he came here, and we didn't give him anything special."

"Is it true that wherever he goes he brings his own claret?"

"No, but he brings his balloons."

Deciding what to give him wasn't easy. As Monica remarked, it could be anything except bacon and cabbage and marrowfat peas, but finally they decided on *médaillons de veau au vin blanc* (Monica insisted on the French). The wine was the next problem. Since Robert behaved more like a bon vivant than a half-impoverished teacher, Monica feared a catastrophe. The last time he took her to a restaurant, he complained loudly that the wine had no shoulder. This phrase so flummoxed the head waiter that he went off to consult the manager; and when they both came to the table, Robert told them with a great display of patience that he did not mean that it was claret in a milk bottle but that it was utterly inarticulate, that it had not uttered a word since it was poured. The manager tilted the bottle to read the label, sighed knowledgeably, and suggested that they have "one of his more judicious wines" on the house. This pleased Robert so much that when they were leaving he told the manager that he had never drunk a wine with such an extravagant vocabulary.

"What I liked most about it," he said, "was that it did not merely speak, it sang. As my lady friend here remarked, it was positively *cantabile*."

"I still think there's no need to worry," Patricia said. "Robert isn't a stuffed shirt. Though he laughs little, he's got a sense of humor."

"I think we must have a dry run," said Monica.

"Dry as opposed to sweet?"

"No, a rehearsal. We'll cook the meal for ourselves first and try out the wine. Then we'll be confident that all will go well on the evening."

"I think we should consult Bernard Baggotty," Patricia said.

"I don't know how you can go out with him when it's plain as a pikestaff that he's a—"

"He knows his wines. When he was in Fleet Street, he ate at the best restaurants in London without ever spending a penny of his own."

"That means that he was always the guest. Guests don't choose. They eat and be thankful."

"No, Bernard had an expense account. He was host as often as he was guest. I think we should get him to choose the wine. In fact, it might be a good idea to invite him to dinner. He's an amusing conversationalist when he's had a few. Besides, it would make the evening more interesting for Robert. A man who is left alone for three hours with two women, even a brave man, will soon find himself on the defensive. Robert will appreciate a comrade in arms, and Bernard will enjoy his company. It might even encourage him to smile—he's been so morose since his wife died."

"Was murdered," said Monica. "I must say the idea doesn't appeal to me, but I'll mention it to Robert."

Monica made no mention of the dinner for a week, and Patricia didn't press the point. She saw Robert every day at school, but since he had stopped taking her for drinks, she saw him in the company of the other teachers, who talked only of Mr. and Mrs. Elsynge. Patricia had come to miss Robert's deadpan humor in McGuffin's. Compared with him, Bernard was an intensely private man, haunted, ambiguous, and moody.

One afternoon, as she came in from school, the telephone rang again. She knew before she picked it up that it would be the "relagger with the enunciation of a lector," and she hesitated; but then she thought that it was in her interest to try to recognize the voice, which haunted the ear as the taste of syrup will haunt the palate after it is consumed.

"I know," the voice said, "that you have come to Dublin from the country and, believe me, I know how you must feel. You have come among Parthians, and Medes, and Elamites, and the dwellers in Mesopotamia, and in Judea, and Cappadocia, in Pontus, and Asia, Phrygia, and Pamphylia, in Egypt, and in the parts of Libya about Cyrene. The city is a madhouse, a babble of different tongues, with men from Connemara trying to overcrow men from Kerry and Clare, and overcrowing them all are the native Dubliners, the detested gurriers. And so you can imagine how refreshing it is to walk in your shadow down Pembroke Road and Upper Baggott Street, the swing of your pleated skirt like the swing of the open sea, bearing the breezes of the country until you pause by the Grand Canal. I stand at your shoulder, breathing the fragrance of your hair as you watch the lock gates spill and spew. You walk on smooth stone with edges worn by a thousand tow-ropes, and you sit with an old man on a wooden seat and again you watch the water spout from rotting timber, making fine foam below, cream streaked with brown like the grain of planed pine-wood. And the water spilling, like the staling of many horses, brings to your nostrils the aroma of the country, because the canal, as you know by now, is the country in the city, bringing lime-laden midland water for poetry-parched gurriers to spit into. You turn for home, and again I follow you, envying every pavement slab that bears the pressure of your heel. I steal closer, inhaling your rural perfumes, and I whisper, hoping that you will hear, while on tenterhooks in case you should: Who is she that 'comes this way sailing like a stately ship of Tarsus, bound for th' isles of Javan or Gadire, with all her bravery on, and tackle trim, sails fill'd, and streamers waving, courted by all the winds that hold them play, an amber scent of odorous perfume her harbinger.' You turn into Lazar's Park, magnificent in your muscularity, and I wish for the pilliwinks and you to turn the screw."

"Who are you?"

"It doesn't matter. What matters is that I live for your rural airs in the miasmatic cloaca that is Dublin."

"Please don't ring me again."

"You can't bear a voice without a face? My face is nothing. It's ravaged by life, but my voice is the voice of innocence inside you."

"I want you to forget me, never to ring me. I—"

"And I want to walk so close behind you that I can take the place of the air that you have displaced before it is sullied by the inrush of exhaust fumes from buses marked An Lár."

She put down the phone and again knocked at Bernard's door, but he wasn't at home. A coincidence perhaps, but then again perhaps not. The mesmerizing timbre of the voice pursued her up the stairs. She sat by the window, looking across the street, wondering if he lived in one of the houses opposite, because he seemed to know the precise moment she returned from school.

The afternoon was dark after rain, the houses black blocks before the lights came on. A magnolia tree in blossom almost glowed, a single flower in a wasteland of brick, and she remembered trees in Cork at the end of March, black against the light except for a flowering cherry, the small leaves pink as salmon flesh, slightly unreal as if they were a trick of the light. She saw prunus trees in blossom in mid-May, a windy day and six of them in a cul-de-sac, the blossoms falling like snow, hopping and scurrying in the street until a whirling gust blew them up into the branches again, and she breathed fitfully as if it were a real snowstorm.

Her life was a modern stained-glass window, a hundred random translucent fragments, each admitting its own distinctive light. She watched the house opposite until the curtains were drawn against the night, then she got up and made a cup of coffee, determined not to weaken, determined not to mention the phone calls to Bernard.

During the third week of March, the weather took a turn for the better. Even the early mornings were warm; and, though Elsynge was still confined to bed, his bedroom window was open at the top to admit the gentle air. In the afternoons Patricia paced restlessly between the desks, up and down, up and down, like a tigress in a cage, and now and again she would think of walking along a headland with Uncle Lar while he pointed with his stick to a scatter of bluebells. One morning after a night of rain, she was so intoxicated by the freshness of the air that she decided to play truant for the day. She rang Mrs. Elsynge and told her that she had caught a chill and that the doctor had recommended a day in bed. She had decided to spend the day in Bray, with the sea idle and grey and a smoking steamer in the offing going south. She would find shelter under a rock and read a novel with her cardigan over her shoulders, and she would watch mitching boys digging for bait in places where no one ever found a worm.

From the bathroom window she looked down into the back garden. Bernard was high in the branches of the pussy willow, sawing wildly. She watched the driving of the bow saw and the branches falling, entangling in the lower branches before they reached the ground. His feet were in different forks, far apart, and he was so absorbed in his work that she felt he believed that the world was made to be destroyed. He was wearing old trousers, ones with a broken zip, and he held on to a branch with one hand while he sawed with the other. As she watched, she wondered whom he was dismembering—his late wife, Sean De Barra, Tom-Tom O'Malley, or herself? Whatever he was cutting, it was not a tree. He was no longer a writer, not even a journalist; he was a butcher jointing a carcass and, what is more, enjoying the work.

She turned away with an effort and went downstairs to ask Mr. Mullally about the tree. He was sitting by the fire with a bowl of mulligatawny soup balanced on the arm of his chair. As a young man he served with the British army in India, and he now ate mulligatawny soup, which he called "pepper-water," every day in memory of the late Mrs. Mullally, whose soup was the envy of every wife in the regiment.

"Why is Bernard cutting down the pussy willow?" she asked.

"No, it's Willow Pattern for the 3:30 with Calico Boy a close second." Mr. Mullally coughed so violently that a spoonful of soup dribbled into the spittoon between his legs.

"Do you want me to place a bet for you?"

"Mrs. Mullally, God rest her, made mulligatawny hot-pot for Larry Olivier and after he'd eaten it he said, "I'll purge, and leave sack, and live cleanly, as a nobleman should do.""

"But that's not *Henry V,* that's *Henry IV.*"

"Fourth Estate will never win a race. Yes, you go out into the garden."

"Why are you cutting down the tree?" she asked Bernard, who did not pause in his butchering.

"If you look, you can see the difference between the heartwood and the sapwood. But heartwood or sapwood, the bow saw is going through it like butter."

Her dream returned as she watched. She was living in the country with Desmond Deeny and he came back from work every evening to tell her about The Forestry. No matter where she turned, she could not put The Forestry from her mind. She bore the weight of it on her back, and he gripped her round the neck like the Old Man of the Sea, and the forest on her back swayed in the wind until she could barely keep her balance. He was lying on his back over the bedclothes, his trousers open and his shirt on the chair. She knelt over him on the bed, raised the bread knife with both hands, and brought it down over his heart. He uttered no word of love or hate, but rose slowly to kiss her with his mouth open. Then he fell back and his red blood spurted through her cotton dress into her groin.

She took a train from Lansdowne Road and tried to leave her dream behind with Bernard in the garden. The wash of the sea would drown its heavy insistence. She would watch boats on one side and passing trains on the other. The salt of the sea would stiffen her hair and she would absorb the light of sanity, of normality, from men and women walking well-fed dogs on the shore. Between Merrion Strand and Dun Laoghaire the railway ran along the sea, then it turned inland and the sea lay somewhere on the left until it appeared again as Killiney Bay. Killiney didn't matter. All that mattered south of the city was Bray, because Uncle Lar had taken her there when she was ten. They sat on a long stone seat on the seafront and a thin little man with a moustache sat beside them.

"Good day," he said to Uncle Lar.

"I've seen worse," said her uncle.

"Captain Bass, ex-RAF, now retired." The stranger extended a hand across her lap.

Uncle Lar took it and turned it over as if to study the green signet ring, then released it without giving his name.

"Your daughter?"

"Only for a week."

"Ah, a relation?"

"Her uncle."

"She'll break hearts, mark my words." Captain Bass pressed a sixpence against the palm of her hand.

A young girl in a tight cotton dress passed between them and the sea, her shoulder bag bobbing behind her, the strap vanishing with each left step into the cleft between her buttocks. Captain Bass licked his moustache.

"A flimsy get-up," he said. "My godfathers, I'd pay entertainment tax to walk after her. Wouldn't you?"

"It's a grand walk to Greystones and back," said Uncle Lar.

"A beach draws all kinds of women. Yesterday I saw a half-naked—"

"It's tea-time," said Uncle Lar. "We must be getting back, Patricia."

"With whom have I had the pleasure of conversing?" The Captain got to his feet.

"Lawrence Teeling."

"Captain Bass, ex-RAF, now retired. Haven't we met before? At the Curragh last summer? The Irish Oaks? Or was it Fairyhouse the season before last?"

"Wrong man, I think," said Uncle Lar.

"Pleased to have made your acquaintance, little lady." The Captain bowed low.

"Some men are mules and some are jackasses. Only a few like myself are horses," said Uncle Lar when they were gone.

"Why didn't you give him your real name?"

"But I did."

"You didn't say Lar."

"He gave me a false name."

"He's Captain Bass and he gave me sixpence."

"He's Captain Cuttlefish, he lives in the sea, and he has a little bag of ink under his chin."

"Tell me a fairy story, Uncle Lar."

"When he's attacked, he releases the ink into the water to confuse his enemy."

"Will we see him again?"

"No, and now I'll have a look at that sixpence."

She gave him the English sixpence, a worn coin but still capable of being changed into ice cream. Uncle Lar flung it into the sea and gave her a shilling instead, an Irish shilling with a bull on it.

"Why did you throw it away, Uncle Lar?"

"It wasn't a good sixpence, it was discolored by sepia," he said. "According to my reckoning it was worth only fourpence-ha'penny."

She got off at Bray and listened to the departing train shake the back of the hotels that faced the sea. She sat again on the stone seat and looked through iron railings at the flatness of the water while a solitary cormorant fished with its neck above the surface like one of nature's periscopes. To the left of her was the harbor wall, and to the right was Bray Head, grassy to look at but covered, she knew, with ferns and heather. Behind her was a straight row of hotels with names like Marie Coeli, Sancta Maria, and St. Philomena that caught at her throat like raw whiskey. Uncle Lar stayed at the Blue House, a hotel with bow windows and the railway like a lesson in Euclid at the back. Now the Blue House was gone, and in its place was a yellow-and-brown hotel with no dormer windows, no bow windows, and no white stones in the concrete of the gateposts.

She leaned over the railing above the beach. It was smaller than she remembered, but the dark sand strewn with blue-grey pebbles like birds' eggs had not changed. On a breezy day she and her uncle leaned over the railing and watched the waves breaking at the foot of the wall. In two places they broke with greater force because, he told her, of the submerged rocks she could not see. She moved down to where the spume was rising along the wall, but whenever it threatened to strike her face it fell back exhausted into the sea.

"It's magic," she called excitedly to her uncle. "It climbs up the wall, but before it washes my face it falls back into the sea."

"That's because the breeze from the land catches it as soon as it rises above the wall."

"You know everything, Uncle Lar."

"And so will you when you grow up," he laughed.

She skirted the edge of the water, watching the breaking waves turning to black because of the sand they bore and then to white froth as they washed the nervous pebbles. The sea inhaled again like a smoker who despises cancer, and the backrush of the water over rolling pebbles made guggling music like the noise of pebbles in a bottle being washed by her mother to take milk to the bog. Unknown to her uncle, she collected five perfect pebbles and when she got home she put them in an empty nest in the garden to see if they would encourage a blackbird to add to their number. And a week later she watched them as fine rain began to fall, spotting them till they looked like real eggs. Now she cursed Mountmellick and Cork for making birds' eggs into limestone and granite, and she crossed the shelf of pebbles at the far end of the beach, pebbles without sand cast against the grey wall. She would now walk to Greystones and, with a backward look after every turning, hear again his short, bright laugh; and she would take the train back to Bray and listen for the hammering of blacksmiths in the echoing tunnels.

The sea looked brighter from Bray Head, perhaps because she was above it, or because the light had changed with clouds racing wildly from the sun. She walked along the cut-out path, grey rock, ferns, and heather rising on her right and the single-track railway following the edge of the sea on the left below. The steel of the rails glinted in the sun while the sleepers and the ballast between them were rusty-brown like smoked mackerel. The wind played in her hair, blowing it from behind over her ears, and then, as she turned the corner of the headland, it suddenly fell away. The path climbed the side of the hill, the sea became bluer, and she turned into a frolicking schoolgirl stirring the barrel of bluestone with which her uncle used to spray potatoes.

As she neared Greystones, she looked back at the railway tunnel emerging from solid rock. When she came with her uncle, it had been for her "the eye of the hill," but now it looked like some kind of anal orifice, and she stared at it for a long time, trying to see it as an eye, but life's burden of negative experience had transformed it forever. She tried to find the guest house where she and her uncle had tea and scones, but only the La Touche Hotel looked sufficiently familiar to attract her.

She lunched off two grilled mackerel in the bar of the La Touche, stumpy mackerel with firm flesh that melted in the mouth and gave a darkly ambiguous flavor to the pint of stout with which she washed them down. An old man with a military moustache sat opposite, dealing expertly with the backbone of his mackerel, leaving it like a fine-tooth comb, clean as if it had been washed ashore by the sea.

"You're fond of mackerel?" he asked as he completed the surgery.

"I don't eat it often, but when I do it's always good."

"The love of mackerel, like the love of music, is a gift which not everyone is given. The mackerel should be king of fish. In this world of dog-eat-dog he would make a more fitting king than the herring, who has never yet been caught with a bait. How do you like your mackerel?"

"Grilled and basted with melted butter."

"You have a greater treat to come. He is most kingly when poached in a *court bouillon* flavored with fennel and best eaten with hot gooseberry sauce. At the risk of being indelicate, I would say that it is a dish that never fails to make a healthy man burp."

He laughed with a show of worn teeth, little brown teeth, not sharp but blunt from masticating military repasts. She could no longer contain her curiosity.

"Excuse my asking, but are you Captain Bass?"

"Captain Bass? Certainly not. I'm Captain Deverel."

"Over ten years ago I came to Bray on holiday with my uncle and we met Captain Bass. I was only ten but I've never forgotten him."

"I knew him myself. Lived here in Greystones and believed that mackerel was bad for the gastrics."

"Is he still around?"

"He died last year and left his widow without a penny. A rum one was Captain Bass, not a man to discuss with a lady. He had no ear for mackerel, and that was the root of his trouble. If he had eaten less trout, he might be alive today with a bank balance to keep him in creature comforts. But the price of mackerel is rising. More and more people are jumping on the bandwagon."

"I must catch the next train back. It was nice meeting you."

"Captain Deverel at your service." He rose and bowed.

As she waited for the train, a thin veil of rain billowed between the two platforms. The twelve-minute journey would be different in this grey light, no longer slightly frightening, but already she felt an eerie sense of anticipation.

The train came in with a halting clank, and she sat on the far side because she wished to look down on the water. The wheels jolted over points. We are back on the single track, she thought, and looked up to find Detective Inspector McMyler about to sit down beside her.

"Ah, Miss Teeling! We meet again!"

"By accident or design?" she smiled.

"In detection, as in football and war, the best moves are made by accident, and the best detectives, strikers, and generals have the knack of making them look like design."

He pushed his corduroy hat farther back on his head and placed his blue shoulder bag on the floor between his whetstones. She wanted to ask him what instruments of detection he carried in it, but he spoke before her.

"Have you heard again from our friend the lector?"

"Yes, I've had another call, somewhat longer than the first. I listened carefully to every word, and I'm certain I never heard his voice before."

"A classicist or a romantic, would you say?"

"A countryman who detests Dublin. He says he follows me down Pembroke Road for a whiff of rural air."

"Undoubtedly a romantic. Classicists are ill at ease with nature, they feel themselves only among the works of man. That is why the greatest lovers are romantics. But speaking of lovers, are you certain it isn't Mr. Baggotty?"

"I think I am."

"You didn't take my advice," he smiled. "I've seen you together in pubs."

"I'm convinced that I have nothing to fear from him."

"Have you told him about me?"

"I followed your advice and said nothing."

He had a pleasant habit of smiling at the end of each sentence as if it contained a cryptogram for himself alone. He turned to her as the train went into a tunnel, stopping in mid-phrase while the blacksmiths' hammers fashioned a horseshoe at speed above their heads. The scent of sweet basil thickened the dark, her knees trembled helplessly, she half turned to him as if to ask a favor, they came out of the tunnel, and grey light glinted sanely on the sea. He was talking again, but she heard words, not ideas . . . Vedanta . . . the King of Death . . . the pleasing and the good . . . the knowledge of Brahman.

137

She had often ached for a man, a big-boned, fair-skinned, fair-buttocked man, but she dreamt in the night that when he came she fled from him. In the morning she would ask herself if in the twilight between mind and body there was a condition, sexual anorexia nervosa, which drove women to long for men and at the same time to shrink from their hirsute touch. But *she* had never shrunk from the man she longed for. He had, quite simply, never touched her. And he had never touched her because he had never met her. A poet like Tom-Tom O'Malley would understand:

> A man who does not exist,
> A man who is but a dream.

But now she knew that he walked on the earth. They came out of another tunnel, McMyler conversing pleasantly as if it were the morning, not the late afternoon, of the world. She leaned toward him, willing him to put a hand on her knee. The train stopped at Bray. He put his shoulder bag on his shoulder and, with an ambiguous wave, said goodbye. Burning, she watched his birdlike walk, and he vanished through a grey door, elusive as the mysteries that were his daily companions.

When she got back to the flat, all that remained of the pussy willow was the stump and a pile of logs with a larger pile of branches in the middle of the garden. She picked up one of the logs and touched the horseshoe which some child had once hung on a branch and which was now embedded in the wood. Then she noticed a forked log at her feet, a lignified human body cut off at the waist and knees. All the features were there, even the cleft of the buttocks, and she shuddered at the violence of her thoughts. She felt herself sink into the solid turf as if it were a quagmire. The evening sky was rosy in the southwest, but in the east was a black stratus, a thick plank in a scaffolding that could come crashing down on rooftops at any moment. She turned to Bernard, who was drilling holes in the stump with a brace and bit.

"What are you doing now?" she asked, amazed at the seeming sanity of men.

"Drilling holes, as you can see."

"Why?"

"I'm going to pour spirits of salt in them to rot the stump."

"Copper sulfate would be better."

"Do you speak as a woman or a scientist?"

"Get stuffed, sir!"

"To please you, I'll drill thirteen holes, and I'll put spirits of salt in six and copper sulfate in seven. How is that?"

"Did you enjoy cutting it down?"

"It was good exercise. A writer must know when to write, when to take exercise, and when to rest."

"You're beginning to sound like Hemingway on a bad day—not a good augury."

"If I placed a piece of blue litmus on your tongue, do you think it would turn red?"

"I preferred the tree as it was. It looked better growing."

"It was the catkins that brought the death sentence. They were falling into the garden next door. Mrs. Goode complained to Mr. Goode, and Mr. Goode complained to Mr. Mullally."

"I'm surprised he heard him."

A cackle and a hoot made her turn. Mr. Mullally, wrapped in two overcoats, was advancing down the garden, testing the ground before each step with the rubber ferrule of his stick.

"We'll have smoke," he said. "If only Mrs. Mullally were alive. There was nothing she liked better than a good burn-up."

"Did you have anything on Barleycorn in the heel of the hunt?" Bernard asked.

"There was nothing she liked better than smoke, and the way to get the best smoke, she always said, was to burn wet weeds. She used to say that a fire without smoke was like a hat without an ostrich feather."

"It's rather late to start a fire, but we'll get no peace till we do." Bernard tugged at his sparse hair.

He got an armful of old newspapers from the shed, made twists from the pages, and laid them in a ring on the ground, while Patricia got a chair from the kitchen for Mr. Mullally. Bernard built the fine branches and twigs over the paper, and when the fire was burning well he threw the logs on top. Arrows of flame explored the bark of the logs, sparks shot and flew, and Mrs. Goode came running out of the house and took in her washing.

"There isn't enough smoke." Mr. Mullally spread his hands. "If only we had some grass cuttings—"

"Or wet weeds," Patricia laughed.

There was more than enough smoke for her taste. The uncertain wind kept blowing it in different directions, under her clothes and into her hair and eyes. Bernard caught the "human" log by the left leg and held it up before her.

"It's only now I see the resemblance. A man's body, not a woman's. We'll burn the evidence while we can." He flung it into the center of the flames.

She watched him smile as the flames licked the crotch, then turned quickly and went into the house. It was five o'clock. The school day had ended. Her pupils had gone home. She was now living in her own time and the ache of guilt she had felt in the morning had gone. She sat down to read the letter from her mother that arrived while she was out.

Dear Patricia,
I have to write again to tell you how worried I am about Lar. He caught cold on the moor three weeks ago and took to his bed for the first time since he came home from Australia. I think he's getting old of a sudden, and Hugh knows it. That fellah never misses a trick. He brought Lar home a bottle of brandy and a bottle of port from the pub, and Lar drunk the brandy and asked for more. But

that's not the end of it. While he was sick, Hugh vacci-
nated the calves against hoose without even telling him,
and then he went to the mart with four bullocks, and Lar
said that he got a better price for them than he would
himself. He trusts Hugh more than he'd trust our Austin
or Patsy, but worst of all he's going to the pub with Hugh
every night—the man that didn't look at a drink since he
was twenty. Desmond Deeny says that Hugh has dug
himself in, and Austin said to me when we were alone
that it's an unnatural relationship, two men, one old and
one young. Only you can save Lar from Hugh. Come
home before it's too late. Come home next weekend and
talk some sense to him before he's too far gone to hear.
The cattle are on grass for the last fortnight. Lar has
been on grass in the day since the last week of February.
The herd got over the bad winter well, though a few of
the cows have lice infection with bald patches on their
necks and shoulders. Lar has bought a pneumatic fertil-
izer spreader—another machine for Hugh to practice on.
Austin finished sowing the wheat, the wet weather left
him late. I hope you're saying your prayers. Say one to
St. Jude for Lar and don't forget, next weekend.

> *Good luck and God Bless,*
> *Mammy*

She wrote to her mother, reminding her that Uncle Lar
was well able to look after himself. Then she washed the
smoke out of her hair, remembering Uncle Lar in the lane, a
spare, craggy man with one bowleg and a stick, realizing
that wherever she went, the short white hair, the bony
skull, and the high cheekbones with deep hollows beneath
would represent for her goodness, simplicity, but above all
the mystery of a life at once lucid and dark.

He had about him the quality of silence. He never
interrupted another man in conversation, but when he

suddenly looked up at the ceiling or the sky everyone knew he was going to speak and waited for words that seemed too slow to come. He was a man above the ordinary run of men, a man of moral and physical strength who never willingly gave pain to anyone. She reread her mother's letter, tore it into little pieces, and put it in the dustbin.

10

After the felling of the tree, Bernard kept to himself for a week, then suddenly one evening he appeared at the door to ask her out for a drink. The Inkwell was more crowded than usual. They failed to find stools at the bar, so they sat at a table in the darkest corner under a smoky picture of ruined Ross Castle, silent while she rolled a cigarette. She was aware of him beside her, smoking sniffily, his buttocks pressing on the seat as he waited on his coign of vantage for her to give form and color to the evening. She longed to surprise him out of his unquestioning egotism, to make him see that she was not a ladybird to be studied and classified or a well into which he could peep every so often to admire his reflection.

"You're silent, Patricia, because you have no tales of horror to relate," he said at length. "What's wrong with you is that you haven't been to hell and back."

"Why should I want to go to hell?"

"Because it's the last stop before Parnassus."

"Some people keep quiet about hell, but you talk as if you'd invented it, as if it were an occasion for self-congratulation."

"You misread me. My greatest regret is that I haven't suffered the true degradation of life. My hell is a clean, well-swept room with white tiles on the floor and white emulsion on the walls."

"A very English hell, in fact, with the plumbing in excellent order."

"I let that pass. For a writer to have been to hell is wasted time unless he brings back something in his briefcase. My journey wasn't altogether in vain. I did discover that hell exists. I tried to transmute the experience but in my haste I broke the crucible to be left with nothing but a stinking caput mortuum."

"Bernard," she laughed, "you're so English. You make it all sound like a tiresome accident, like getting a puncture on the way to a dirty weekend in Brighton. You were left with your stinking caput mortuum, not because you accidentally broke the crucible, but because you lack the mystical quality. Mysticism is as important in the effort to see the Diabolic Vision as it is in the struggle to glimpse the Beatific. You're too sane, Bernard. You long to be a *poète maudit,* but the only thing remotely *maudit* about you is your obsession with slow horses. A horse, even a slow one, is clean-limbed and sleek. He is not an animal of the dark. He is at his best in the glare of early afternoon at Epsom, Fairyhouse, or Longchamp."

"I can see that this is Be-Nasty-To-Bernard Evening, but for all your science—or is it alchemy?—you got the analysis wrong. I came back empty-handed because I left before my eyes had time to become accustomed to the dark."

"Then you must pay another visit. *The New Yorker,* if not literature, will be the richer for it."

"The only civilized answer to that is to heap confusion on you by offering you another drink."

She smiled as she watched him at the bar waiting for the barman to top the pints. He looked impatient and slightly baffled as if the topping of pints were an antiquated ritual like swan-upping. He once said to her that what puzzled him most about Dublin was that when he asked for a pint of Guinness, barmen invariably said, "A pint of stout," and when he asked for a pint of stout, they invariably said, "A pint of Guinness." And then he said that though the nuance, cultural or religious, escaped him, it would provide a telling aperçu for his next *New Yorker* story.

"You heard Mullally say that a fire without smoke is like a hat without an ostrich feather?" He placed a pint before her, an imperfect pint with a dimple in the top like a crater on the surface of a dead planet.

"Yes, but I don't agree with him."

"And do you remember the poets talking about ostrich farming and making use of every part of the ostrich, including its feathers?"

"Yes."

"It isn't just coincidence, you know. There's more to it than meets the eye."

"I don't understand."

"You obviously don't subject what people say to close conversational analysis. Mullally must have known the poets."

"So?"

"He invited them to the house. They just didn't hit on us in their much-advertised search for lute music."

"Don't be silly. How could Mr. Mullally have met the poets? He hasn't stirred out of the house in years."

She looked at him to see if he were making fun of her, but he was staring unseeingly at his pint, his eyes blue as the smoke from his pipe, his eyebrows so fair that you could hardly see them.

"We must all try to make sense of the things that happen to us," he said. "For me the choice now lies between the coincidence theory of life and the conspiracy theory."

"There is no need to explain such trivia."

"The trouble with you, Patricia, is that you don't observe. Now, look round and ask yourself if you see anything fishy."

"Why should there be anything fishy about The Ink-well?"

"Do you remember how I told you a month ago that I was out of the woods, that I was no longer being followed? Well, I was wrong. There's a gentleman in this bar who's been keeping an eye on me for the past fortnight. He's sitting opposite, in the other corner, looking as if he were engrossed in his hat, but, believe me, all he's interested in is yours truly."

Patricia held her breath. On the other side of the bar, flicking what she took to be imaginary fluff off his hat, was Detective Inspector McMyler. He took a sip of his pint and moved the hat to the other side of the tumbler as if he were castling at chess.

"Your move," she said to Bernard.

McMyler patted the top of his hat, a kettle of boiling water too hot to touch.

"Have you noticed him before?"

"It's the first time I've seen him here."

"I've been studying him while he's been studying me. He always carries a shoulder bag, which he never opens, but it's obvious to me that it's a game bag and that the notebook he occasionally draws from beneath his hat is a game book."

"Where is the game, then?"

"What a naive question! To complete the hat trick he's got a game leg, as you will see when he gets up to go to the bar. He walks like a barnacle goose, bringing his whole body round with each step. As a measure of revenge, however schoolboyish, I've begun calling him Goosefoot."

"You should write him into a short story for *The New Yorker*. A character with a game bag, game book, and game leg must surely have symbolic possibilities."

"You refuse to believe me? Then we'll conduct a little experiment."

"Not with your dowsing rod, please. I've seen enough of that."

"We'll go down the road to The Noggin an' Piggin and see if he follows. If he does, will you believe me?"

"We'll see."

They finished their pints and on the way out passed McMyler's table without looking at him. The Noggin an' Piggin was spacious and bare. All the customers, about ten or eleven, were sitting at the bar with their backs to the tables round the walls.

"I'll bet you a fiver that before I've finished my pipe and pint he'll be here." Bernard chose a table in the corner behind the door.

He was right. Within ten minutes, McMyler entered with his hat pulled well down, the brim casting a shadow across his handsome nose. When he had secured his pint, he looked neither to right nor left but walked with exaggerated care to a table at the far end of the bar.

"He's trying to conceal his game leg," said Bernard.

"He's trying not to spill his pint, more like."

"He's been chosen because he's so conspicuous. Everything about him is calculated to attract attention. You are meant to ask yourself what he carries round in his bag and why he's afraid his hat will leap up off the table. His purpose is to rattle me, to goad me into showing my hand. But I've got low animal cunning too."

"You're obsessive, Bernard. You're like a dog that won't let go of a bone."

"He's just an ill-educated policeman. We'll go over to his table and confuse him with light literary badinage."

"You must be mad."

"Watch me take the mickey in the subtlest possible way."

Unwillingly, she followed him across the room.

"Do you mind if we join you?" Bernard asked.

"Not at all." McMyler transferred his hat from the table to an empty chair. Then he removed a silk scarf from under the collar of his overcoat and laid it neatly over the hat as a priest might drape a corporal cloth over a chalice. He looked at Patricia without a hint of recognition, and she noticed that his right eyelid was weak, that it tended to droop as if he were trying unsuccessfully to wink.

"We were having fun in the other corner. We saw you alone, and we thought we might spread a little sweetness and light."

"Two elusive but inestimable commodities." McMyler smiled. "You might feel you had them in abundance in one corner and find that they had deserted you by the time you crossed the room. There is another complication. Not everyone appreciates them. There are men—why, we all know them—who prefer bitter aloes in the dark."

"I knew you were a philosopher. I said to my lady friend, 'That man drinks alone, that man has time to think.' You see, I'm of the opinion that there's far too much talk in this city. There is so much talk that you can barely hear the Mass bells above the hum of conversation."

"I think you mean the hum of traffic."

"Talk is fine provided it is preceded by thought. That is why I believe the English licensing laws are more civilized than the Irish. In England, because the pubs close for longer, there is more time to think. Here there is less than an hour to recharge the batteries between ten in the morning and eleven at night."

"Is there more matter in English conversation, then?" McMyler inquired.

"Oh, yes, more by far."

"More matter with less art," McMyler smiled while Bernard lit his pipe rather defensively before trying a different tack.

"Have you ever heard of goosefoot?" he asked.

"I've heard of goosefooting, a variant of first-footing common in Northern Ireland. Presbyterians who keep up Scottish traditions by going first-footing at Hogmanay sometimes mistake a Catholic house for one of their own in the dark. They cross the threshold expecting to kiss the lassies inside but are promptly goosed by the paterfamilias for their pains. This is called goosefooting, a serious business, if I may say so. Why, I once heard of a first-foot who got such a goosing as he retreated that he developed an anal fistula, which here in Ireland, as you may know, we call *fistula in ano*."

"The goosefoot I had in mind has nothing to do with Irish tribal warfare." Bernard breathed heavily. "It is a weedlike, evil-smelling plant with leaves like the foot of a goose, the botanical equivalent of animals that farmers shoot as vermin."

"Well, of course, I've heard of it. The Germans, who used it to fatten poultry, called it *Fette Henne,* but when you English translated it as Fat Hen, they understandably changed the name to *Gänsefuss*."

"I didn't know that, but I do know that it's also called pigweed because it's fit only for swine."

"The French call it *la patte d'oie,* but, typically, they confuse it with those little wrinkles which women conceal and brave men openly call crow's-feet."

"Here's to *Gänsefuss*," said Patricia to relieve the tension.

"And here's to Goosefoot, alias Pigweed." Bernard raised his glass.

"To *pes anserinus*," said McMyler. "I prefer the Latin."

"It's time we went," Bernard said to Patricia.

"A light-hearted question before you go," said McMyler. "Which medieval king developed an anal fistula from sitting too long on his throne?"

"You're obsessed with the anus," said Bernard, and he marched to the door with his right hand over the seat of his trousers. He paused on the threshold and looked back.

"It might interest you to know," he shouted, "that the Latin for barnacle goose is *Anas leucopsis*."

"That was a very un-English exit, dear Bernard," Patricia said when they got back to his flat. "You grow more like the natives every day."

"Now you know I'm right. Goosefoot is a hunter. He

sees himself playing cat and mouse, and he sees me as the mouse."

"Nonsense, he was just engaging in light-hearted literary badinage, and doing it rather well, I thought. He struck me as a man of immense detachment, who would as lief do one thing as another."

"Come to bed, it's the only connection."

"You already know my answer to that."

"Look, Patricia, I'm in trouble, and only you can redeem me."

"Be brief and I'll listen."

"My problems are metaphysical. You would think them flimsy if I defined them, but they are nonetheless very real."

"So you wish to be saved by sex, not philosophy."

"By you."

"By sex with me."

"I want to possess you in a full, unstinting relationship. I want you to come down and share this flat with me. I want to be with you every hour of the day. I want you to share my bed, my table, and my dreams."

"But I have all-too-insistent dreams of my own."

"You'd be good for me as a living, giving, taking woman. Without knowing it, you're a cornucopia of life's riches, the greatest of which is your country upbringing—your mother, your brothers, Uncle Lar, and the river. They are as real to me from hearing about them as they are to you from having lived with them. For you they are a spiritual soakaway that drains the poison of urban life from your system. I don't have a soakaway of my own, but yours would do if we were sharing a life together."

"What nonsense! In the great crises of life we are alone. No one can help anyone else."

"I'm surprised to hear such pessimism from you. Is it because you're searching for a father and can find only sons?"

"Which means?"

"If you'd seen me as a father, you'd have found your way to my bed by now. My tragedy is that I'm a son."

"I'm going to bed to work that one out alone."

She paused at the door and turned to him.

"Incidentally, stop calling me your 'lady friend.' I may be your friend but I'm not your lady friend. I have an intense dislike of the phrase."

"What shall I call you? My leman?"

"When you discover the *mot juste*, I'll let you know."

As she waited for sleep, she felt excluded from his vision of the world. He talked about the essence of one day as opposed to that of another, about the past in the present and the unremitting malignancy of human experience, but though she understood each word she did not feel the force of them as a totality. Is he a genuine philosopher or is he a fraud? she asked herself. Is he truly concerned with matters of the spirit, or is he badly in need of a good ride? Are his problems rooted in the intellect or are they spindrift from the black sea of guilt in his heart? The answer would not come, so she decided to sleep once again on his wound.

A week later Monica mentioned the dinner. "We'll have it on Palm Sunday and you can invite Mr. Baggotty if you like," she said.

"What made you change your mind?"

"I told Robert about you and Baggotty, and naturally he's curious to meet him. He reads detective stories, does Robert. He's deeply interested in crime!"

"Monica, how can you suggest such a thing?"

"Maybe I say what you only think."

"I know I say less than I could, but I never say less than I should."

At times she found the primacy of Robert in all that Monica did and said extremely irritating. He had taken possession of her as many husbands take possession of their wives, transforming them into humorless old hens preoccupied solely with nesting.

"I've had second thoughts about the veal medallions,"

Monica said. "They're too prosaic. I think we'll give him *cassoulet de Castelnaudery* because of his taste for alliteration."

"Aren't haricot beans rather a risk in mixed company?"

"Never mind, we'll all share the same boat. More important, have you thought about the dessert?"

"I think I'll do caramelized oranges."

"Good, and get Crippen to choose the wine."

"Monica, I wish you wouldn't say these things."

"It's only between ourselves. I don't say them to Robert."

Patricia moved into the kitchenette to conceal her irritation. She stood by the curtain, tapping the seal of a new coffee jar with her forefinger, then suddenly collapsed in laughter.

"Have I said something funny?" Monica asked.

"I was once at a party in Cork and two young men laughed their heads off over a jar of instant coffee. They were alone in the kitchen and they didn't know I was outside the door. One of them was tapping the seal like that, but not sufficiently hard to break it, and then he gave it to his friend, who put his finger through it in one jab. 'Rape! Rape!' shouted the first, and they both nearly choked with laughter."

"But what did they mean?"

"They were pretending that the seal was a maidenhead, and that they were deflowering a virgin. Here, tap it with your finger and see."

"How can you, Patricia? How can you laugh at coarse, insensitive men?"

"Laughter is healthy. It's what keeps me from going mad. But if I weren't a virgin, I'd probably think it childish."

"Well, I'm a virgin and I think it disgraceful."

"I like to think that somewhere in the world is a man who would love me for laughing, if he knew."

Monica marched off into the bedroom as if it were not a conversation for a woman with the gravitas of a man. She had stopped romancing about the circumference of men's necks and the market value of a long-preserved virginity. Perhaps she had paid what she used to call the premium that would ensure a husband, a house, and emotional and financial security. Or perhaps what she had lost was her girlhood, sunk in the muddy shallows of Robert's fanciful conversation. Why a man who thought it amusing to say that he played the saxifrage should have such an effect on her was hard to tell. All Patricia knew was that she and Monica had lost the sense of sorority that had once made midnight conversation sparkle in the *grand lit*. In losing it, however, they had gained something else, more real and lasting perhaps, but something that closed a door that would never reopen in their lifetimes.

The dinner on Palm Sunday was a gastronomic success, but conversation failed to flower. Robert and Bernard struggled to be humorous, but everything one of them said seemed to have a serious side which was immediately seized on by the other. Bernard, in one of his I-am-a-writer moods, spoke with the self-conscious care of a man giving directions to a tourist with only a rudimentary knowledge of the language. His patronizing manner irritated Robert, who, finding that his jokes met with incomprehension, refused to be daunted and addressed himself to invisible interlocutors who understandably failed to answer the questions with which he peppered his conversation. Over the brandy he drew from his pocket four gaudily colored balloons and gave one each to Monica, Patricia, and Bernard.

"What are we to do with these?" Bernard asked.

"Blow them up of course," Monica laughed uncertainly.

"You're not doing very well," Patricia said to Bernard, who had placed his balloon beside a half-eaten biscuit on his plate.

"What, if anything, are they supposed to denote?" Bernard asked loftily.

"Why, nothing," Robert replied. "We do but jest, inflate them in jest; no offense in the world."

"Are they meant to be symbolic?" Bernard asked.

"They are meant to be filled with hot air." Robert released his balloon, which curved over their heads with an unpleasant farting noise before coming to rest on the mantelpiece. Monica then released hers, followed closely by Patricia's, and they all laughed like children, all except Bernard.

"Don't you think the blowing up of balloons becomes a child better than a man?" he asked without a trace of humor.

"If you must know, my balloons are an indication of my life-long interest in the diffusion of gases, particularly in Fick's and Graham's laws. I myself am not a scientist, but I feel certain that Patricia will be only too pleased to explain to you the principles involved."

Patricia tried to laugh, and Monica, sensing tension, offered Bernard more brandy.

"What is Fick's Law?" Bernard asked Patricia. "To begin with, is there such a law?"

"Oh, yes, it's a law which says that the rate of diffusion of gases depends on the difference in their concentration."

"And what has that got to do with balloons?" Bernard asked Robert.

"I must confess that my own interest in the miscibility of gases is rather more light-hearted than Fick's. You see, I'm trying to perfect the use of balloons as a means of diffusing undesirable body odors as far as possible from the body. By no means an academic exercise after a dinner which, I am told, included a pound of haricot beans."

"What are you trying to say to me?" Bernard asked.

"Merely what you heard. Or did you mishear the word 'Fick'?"

"I sense that you have a statement to make, a statement to which this whole evening has tended."

"About balloons?" inquired Robert.

"I leave that to you."

"I have told you all I know."

"About the poets, for example?"

"I read only three poets for pleasure: Blake, Hardy, and Yeats. The rest are just fodder for curricula."

"You told us earlier that you like lute music."

"Yes, as a change from poetry."

"You gave Patricia a Weiss record, didn't you?"

"In a moment of unwonted generosity." Robert looked at Monica.

"It's a lovely record, I'll return it if you like." Patricia smiled uneasily.

"I don't take back gifts."

"Do you always publicize your good works?" Bernard asked.

"I don't know what you mean."

"You told the poets, didn't you, and they came to my flat in search of lute music. It was an ingenious excuse."

"Now you've lost me utterly, old boy," Robert laughed.

"Well, perhaps they're not poets. I'll put it another way. Do you know two peasants who call themselves Tom-Tom O'Malley and Sean De Barra?"

"I've never heard of them. Should I have?"

"I do but jest, interrogate in jest; no offense in the world."

Bernard picked up the balloon from his plate and with a few puffs transformed it into a long, ugly phallus that reached across the table toward Robert, who filled his pipe and pretended not to notice.

"Release it now and see if it goes higher than ours," said Monica, but Bernard gave another vigorous puff, the balloon burst, and a wet strip of it struck Robert in the face.

155

"Have you ever met Satan, Mr. Foxley?" Bernard asked.

"I've often heard his whisperings but I've never actually seen him."

"I saw him a week ago, drinking a pint of stout in a literary pub and affecting a knowledge of semiotics. Curiously enough, he didn't have a cloven hoof but a goosefoot. Now, does that interest you, Mr. Foxley?"

"There's nothing tastier than a stubble goose and apple sauce at Michaelmas."

"You depart from the point, Mr. Foxley."

"What is the point?"

"Satan."

"Satan, you say. Did he walk with a limp?" Foxley asked.

"Not with a limp, as you well know, but with what you Irish call a gimp."

"Did you have a word with him?"

"I told him that I didn't think much of his foreign policy, that he was losing the struggle with the Great Adversary because he was reluctant to delegate enough power to his followers. I told him that if he bestowed on them the diabolical equivalent of grace—"

"And what did he say to that?" Foxley affected an all-consuming interest.

"He said that it's the end game that matters, that though he'd lost a few battles he'd win the war."

"I'm surprised at such a lack of self-knowledge in a man who seems to understand everyone else all too well."

"What worried him most was something simple. He bemoaned the dearth of good musicians among his followers; he said he'd consider paradise well lost if only he had a composition to match the *St. Matthew Passion* or the *Messiah*. 'Why,' he wanted to know, 'should God have all the good tunes?' Finally, he told me that the latest news from hell was that the Great Adversary was a pervert, and that he, Satan, had him where he wanted him."

"So the devil like the rest of us succumbs to wish-fulfillment!"

"I told him as much, but he laughed and said I didn't know my Scripture. The Great Adversary quite simply gave the game away. He said 'Get thee behind me, Satan.' "

Bernard gave a nervous screech of a laugh and blew the ash from his pipe all over the tablecloth. He pushed back his chair and the laugh turned into a smoker's cough that seemed to steal the very breath from his lungs. Patricia slapped him on the back and Monica turned to Robert and said, "Coddin' is catchin'." At last Bernard got up, swaying between coughs.

"You've heard my description of Satan. Do you recognize him?" he asked Foxley.

"I recognize the manner but not the man."

"You're a liar, sir. I say it to your face: you are in league with him." He stormed out of the room, and they heard his stumble on the stairs.

After a while Patricia followed him to make sure he came to no harm.

"You're obsessed with those two poets. You must try to forget them," she said.

"You have no idea how difficult it is to keep your self-control when you're goaded on all sides."

"You didn't keep your self-control this evening."

"I didn't take to your pedagogic friend. He's a tiresome fraud, all froth and no body like a badly poured bottle of stout. One look at him, and I knew he was in league with the enemy."

"What enemy?"

"Satan."

"I wish you'd use the same language as the rest of us."

"It's my language, not yours."

"Good night."

After Robert left, Patricia helped Monica to wash up, then they both sat over a cup of coffee while Patricia rolled her last cigarette of the day.

"I'll be leaving soon," Monica said. "Robert has asked me to share his flat. It's got two bedrooms, one of them never used."

"When are you leaving?"

"Not for another month. It will give you time to find someone else for the flat—if you want to keep it on, that is. I'll be sorry to leave, though. We've had some good times."

"It had to end some time."

"Don't think I'm going to live with Robert. We'll use the same living room and kitchen but different bedrooms. I know he sees all this as a first step toward what the newspapers call cohabitation, but I'm determined to be strong. He'll thank me for it later when he finds out that it was worth waiting for."

"You expect virtue to be rewarded?"

"Don't you?"

"I suppose I do," said Patricia.

11

On Holy Thursday she drove down the country for Easter. Bernard begged her not to go, and, when she told him that she must see her uncle, he said that he would like to see him too, that the city had driven him to the end of his tether, that only fresh air and open fields could heal him now. She decided to be firm, however. She told him that she did not wish him to come, that she too needed a change, and that above all she needed to be alone.

It was a bright, cold day with a ragged paling of white cloud on the western horizon. She was relieved to be free of the school and flat for a fortnight, and glad to be alone in the car with her suitcase on the back seat, the tang of regrowth in the air, and farmers in the fields busy with the spring sowing. She glowed with the excitement of the drive, passing heavy lorries bound for Limerick and Cork, past the road to Punchestown, knowing that the delights of the Curragh beyond Naas were still to come. At Naas she was more than halfway, so she decided to stop for a drink, a pee, and perhaps a horsy conversation in The Master McGrath, though it commemorated a greyhound, not a horse. The door was open to welcome her but' so little daylight penetrated the windows that the lights were on inside. Nine or ten men were watching racing on the television, while on the walls above them were pictures of legendary greyhounds which they were too turf-intoxicated to notice.

She ordered a pint and sat opposite the door so that she could watch the line of lorries going south. The pint tasted sour, but for that she could not blame the landlord. She'd had too much to drink the previous evening, and the bottom of her stomach was raw. She took another sip, but it was no better than the first. Then she got herself a large Paddy and drank it slowly with just enough water to dull its burning edge. When she had finished the whiskey, she went back to the stout. The effect was electric. Now it tasted smooth and cool with a hint of viscosity that made it linger pleasantly in the hollow of her tongue. With the second pint, she burped but not too loudly, at least not loud enough to be heard above the impassioned commentary on the final furlong. Immediately, she felt better. The rawness in her stomach had dissolved. As Bernard would say, it was coming right; or to quote the Irish master's favorite phrase, *Bhí sé ag oibriú*. Warm with well-being, she read the caption of the picture above her:

Master McGrath, Winner of the Waterloo Cup
1868, 1869, 1871
Sire: Dervock
Dam: Lady Sarah
Bred by: James Galwey, Esq.,
Cooligan Lodge, Dungarvan
Running Weight at Waterloo: 54 lbs.

Two farmers with heavy faces sat at the next table and began a conversation about another farmer who was famous for his dirty cattle. She listened intently while pretending to watch the racing, and suddenly she found herself laughing as she remembered that she'd heard the same conversation in this pub the previous October. She felt grateful for her midland upbringing. She felt in collusion with the farmers, a party to the secret life of the country, a life of unspoken assumptions and beliefs that gave color to both work and play. It was a gift from heaven that no amount of negative living could now take away from her.

Beyond Naas were Newbridge, Kildare, Monastrevin, and finally Portlaoise, dull towns with evocative names which she pronounced to herself aloud in both Irish and English as she read the hurrying signposts. About a mile outside Portlaoise she found herself driving behind a tractor with a load of dung, the first she had seen since she had gone to live in Dublin. The road was winding, and the tractor, wandering from side to side, made it impossible for her to pass. Every time the tractor swerved, a dollop of dung would fall on the road, but she did not blow her horn—she rolled down the window and inhaled the purest smell in the country, the smell of fresh manure. She felt the muscles of her neck relax; she had come into her own territory.

The house was empty when she got home. She went out to the yard and into the shed, noting what was new and what was old and what had changed position since she last looked. Patsy, her twin brother, came through Cape's Gate with a swing, stepping in time to his tuneless whistling.

"Where's everyone?" she asked.

"Mam's gone to confession and Daddy and Austin are sowing beet in Dick's. I've come back to make a drop of tea."

Whenever their mother was out, it always fell to Patsy to do the cooking, and when she was in the house she would ask him, not his father or brother, to lift heavy pots off the range.

"Don't worry," Patricia said, "now that I'm here I'll make something ready."

Within half an hour her father and Austin came back from Dick's and her mother came home from the chapel. Tea, as always, consisted of thickly sliced bacon, tomatoes, soda bread, butter, and cheese. The bacon joint was left in the center of the table and anyone who wanted seconds helped himself. She ate with cholesterol-conscious care, cutting the strips of fat off the bacon and piling them on the edge of her plate, while her father and brothers ate both meat and fat indiscriminately. Her mother, who never ate meat except for a piece of turkey breast at Christmas, had two poached eggs with plenty of bread and cheese. As usual her mother did the talking. The men ate and listened while she rehearsed the ever-engrossing saga of Hugh and Uncle Lar.

After tea Patricia walked across the fields to her uncle's, recalling her girlhood and the weekend "holidays" she spent on his farm, in particular the morning milking before breakfast with the sun barely up over the trees. First she would milk Polly Famous for the house. Then she would let the two youngest calves into the cowhouse to suckle the cows for ten minutes. When they had satisfied themselves, she would let in the older calves, apart from the three that were on powdered milk. They had been on powdered milk from birth, her uncle said. They did not know the taste of real milk, and when their half-brothers rushed across the yard to their mothers, the three would poke their noses through the gate bars and stare with unblinking eyes at the incomprehensible confusion in the cowhouse.

She liked to watch the suckling calves standing with their forelegs apart, their rumps higher than their withers, their necks outstretched, and their tails swishing with innocent well-being. Some of them suckled more gently than the others, but all of them "frothed" at the mouth—slavers of milk and saliva hung from their chins and formed pools on the concrete floor between the cows' legs. The mothers stood still for the most part, staring placidly at the bare walls of the stalls, but now and again one of them would lift a leg in warning if a calf butted her too strongly with its snout. When they'd had enough, Patricia would drive the calves through the farmyard gate into the paddock, and she and Uncle Lar would laugh to see them lick the froth of the milk from one another's faces.

As she walked, she paused every so often to judge the flesh of a newly plowed furrow or examine the buds on the hedges ready to explode. Then she looked all round and squatted in a sheltered corner of a headland for a pee. Though she had drunk three pints in Naas and two cups of tea in the house, she hadn't made water since she left Dublin. She watched a beetle on the ground trying to climb over a straw and falling on its side each time, and she thought of the minute world of insects and of how she used to spend hours watching the movements of ladybirds as a girl. The countryside was a poultice that warmed, softened, and soothed. She thought of Bernard and how pleasant it was to have left the life-in-death of Dublin behind.

Her water came with a rush, prolonged and satisfying, forming a pool on the hard ground in front of her and running downhill in a rivulet in which the beetle swirled with atoms of dust and pieces of straw. She watched it vanish into a crevice in the poached earth, disappointed that it had stopped, wishing for a larger bladder and more water, not a rivulet but a river.

She looked up as she heard the swish of a bending branch on her right. Hugh came through the hedge. She made as if to pull up her knickers, but realizing that he'd already seen her, she decided to hold her ground. Bernard Baggotty, like most men, would have looked the other way, but Hugh bore down on her with his ashplant under his oxter like a gun and a look of amused devilment in his eye. She watched him approach, determined to conceal her embarrassment.

"When did you come?"

His head was a block of basalt with a sparse patch of lichen on top.

"Only an hour ago."

"I won't offer you my hand. I can see you're occupied—or maybe preoccupied."

"I'm going to Uncle Lar's. I'll see you there."

"You're sure you don't want me to wait for you?"

"Certain. I'm not in any hurry, I want to take in the scenery on the way."

"You're part of the scenery yourself," he smiled.

He tapped the toecap of his boot with his ashplant, waiting for her to give something of herself away, but she reached out and plucked a blade of couch grass, pretending that he wasn't there.

"I never go in the house myself," he said. "The influence of the Australian outback, I suppose. Though the choice of terrain here is more limited than in the Northern Territory, what there is of it is more varied."

He laughed but she did not respond, so he stuck the tip of his ashplant into the crevice where her water had vanished and looked at it as if it were a dipstick.

"I'll see you at the house."

He slapped his boot with the ashplant and off he went whistling. She watched the lilt of his shoulders from where she squatted, broad and strong and heavy like a bull's. Compared with him, Bernard was a mere bullock, his sexual presence veiled in middle-class English faineance. Hugh's, on the other hand, was so insistent that it gave off a kind of smell that reminded her of rank grass growing on the remains of an old dunghill. She waited until Hugh had vanished from sight, then continued her walk through the fragrant fields, trying to put from her mind the bulge in the crotch of his tight trousers.

Uncle Lar, who was waiting at the farmyard gate, took both her hands and held her at arm's length to get a better look at her. He smiled with unfeigned pleasure, but she thought she could detect a hint of withdrawal in his eyes. He was finally beginning to look his age. Perhaps for the first time he had come to realize that the world would go on without him. With such knowledge must come the wisdom of detachment, she told herself, but she saw not so much wisdom as a lessening of the transparency of the spiritual lens, and neither drugs nor surgery, only rebirth, could cure this particular form of cataract. She felt like hugging him to get his dry, outdoor smell, but he let go of her and said:

"You've lost some of your color—nothing that a week of fresh air and country food won't cure."

She spent the rest of the afternoon ironing his shirts and darning socks while he told her about the farm and the herd. As she listened, she was aware of noises in the yard, Hugh doing a last few jobs before nightfall, moving between the dairy and the cowhouses, clanking buckets and calling to the dogs. She could feel the weight of his presence in the gathering twilight and the shape of his foot in the sock in her hand, and she wanted to ask her uncle about him, but her uncle was talking with his eyes closed as if Hugh were not in the yard but in another hemisphere.

At half-past nine the three of them drove to the village for a drink. It was the first time she had been to a pub with Lar, and from the way the other men waved or called to him she could see that he had become a local character. She decided to drink brandy because she did not want to shock her uncle or amuse her cousin by drinking pints. The two of them drank their stout steadily and unhurriedly like confident men for whom tide and time, at least for an hour, were obsequious flunkies. They began telling yarns about the Australian outback, one capping the other's tall tales, and she sensed an instinctive concordance between them, which made her think that in losing his grip on the present Lar had, through Hugh, strengthened his grip on the past. After a while he asked her to tell them about Dublin, if she were lonely, if she liked teaching, and what she did in the evenings. He began making fun of her, pretending that she had picked up the Dublin accent, and meanwhile Hugh drank his stout and pressed his thigh against hers under the table. She responded light-heartedly to her uncle's badinage and firmly to the pressure of Hugh's thigh while wondering about the strange thing he did to Desmond Deeny's sister. Desmond and her mother were biased. They both saw Hugh as a threat, but she would see him as Lar saw him, because it was Lar's view, not her mother's, that mattered.

Her uncle went to the bar for a round of drinks and Hugh picked up her hand like a glove from the table.

"It's a strong hand," he said. "Strong enough to hold a pair of plow horses."

"Is is a perfect hand?" she teased him.

"No, it's a shade too small for the wrist." He replaced it beside her other hand on the table.

They left the pub at twelve, and she offered to make them tea when they got home.

"It's bed for me," said Lar. "I'll see you both tomorrow."

"We'll have a nightcap, then," Hugh said to Patricia. "After all, it will be Good Friday in the morning."

He produced a bottle of brandy and two half-pint tumblers from the dresser and poured the equivalent of two pub doubles into each glass. He sat beside her on the settee and moved the sleeping dog so that he could stretch his legs.

"You've taken after Lar," he said. "You never lose control."

"What do you think of Lar?" She tried to sound indifferent.

"He's as solid as Ayers Rock, and like the rock he changes color depending on the time of day. In the morning he can only think of farming but in Dartry's in the evening he's got a thought on every subject under the sun."

"He's an innocent man," she said seriously. "He spent most of his life in this house on his own. He's had time to think, and curiously he thinks well of everyone else. That's why I say he's innocent. I've never heard him laugh in malice."

"You mean he's a poor judge of character."

"No, I just mean that he sees the good in life before he sees the bad. Life is like an optical illusion, a geometrical figure that changes shape depending on how you look at it. Uncle Lar sees both shapes but he sees the good one first."

"He's to be envied, then," Hugh said. "He's well off. Round here he's thought of as a successful man, and he still can see both shapes. Most men who make a go of it convince themselves that there's only one."

He put his right arm over her shoulder, but not before she had come to expect it. Then he asked her if she would like to see Australia, and she wondered what and where his next move would be. His arm lay like a deadweight on her shoulder, and suddenly he kissed her with the speed of a woodcock breaking cover at dusk. She was reminded of a woodcock because the flight of a woodcock frightened her into crying when she was five. Though his kiss did not frighten her, she had not expected the raw force of it. She had expected it to land on her cheek and neck and finally on her mouth, but it fell straight between her lips like a cleaving shaft of lightning, while his stout-laden breath came in short snorts through his nose and his broad hand felt the weight of her right breast.

After twenty minutes he got up and switched off the light, and the kitchen was cozy and not altogether dark because of the glow from the open door of the range. The dog, snoring on the mat, stretched in his dream and another dog barked in another town land. A coal fell in the range and her mind planed like a seagull over the liquid silence, dipping and soaring with an uncharted terrain beneath. She wondered what on earth he had tried to do to Desmond Deeny's sister, and before she had ceased wondering he unbuttoned her top and unhooked her bra and was kissing her naked breasts, the weight of his basalt head pressing down on her, heavy and powerful and butting like a bull calf suckling. He was licking her nipples, making a lapping movement with his tongue, causing her to float upward on a quiverful of shooting sensations. She ran her hand through his short hair. It was fine, almost silky, certainly not spiky to the touch like lichen, and his scalp, though hard, was warmer than a block of basalt in the sun. She ran her hand down his back inside his shirt, aware of the warm cloud under her bottom bearing her upwards with her legs open while the weight of him moved like warm lightning in her breasts and belly. He had taken off her knickers and he was kissing her on the lips again while the tip of his penis tickled the furrows of her vagina. She wanted him to remain like that for a long time, moving his pestle along the rim of her mortar, sipping her slowly like good brandy with the night all round, the fire dying in the range and time and tide immobilized by a moratorium. He put his hand between her legs and parted the lips with rude fingers.

"I'm not ready yet," she whispered.

"What's wrong? You're dry as a keck," he said thickly.

He thrust a thick tongue between her teeth and she turned her head in sudden nausea. In the urgency of his need he had begun massaging her labia with his forefinger, up and down mechanically and insultingly like a scientist obsessed with cause and effect. She tried to get out from under him but his arms and legs held her like the sides of a coffin. Sensing that he was determined not to be robbed, she put down her hand, got a firm grip on the butt of his penis, twisted it like a chicken's neck, and pulled.

"Christ! You've sprained it," he cried, rising off her with a spring.

When she had buttoned her top and regained her breath, she put on the light. He was sitting on the edge of the settee, bent in two, still hugging himself between the legs, looking ridiculous with his trousers round his ankles and her knickers hanging on his still erect penis.

"I'll have my knickers back," she said.

"No, you won't." He stuffed them into his pocket. "I'm going to hang the fucking things on the highest branch in the garden first thing tomorrow and I'm going to pepper them with buckshot till the gusset is a sieve. And it isn't a twelvebore I'd like to have but a bloody machine gun."

"You're a rough one."

"If so, I've met my match in you, you unnatural bitch."

She walked home slowly, not across the fields, but along the road, half aware of the complaints of drowsy birds in the hedges and the rustle of scampering rabbits in the undergrowth. It was a night of sky-brightness, of cloudless starlight with no moon. The stars were alien and cold, Uncle Lar was stretched in a stout-stupor on his bed, Hugh was nursing his yanked pecker, and she was going back with shame and disquiet in her heart.

In the lane she opened the iron gate and stood on the lowest bar, allowing it to swing inward with a squeal, remembering her schooldays and her mother saying "How many times have I told you not to swing on the lane gate?" She changed to the other side and rode back till the clang of metal told her to shoot the bolt. Her act was a deliberate effort to recover a lost faculty she had missed for the first time in the pub when she found herself looking at Uncle Lar as if he were her father or any other sinful man. When she remembered him in the city, he trailed clouds of glory like a winter sunset, but in the pub what she saw was an old man so desperate in his search for human love that he had pinned his hopes on a man of stone. For that she had only herself to blame. If only she had written more often . . . if she had rung him once a week . . . if she had come down every weekend . . . if . . . if . . . if she were an entirely different woman.

It was two when she got to bed. She tiptoed up the stairs in stocking feet while her brothers snored in the back room, sunk in the sleep of those who await their first awakening. For a long time she lay in the dark, listening to familiar night sounds—the bark of a dog, the whine of a tomcat, a cough from the cowhouse, the rattle of chains from the loose-box—telling herself that for the moment, here in her mother's house, she was safe.

Toward morning she woke in a sweat, clutching the cold

bedstead with both hands. She was being held prisoner in a white-emulsioned room, tied down naked on an iron bed with a ship's hawser that snaked between her legs and across her breasts, while on the wall above her hung a long, thin sword, an inch or two out of reach. Detective Inspector McMyler entered sleepwalking with arms outstretched, hatless and bagless and naked to the world, and with his eyes still closed he caught the sword in his left hand, slashed the ropes that held her, and, as she was about to embrace him, he drove the cold, thin steel through her heart.

She got up late with a sense of defilement as she remembered the word "unnatural" and a longing to cleanse herself in the company of Desmond Deeny. After the three o'clock service in the chapel, she drove to Dunbarron but he didn't appear to be at home. She walked round the house, reading neatness and thrift on every stone, and she told herself that it was a lovely cottage with a rambler rose at the door and that Desmond had everything he could wish for except a landed woman. She went to the kitchen window and looked in. Someone gripped her waist from behind and she recognized the hearty ring of his laugh.

"When did you come?" His eyes danced madly.

"Yesterday evening."

"And you waited nearly twenty-four hours before coming to see me."

"Last night I went with Uncle Lar to the pub."

They leaned over the garden wall and he pointed to the new potato drills and the bank of daffodils at the end. He was wearing green gumboots, old cavalry twills, and a heavy duffle coat with a missing toggle, and he smiled at her, freckled and square-jawed with a chin too heavy for his face. Unlike her brothers, he shaved every morning because he worked for The Forestry, but by noon his face would darken like a winter sky as a thick stubble sprang from every pore. Though physically he was far from perfect, she liked him for his infectious enthusiasm. In company he said little, but alone with her he would wax lyrical about trees and plants, birds and animals, and on less inspiring days about his secondhand Land Rover. He wasn't overtly intelligent. At primary school he had been slow, but now in manhood he seemed merely wide-eyed and somewhat naive. Someone who had not known him as a boy might think that the connections he made were those of a poet, but Patricia knew that they were those of a man who lacked a capacity for dispassionate analysis. He once said to her that we make fun of those we secretly admire, and when she told him that we are more likely to laugh at those we secretly fear, he argued for an hour without budging from his, to her, strange, almost naive belief.

Though at times she found herself in the act of patronizing him, she could not help envying him his male intuition and male impulses, which were seldom negative. Most of the men she had met lived their lives on the assumption that they themselves knew best, that they were born to take life's measure, and that the doings of other men must at best appear slightly ridiculous. Most men were plane surveyors, armed with ordnance maps and theodolites, strong on "how" and weak on "why." Their philosophy, if they had one, must perforce be prescriptive, at its most characteristic in domestic judgments made for the greater happiness of a wife originally chosen for an intelligence and imagination which would not threaten the pre-eminence of her lord's. Desmond, as it happened, had actually studied plane surveying, but he had also seen the stars. Though he knew how to get to a given destination, he did not become so engrossed in measuring the relative positions of points that he forgot the reason for the journey. She followed him into the cottage, glad of his uncomplicated affability.

They spent the evening in the cottage. First she cooked a simple meal, and then they sat side by side in the living room listening to a German performance of the *St. John*

Passion on television. It was an evening of serious, though largely unspoken, thoughts that could only strive unavailingly for the purity of Bach, and she left before ten with the feeling that Good Friday was not a good day to visit Desmond Deeny. She took her mother shopping to Roscrea on Saturday and spent the evening at home, reluctant to revisit Lar because of Hugh.

Easter Sunday was cloudless and calm. She woke at half-past seven and decided to go to eight o'clock Mass like the rest of the family. Austin left early with her father and mother, and she waited for Patsy, who was still polishing his boots with an old cap at ten to eight. As they came up to the first crossroads, she spied Uncle Lar's car ahead of them.

"We're in time," she said.

"We're not early," Patsy replied. "No one was ever in time who was later than Lar."

"But he's always on time."

"Only just is what I mean."

She drove quickly, taking outrageous risks at crossroads, but she did not gain an inch on Lar. The chapel was only half full, and the low morning sun filled the empty seats with glorious light. A solitary altar boy emerged from the sacristy, rubbing the sleep from his eyes, arousing a sense of expectation which was reinforced by the clarity of the air. A pale priest in white vestments appeared from behind the brick screen and began the Mass without once looking at the congregation. He must have been new. She had not seen him before, and as she listened to the music of his reading she wanted to be like Desmond Deeny and the other members of his untroubled flock. She felt vulnerable and weak, perhaps because she had not eaten, and she listened to his simple sermon on St. John's account of the Resurrection with longing for past Easter Sundays and anguished bewilderment at what life was doing to her. She heard little of what followed the homily. She just knelt in her seat reading and rereading St. John:

So they ran both together: and the other disciple did outrun Peter, and came first to the sepulchre. And he stooping down, and looking in, saw the linen clothes lying; yet went he not in. Then cometh Simon Peter following him, and went into the sepulchre, and seeth the linen clothes lie, and the napkin, that was about his head, not lying with the linen clothes, but wrapped together in a place by itself. Then went in also that other disciple, which came first to the sepulchre, and he saw, and believed.

She found tears in her eyes. She realized that she was standing, that people were leaving the church, that Mass was over. Outside, neighbors were sitting on a wall, laughing and smoking, while a row of cars queued at the only petrol pump. The sun was brighter now and suddenly she felt overjoyed to be surrounded by sane men on a day that looked like any other.

"I saw you behind me in the mirror. You never lost an inch, fair play to you." Uncle Lar squeezed her arm.

"But I never gained one either," she smiled.

"Your car doesn't know the corners like mine."

"He's a very holy man, the new parish priest," she said to test him.

"He's a slow man. He never says Mass in less than an hour."

"A sure sign of holiness."

"It's an occasion of sin," said Lar. "He makes everyone fidget and wonder about the time. The young curate is your only man. He's so fast that you've got to work hard to get in a prayer or two before the final blessing. Everyone likes him because he makes them feel holier than himself. It's a charitable trait in a priest."

Uncle Lar crossed the road to his car, Patsy told her that he was getting a lift from a neighbor whom he wanted to see about fodder beet, and a friend from her schooldays came up and shook her hand. She rejoiced in her uncle and the farmers round her. They weren't philosophers, but they knew a trick or two that enabled good humor to serve the purpose of serious thought. Driving home alone, she felt better. She decided to visit Desmond Deeny in the afternoon.

He was tinkering under his Land Rover, and he looked up like a black minstrel as she approached.

"I was expecting you yesterday," he said. "If you hadn't turned up, I was going to fetch you after tea."

"It's a lovely day, but I suppose it's too cold for swimming."

"We'll go to the woods. I'll give you a Cook's tour, and we'll have a drink in Dartry's on the way back."

"And after that we'll go to a dance in Abbeyleix."

"If you like." He went into the house to wash.

They drove up the mountain in his Land Rover with the roof off and the bright countryside unrolling like printed calico behind them. Desmond was at his most innocent, telling her about wood and its uses: that in the old days elm was used for mill wheels but that it was now used for coffins; that ash made the best oars and hurleys; and that spruce made tall masts for sailing vessels. He continued his disquisition as they walked beneath the trees, the sun cleaving avenues of light between branches, the slightly sour smell of the earth mingling with the resinous smell of pines.

"Spruces are like men and larches are like penguins." He pointed eagerly.

"How is that?"

"Look how the branches of the spruce point upward and those of the larch point to the ground. Man raises his arms to the heavens in prayer and the penguin points with his flippers to his toes. It is not the only curious thing about the larch. I'll bet you didn't know that it's one of the few deciduous conifers."

He spread his duffle coat on a dry patch under a lodgepole pine (a Sitka spruce, he said, wouldn't do), but she didn't feel like sitting down. She wanted to skip and dance over the needle carpet, running from one shaft of light to another to express her joy in the day and the wonder of being together where they were.

"Have you seen Hugh?" he asked.

"Only once."

"It can come to no good, you should stop it while you can."

"Everyone says that, but there's nothing I can do."

"You can come back from Dublin. If you don't make Lar see sense—"

"I'm tired of thinking about him. I want to forget." She sat down on the coat beside him.

He kissed her first on the neck, then on the lips, and they lay in each other's arms while he explored the curve of her bottom through her dress in an intimate form of geodetic surveying. A lark singing above them transported her to an empty cathedral with spring sunlight pouring through the clerestory onto grey pillars while plainsong rebounded off the walls. There was no one in the cathedral but herself, neither priest nor choir, yet the very air trilled with the purity of never-before-sung music. The music swelled in her breast and then she lost her awareness of it in her desire to give herself to Desmond Deeny.

He was fumbling with her dress, undoing buttons, and she closed her eyes as if daylight had already died and she had surrendered to the ambiguities of the night. Desmond often caressed her legs but she always stopped him before he could touch her in between. It was a ritual which had been sanctified by usage, so that he never embarked on it without certain knowledge of where it would end. This time she failed to arrest his advance with the customary signal, and he dithered in disbelief while she feigned unconscious impassivity. After what seemed an eternity, and with much huffing and puffing, he pulled down her knickers and placed his right leg as a kind of bridgehead between her knees. While executing these delicate maneuvers, he had stopped kissing her, but now he started again as if he had suddenly realized that it was possible to do more than one thing at a time. Though she found the lack of ease in the negotiations distracting, she wanted him desperately and she dared not open her eyes in case he should see in them the demon calculation, the archenemy of romantic love.

At last he rolled her over and lay on top of her, and she wanted him to take her quickly, to overcome without further perambulation her invincible virginity. She could not help him because she was not supposed to, and anyhow it was so ridiculously unreal because they were over-dressed above and naked in the devil's domain below. He was moving like wildfire along the edge of her vagina, but with a lack of purpose that made her bite her tongue. Then, as she thought the tension would never end, the breath left him with a rush as if someone had slapped his back, and she felt the throb of his penis and the trickle of broth between her thighs. She thought of asparagus soup as he lay like a pork carcass on top of her, and she kept her eyes closed against the light and tried to recall the plainsong, the cathedral, and the lark.

"You're too heavy," she said at last.

"I was too nervous."

"Maybe it's just as well."

"If you wait for half an hour, I'm sure—"

"I think it's time we went home." She plucked her knickers from the branch on which he had hung them and stuffed them in her pocket. She got to her feet, pulled down her dress, and buttoned it in front while he rubbed a grey stain off the inside of his duffle coat.

"You're a changed girl." He tightened his belt.

"Why is that?"

"You never let me do that before."

"I never wanted you like that before."

"It's the city, I suppose."

"It has more to do with the country and the spring air."

"Do you go out with other men?" he asked.

"You're the first to touch me there—if that's what you want to know."

He was busy brushing pine needles off the nap of his duffle coat, and then without looking at her he said:

> The Noble Duke of York,
> He had ten thousand men,
> He marched them up to the top of the hill,
> And he marched them down again."

"Wait for me here." She walked away unsteadily, wondering if what had or had not happened to her were real.

Behind the cover of the trees she took her knickers from her pocket, and as she stepped into them staggered and fell backward into a bed of moss. She felt helpless as an overturned beetle, but she picked herself up and leaned weakly against a tree, convulsed by tearless sobs. Her shoulders shook, her breath clawed at her windpipe, and her breasts heaved painfully. She felt chafed and bruised, she wished for nothing but the soothing touch of sleep.

Desmond was cutting a blaze on the lodgepole pine when she got back.

"Vandalizing trees is a strange thing for a forestry man to do," she said.

"It's a form of magic. Now the tree bears the wound, which mercifully time and weather will cicatrize. Come on, we'll go for a drink."

"I don't think so. I want to get to bed early."

"What about the dance in Abbeyleix?"

"We'll go another time."

He drove her home in silence, and she sat emptily beside him like one of Foxley's collapsed balloons. She used to tell her pupils that the average living room has a volume of about 30 cubic meters, that each cubic meter of atmosphere has a mass of nearly 1.3 kilograms, and that therefore the air in the average living room has a total mass of 39 kilograms. She now felt that a 39-kilogram sack of stones was pressing down on her head and shoulders.

"I'll call for you tomorrow," he said at the gate, but she knew already that by tomorrow she'd be in Dublin.

"Where are you going?" her mother asked as she came down the stairs with her suitcase.

"I'm going back to Dublin."

"Tonight? I thought you were staying for a fortnight."

"I'm going back now, Mother."

"But what will Lar think?"

"Uncle Lar, like the rest of us, thinks what pleases him best."

She left at seven, just as her father and brothers were sitting down to tea, and she drove steadily as a robot without stopping for a drink in Naas. Tired and tense, she reached Ballsbridge at a quarter to ten and knocked at Bernard's door.

"What happened?" He made no attempt to conceal his joy.

"Nothing happened. Country life is just not what it used to be."

"Did you have a row with your uncle?"

"No."

"With your mother?"

"No, I decided that the pint is better in town."

"What a girl you are, Patricia. Do you realize that tomorrow is Easter Monday? We won't start a Rising, we'll go to Fairyhouse and the Grand National."

"I don't care where we go provided it's in the open air." She flopped down on the sofa and wished she were in bed alone.

12

At first sight Fairyhouse was a field full of stereotypes—suntanned men in brown suits and soft hats with expensive binoculars beating their breasts and women in softer hats with white gloves affecting an inordinate interest in their race cards. She had not expected such a crowd, and it was only after ten or fifteen minutes that she realized that the stereotypes were in the minority. The majority were ordinary Dubliners and their families, out to enjoy the good weather and the controlled disorder that mixes the blood with madness at a race meeting.

Bernard had spent the morning studying form. He had already decided to eat out that evening and said he knew which races would pay for his dinner. He was not content, however. He was still looking for the coincidence that would give the day its characteristic piquancy. She could see why he always lost; he was far too excitable, too easily intoxicated by sudden commotions, rumors, announcements, and the thud of hooves on turf.

"There's only one thing the Irish do better than the English," he told her loftily on the way to the paddock.

"And that's racing commentaries. The soft Irish speech is particularly suitable for the first few furlongs of a race like the Grand National while the field is settling down. I always think the start of a race is like a summer morning before the day takes on the serious cast of inevitability. Your Irish commentator is at his best then because he resists the temptation to give the race the bogus urgency you get on the BBC. 'And now they're off,' he'll say quietly, as if he already knew the result. 'And it's Sandy Lady, Saucy Samuel, and Adam's Apple making the running, followed by Tagliatelle, Shancoduff, Gregorian Chant, Aberdeen, Et Tu Brute, English Mustard, Surface Tension, and Quick As Lightning.' It isn't the speed of the commentary that tells, it's the rhythm. In the mouths of the best commentators, the names of horses become poetry, like a passage from Milton full of musical place names. Do you see what I mean?"

"Yes, Bernard," she said, not wishing to encourage him.

"First, we'll do some eavesdropping," he said. "At the races all is coincidence. The best tips come from the air—they are the punter's *donnés*."

For a long time they watched the horses being walked before each race by stable lads, horses that snorted nervously, horses with delicate ears cocked forward, horses with delicate veins in their necks, horses with thick veins in the inside of their thighs, horses that showed well-brushed teeth as they neighed, and one horse with a mouthful of brown teeth, as if he'd been reared on black tea.

"I'm going to bet on him," she said. "He's more plebeian than the others."

"No," said Bernard. "Simple anthropomorphism will get you nowhere. You must judge first with a cold eye, and then you must temper science with intuition. You must ask yourself, 'Does he move me? Do I like his style?' If the answer is yes, you'll go wild to see him win, and even if he doesn't, you'll still get a good run for your money. But if you must know the true secret of betting, it's the balance of form and coincidence. Always place two bets on every race, one on form and one on coincidence."

Two middle-aged men in dirty raincoats pushed their way through the crowd to the railings.

"The going's just right for him," said the first.

"If that scutcher of a jockey doesn't lose his irons again," said the second.

"He jumped like a cat at Leopardstown, and he'd have won if it hadn't rained in the night."

"I was talking to his stable lad this morning and he said he was a very genuine horse. 'A very genuine horse'—those were his very words."

"A genuine horse?"

"A horse's horse."

"Like a man's man?"

"That's right. But he has a human side too, I'm told. He wanders round the yard and puts his head in the kitchen door. This morning the trainer's wife burned the toast, and—would you believe it?—he had a bit of it for breakfast."

"What was that all about?" Patricia asked when the dirty raincoats moved off.

"Didn't you hear? They were talking about 'horseness,' " said Bernard, following them. "Horseness, not horsiness, is the essence."

"Where are you going now?"

"I'm following them. I myself had burned toast for breakfast, and I must find out which horse they're talking about."

They followed the two men to the betting window, and Bernard waited for an opportunity.

"Excuse me," he said. "Do either of you gentlemen happen to know which horse likes burned toast? I read about it in one of the papers and forgot. My wife says it's Cock-a-Leekie—"

"Never," said the first dirty raincoat. "It can only be Papal Slipper."

"What a coincidence!" said Bernard when they were alone. "We'll eat out this evening, Patricia. Papal Slipper's thirty to one."

"We meet again, so we do. The world and his floozie must be here." Voices of self-mockery came from behind.

Patricia and Bernard turned, and there stood Tom-Tom O'Malley and Sean De Barra, each with a sheaf of typewritten sheets in his hand.

"Selling race cards?" Bernard inquired. "Sorry, not today."

"We're hawking poetry," said Tom-Tom. "All we had was the bus fare, and my friend here had the bright idea of flogging a few love poems to raise enough for a bet. I'm afraid we've had only a modest success so far. A young physicist bought a Petrarchan sonnet for his light-o'-love."

"We make a point of selling only to the semiliterate professions," said De Barra. "Doctors, lawyers, accountants, architects, engineers, surveyors—anyone in fact who hasn't read a language at university."

"What snobbery!" Bernard hooted.

"Snobbery, my foot," said De Barra. "We find on the contrary that their literary tastes have not been calcified by prejudice."

"How about you, Patricia?" said Tom-Tom. "Would you like a love poem for as little as a pound? It's a period piece, a pastiche of the Bard that will thrill you to bits:

> *It was a lover and his lass*
> *With a hey and a ho, and a hey-nonino!*
> *That o'er the green corn-field did pass . . ."*

"Or how about this?" said De Barra:

> *Shall I compare thee to a summer's day?*
> *Thou art more lovely and more temperate . . ."*

"But that *is* Shakespeare!" shouted Bernard.

"We do believe in giving value for money," said Tom-Tom.

"Excuse me," said De Barra, turning to run after a young man and his lady, both of whom were engrossed in the brim of her enormous hat.

"See you," said Tom-Tom, hastening after his friend.

"Those two need watching," said Bernard. "I'll bet they'll steer clear of us now that I've rumbled them."

"Rumbled them?"

"The game is up. They know I know they're not real poets."

"Well, at least they went to the trouble of typing out real poetry."

"You're an innocent, Patricia. I've blown their cover. Semiliterate professions indeed! No real poet would make such a specious distinction. They're not what they seem, I tell you. They're not even real farmers."

"They're two amusing young men with an ability to laugh at themselves as well as other people. What's wrong with selling Shakespeare? It's better than selling ice cream."

He gripped her sleeve and stiffened like a pointer. She looked down to see if he'd raised one foot, but, to tell the truth, he hadn't.

"Don't look now, but I spy Goosefoot."

"White, Red, or Stinking?"

"It's no joking matter. I caught him looking at us through his binoculars."

"He must think we're horses. Another man that can't distinguish between horsiness and horseness."

"This is serious, Patricia. I'm going to work my way upwind of him. I'll pretend to go to the gents and double back. Don't move a muscle, wait for me right here."

Before she could speak, he had gone. Mad as a hatter, she thought, trying to concentrate on her race card, wondering what to do, wondering if McMyler were studying her face. The thought gave her a sharp little thrill, and she walked toward the parade ring, to a spot from which she could keep an eye on the horseflesh and the place to which Bernard said he would return.

"What a lovely surprise! I had no idea you were an aficionado of the horse."

"I'm only here for the jockeys," she laughed. "Horses take second place."

He was standing beside her in green thornproof tweeds with the same blue shoulder bag but a new dark brown hat. He leaned toward her, warming her with the soothing darkness of his voice.

"Jockeys are a weedy lot," he said. "A tiresome necessity until such time as the horse recovers his glory as the centaur I believe he once was."

"Where are your binoculars, Inspector?"

"I never take them to the races. I see more than is good for me with the naked eye. Looking through binoculars is a form of specialization. In focusing on a single object you miss its relationship to the whole. The horse who is last is as much part of the race as the leader of the field, and both must be seen in a single glance. But you haven't told me your choice for the big race."

"Rum Baba, I think."

"The housewives' choice," he laughed contemptuously.

"Why the housewives'?"

"Because no housewife ever put her blouse on a horse. She bets rather on the color of the jockey's shirt. Housewives love any shade of red. Believe me, I've just seen one of them feeling a jockey's sleeve as if she were in a draper's buying a length of silk. In a nutshell, housewives go racing to find a socially acceptable outlet for their more outrageous sexual fantasies. No, put thy money on Phlogiston and put money in thy purse."

"But Phlogiston is a rank outsider. He's forty to one."

"He's got an inflammable temperament, believe you me,

and in Fred Bunsen he has a highly combustible rider. As for his owner, the less said about that coincidence the better."

"What about Papal Slipper? I believe he's had burned toast for breakfast."

"Not burned toast, Miss Teeling, but a stone of rolled oats."

"Is that bad?"

"It isn't good. But have a care, Mr. Baggotty is returning from the gents, upwind when he should be downwind, as usual."

"Wait," she said, looking round, but all she could see was the brown hat with the black, shiny band vanishing among the other hats in the crowd.

"He's vanished," said Bernard. "Vanished into thin air."

"Never mind. What a pity there isn't a horse called Goosefoot."

"I've made up my mind," Bernard declared. "I'm going to put a tenner each way on Papal Slipper."

"That's a bit rash. While you were gone, I heard a rumor that he had a stone of rolled oats for breakfast."

"A joke, one of the hairiest and hoariest in the punter's canon."

"Please yourself. I'm going to put a straight fiver on Phlogiston."

"You must be mad."

"He'll stay as well as Papal Slipper."

"But he hasn't had burned toast for breakfast."

"More to the point, his owner is called Lavoisier. A nice coincidence."

"He should really be called Stahl, you know."

"No, that would be too neat. Lavoisier is more ironic."

Before going to the stand for the start of the Grand National, they watched the horses in the parade ring. Bernard was quick to point out that Phlogiston was smaller than the others, that he was too nervous, and that his middle-aged jockey had to pat him on the neck for two minutes before mounting, whereas Papal Slipper felt so much at home in public that he bowed several times to the crowd with monarchical condescension. Trainers and owners spoke a final word to light-boned jockeys with the sheen of spring light on their silks. She waited impatiently on the stand while Bernard gabbled about the importance of experience in a big race, reminding her more than once that Papal Slipper had over ninety meetings "under his girths."

In the distance, almost on the horizon, the horses were under starter's orders. They seemed to be out in the country with low, candyfloss clouds behind them, and suddenly they were gliding down the incline with Arenicola, Calico Boy, Surfers' Paradise, and Spanking Progress leading the field. There was no mention of either Phlogiston or Papal Slipper, and she could not make them out in the distance because she did not have binoculars. Someone beside her groaned as his horse fell at the first jump, a burst of sunshine flashed on silks, and as the field passed before her she could not believe that it was Fairyhouse and the Grand National, so disproportionate was her emotion to the ordinariness of the occasion. The grass of the turf was not sufficiently green, the course seemed makeshift as a point-to-point. It all looked so simple that it was hard to imagine the strain on horse and rider, the stress on girth and stirrup. Papal Slipper was lying eighth, pursued by Phlogiston, who was running comfortably with his jockey whispering what could have been one of Tom-Tom's love lyrics in his ear. Again they vanished into the distance. She looked round the crowd, then at Bernard straining every nerve, while the horses approached the fences for the second time. It was a grueling race, and already her excitement was being colored by exhaustion. Papal Slipper stumbled, Bernard cursed in Anglo-Saxon, and the commentator suddenly noticed Phlogiston "coming from nowhere" at the fourth-last fence. She watched them coming into the straight, reexperiencing her dream of the relay race and the crowds cheering her on. Now the race and the commentary were one. Calico Boy had begun to fade and Spanking Progress was failing, as the commentator said, "to make enough spanking progress." Tears came to her eyes. She could barely see the horses, she was so caught up in the relentless commentary: "Phlogiston has found the right gear. He's motoring past Calico Boy. He's gliding like a bird, with at least another three good furlongs in him . . . And he's past the post. Phlogiston from Calico Boy, second, with English Mustard third, and Spanking Progress fourth."

"Just my luck!" said Bernard.

"Don't worry, we'll still eat out this evening."

As she went to collect her money, an announcement saying that there had been an objection aroused excitement in some and impatience and anger in others. They had a drink in one of the overcrowded bars while Bernard told her that he knew Phlogiston was a loser. The objection had put a damper on her enjoyment. She drank without tasting the sour bottled stout, then she hugged Bernard wildly as the announcer said that the result of the stewards' inquiry was "no alteration."

She collected almost two hundred pounds, which had the welcome effect of discouraging Bernard from further attempts to distinguish between horseness and horsiness. Over dinner she tried to comfort him for the "inexplicable failure of Papal Slipper," but finally it was the wine not her words that mellowed him. For one precious hour he forgot Goosefoot and the poets and talked wittily and amusingly about the London suburb in which he was born. He seemed completely at ease. She felt pleased to be with him, and she was delighted when he asked her to have a nightcap in his flat before going to bed.

Fate decreed otherwise, however. When they got back, the poets were waiting on the landing, Tom-Tom O'Malley with a bottle of brandy and Sean De Barra with a bottle of whiskey, both of them obviously the worse for drink.

"Didn't I tell you we'd come back with a bottle. It's an ancient bardic custom," said Tom-Tom. "We sold seven pounds' worth of love poems and put every penny of it on—"

"Phlogiston," hooted Bernard. "The charlies' choice and the true punter's despair."

"Don't tell me you missed the coincidence," laughed De Barra.

"I didn't," said Patricia. "I had a fiver on him to win."

"Aren't you going to invite us in?" asked Tom-Tom.

"Wait and see," said Bernard, opening the door.

"We'll play some lute music," Patricia laughed.

"It wasn't a real coincidence," Bernard told them as they entered. "It's obvious to every schoolboy that his owner named him Phlogiston because he himself was called Lavoisier."

"Where are the glasses?" De Barra asked.

"There will be no drinking till we've heard a poem from each of you," said Bernard.

O'Malley jumped up on a footstool and with wild arms declaimed:

"O many a day have I made good ale in the glen,
That came not of stream, or malt, like the brewing of
men.
My bed was the ground, my roof, the greenwood
above,
And the wealth that I sought—one far kind glance
from my love."

"Enough!" shouted Bernard. "I didn't ask you to quote, I asked you to compose. You will each make up an impromptu quatrain with alternate rhymes. We'll begin with you, O'Malley."

"Haven't you heard that a drink comes before a story?"
De Barra winked at O'Malley.

O'Malley laughingly laid the bottle of brandy on the
table, put both hands to his lips, and after a moment's
meditation came out with the following:

> *"Give me a pint of carotic stout,*
> *And the ear of a drunken gobemouche,*
> *And I'll drink his health and tell him about*
> *A roscid pratt for bonne bouche."*

"Your turn, De Barra." Bernard pointed.

De Barra winked again at O'Malley and between a laugh
and a hiccup recited:

> *"I spied a breast Churrigueresque*
> *In dancing ithyphallic.*
> *I felt a bottom Rubensesque*
> *And dreamt of kissing Gallic."*

"Out, out, both of you," said Bernard, going to the door.

"Why? Don't you like our poetry? De Barra asked.

"That isn't poetry. It isn't even good doggerel. You think
you can palm yourselves off as poets, do you? You may
pass muster in the Bender and Stoker, but not here. You
frauds, counterfeits, and costermongers. You saltimban-
coes, quacksalvers, and charlatans. Out, out, before I
throw you out."

"You're quite mad," said Tom-Tom.

"As a March hare," echoed De Barra.

"Consider yourselves lucky," Bernard yelled after them.
"The money-changers in the temple were whipped for
less."

"I'm going to bed now," Patricia said when they'd gone.

"I told you they were frauds. The poetry is only a cover,
can't you see?"

"A cover for what?"

"I subjected four of their best poems to close textual

analysis and found beyond a doubt that they'd been written by the same man. The real poet is a third man, and they are only his puppets."

"They seem to me to be poets," she said.

"I don't lecture you on physics. You mustn't lecture me on literature."

"You have no sense of humor."

"I have an English sense of humor." He drew himself up to his full height.

"And we all know that English humor is what passes for humor in England."

"It's a jolly sight better than Irish humor, all incongruity and visceral convulsions."

"I think you should sleep on it." She opened the door. "I'm sure you'll feel better in the morning."

13

The summer term began on a calm Monday of fine rain that clung like condensation to the windowpanes. She walked between the desks trying not to breathe the warm steam that came off the pupils' damp clothes, telling herself that in a little over two months she would finally shake the dust of the hated Quad off her feet forever. In the staff room the Irish master, displaying his unerring ear for the asinine adage, told her that "one bite of a rabbit is better than two of a cat," and before she could reply, Robert Foxley entered with the air of an awed disciple.

"He is risen," he announced.

"Have you seen Him?" demanded the classics master.

"I have witnessed the white flash of his socks beneath the black billow of his gown."

"Except I shall see the eaves-drip of his moustache and the grouts in his soup bowl after he has eaten, I will not believe," intoned the Irish master.

At that moment the door opened and the Irish master blushed aghast.

"A word with you in private, Miss Teeling." God beckoned from the door.

She followed him down the corridor to his murk-musty study.

"It's good to see you out and about again." She almost choked over her inexplicable insincerity.

"There are those who would say that that is a matter of opinion." He blew into a handkerchief as if his nose were a French horn with his hand in the bell. "The best teachers, Miss Teeling, are those who have learned not to confuse fact and opinion. That I am out and about is a fact, but that it is good to see me is an opinion. That you were late for school this morning is a fact—"

"I forgot to set the alarm."

"But that you forgot to set the alarm may be a matter of opinion."

"I forgot to set the alarm," she repeated.

He stood with his back to the fireplace. She dared not lick her lips because of the dampness of the room and his moustache. His right hand clutched his gown, the thumb jerking like the tail of a sparrow. She inhaled the smell of old leather and felt her mouth go dry.

"You know Directive I?" he asked. "The teacher shall unfailingly be first in the classroom in the morning and last to leave in the evening. This morning you were last."

"It was an exceptional morning." Her tongue clicked drily on the roof of her mouth, which had been pushed out of its natural shape by the effort of speech.

"It's been an exceptional year, Miss Teeling. You are within your rights to wish for another, but I can tell you now that you won't be spending it here."

"I have no intention of coming back to this—"

She wanted to say "glorified *pissoir*" but her tongue was fixed in her mouth and she thought she heard Elsynge saying:

"One more thing. Tell the other members of my staff that I am not to be sent get-well cards in my own house. I don't like it. It is unnecessary. It is presumptuous. It is a flagrant infringement of my privacy."

"Fuck off like a good man." Her tongue finally broke its binding.

Elsynge's chin dropped weakly. She caught his gown by the lapels and swung him sideways so that he landed on his back on the settee. His shoes and white socks swayed in the air like the legs of an overturned dung beetle. She pulled off both shoes and socks while he coughed and spluttered, and she stepped astride his legs and with her back to him held his feet between her knees like a farrier shoeing a horse.

"I'm a sick man, Miss Teeling."

"You're a madman, Mr. Elsynge." She tickled the soles of his feet with the tip of her red Biro.

Elsynge laughed like a half-choked drain, but still she tickled, wishing the other teachers could hear such unaccustomed jollity in the headmaster's study.

"What are you doing?" Mrs. Elsynge demanded from the doorway.

"He was dying for a laugh, and he implored me to tickle his feet, but now that you're here I'll allow you to take over."

"This is monstrous," cried Elsynge through a spasm of coughing. "I shall never give you a reference now, Miss Teeling."

"You can stuff your reference up your intergluteal orifice. You can then use it to tickle your anal sphincter, and finally you can wipe your ineffable fart-hole with both sides of the paper."

"You brazen hussy!" said the incredulous Mrs. Elsynge.

"A word with you in private, Headmaster. You should wash your feet. They stink of stagnant fen water. Mrs. Elsynge, if she's honest, will bear me out."

She marched down the corridor to the staff room, but the other teachers could not see the joy of triumph in her face for the pall of cigarette smoke over the table.

Monica moved in with Robert Foxley at the weekend, so Patricia had the *grand lit* to herself. At first she thought of advertising for a flat mate, but she decided that while the money she had won on Phlogiston lasted she would pay double for the dubious pleasure of living alone. She was surprised to find that she missed Monica. She felt too uneasy to settle down with a book after school, so she usually sat for an hour by the bedroom window watching nesting blackbirds in the garden.

Bernard took up most of her time in the evenings. More and more he relied on her for amusement. He seldom went out alone, and he seemed to do little or no writing at the weekends. She had come to feel the insistent weight of him on her shoulders, but she went out with him whenever he asked because she could not bring herself to refuse, and possibly because being with him was not so different from being alone.

"I live on the edge of sleep," he told her one evening in The Inkwell. "From the time I get up in the morning I look forward to going to sleep again, because it is the only time I am entirely free of discomfort. Yesterday on the way to the National Library to read an article on narcolepsy I dozed off for a moment on the bus. I have an image in my mind as I fall asleep, a dark sea with a stiff wind wrinkling the surface. Gradually, as the wind drops, the surface becomes smoother, and as the last wrinkle vanishes consciousness ebbs away."

She did not know what to make of him, she could only marvel at his handsome face—at his fair eyebrows, light blue eyes, cleanly drawn nose and jaws, and even, glancing teeth, made for more laughter than he enjoyed. His only imperfection was his hands, the fingers of which thickened rather than tapered at the tips, forming ugly spatulas with flat, thick nails. He was conscious of their ugliness. He seldom gesticulated, and when walking or sitting he kept them in his trousers pockets. He now said little about literature or politics. He only wanted to hear about her childhood in the country, and sometimes she would feel that he was choking her as the ivy was choking the oak in

194

the lane. It was as if the draught of life was too strong for him, as if he needed her to sip it first and report to him on the taste and specific gravity.

On the third Wednesday in May she had a letter from her mother, begging her to come home at the weekend. Uncle Lar was getting worse. He had lost his "last and only stim of sense." He and Hugh were singing their heads off in Dartry's every night of the week. Last Sunday evening they went to a charity concert at the local school and drowned the national anthem with a raucous rendering of "Waltzing Matilda." The police chucked them both out and the national anthem had to be played again.

On Friday afternoon she drove down the country, glad to be on the road again. It was as if she did not know whether to live in the city or the country and could be herself only briefly on the journey from one to the other. Halfway to Naas, black clouds began to gather like Aberdeen Angus bullocks from the west, pressing together to form a black mass that stretched across the sky, leaving only a strip of brightness along the southern horizon. The clouds formed a black cupola above her that threatened to tumble from the heavens, and then between Kildare and Monastrevin rain began falling in great drops accompanied by darting lightning and rolling thunder. She had never seen such rain. It came down in continuous sheets, splashing off the bonnet and windscreen, so that she could barely see five yards ahead. She pulled into the side of the road and rolled a cigarette. A lorry crawled by with its headlights on. Darkness was falling with the rain, though it was only six o'clock in the evening. Then gradually the black cupola began to crack. Chinks of light appeared like veins of fat in Aberdeen Angus sirloin. The black mass broke up and slid down the sky to the horizon. The thunder and lightning stopped, and the rainstorm became a refreshing May shower. Birds began to sing, and the height of the heavens was pure and clear with the cloud now fencing the skyline. Suddenly it was a lovely evening. She rolled down the window and moved off with a hymn to the countryside in her heart. The ugliness of the city was behind her. All that mattered was fields and hedges, wheat and barley, and herds of bullocks grazing. And it seemed to her that she had experienced neither city nor country, that somehow she had become a Flying Leixwoman, condemned to drive endlessly up and down the Naas road without even the possibility of stopping off at Punchestown for the races.

Her mother was alone in the kitchen making scones for supper. For a moment she felt that nothing had changed since she was a girl. Her mother's hands were flour to the wrists and the roasting tin was warming on the range.

"Why do you always wear hobnailed boots like a man?" she asked her mother. "And why don't you buy a wig and fling your beret in the fire?"

"I was out all day and I forgot to take it off."

"You know as well as I do that you never take it off."

"There you are, not back five minutes and you're after me already. Still, I'm glad you've come."

"You worry too much about Uncle Lar. If he wants to sing his head off in pubs, let him."

"I'm not worried about Lar, I'm worried about you. Lar can sing until he's hoarse for all I care. The reason I asked you to come is that Austin saw him and Hugh coming out of the solicitor's last mart day."

"Well?"

"It isn't good, Lar and Hugh together at the solicitor's, and Lar sixty-nine since September."

"What's wrong with it, Mam?"

"He's never in town but he's drunk, and when he's drunk he could sign away the land. You'll have to come down more often, every weekend if you're wise."

"It's Uncle Lar's land, not mine!"

"He as good as said it was yours."

"Why do we always talk of nothing but land?"

"Where would we be without it? In this country if you

haven't got land, you need to have education. If you play your cards right, you'll have both."

"I'm going to wash my hair. The water is softer here than in Dublin."

"Lar isn't half the man he was last year. I never saw so strong a man fade so fast."

"Do you want the water in the kettle, Mam?"

"No, the wheel's come round again. He started as a good-for-nothing and now he's ending his days in soak. The man in between was not the real Lar at all."

"He's more real to me than Daddy. He taught me to laugh, which is more than anyone in this house ever thought of doing."

"Times were hard in this house when you were a girl. Lar could afford to laugh, he had only one mouth to feed."

"Don't talk to me about Uncle Lar. Talk to me about Daddy and yourself, about how he had no time for anything but drink, and how you had no time for anything but land. Between the two of you, you brought up a fine family. Austin as dry as an old stick. Whenever he sees kissing on television, he goes to bed. And Patsy as harmless as a day-old chick, and me searching for God knows what. Why did you bring us into the world? Was it to prove to the neighbors that you could do it, or was it because you didn't know how to stop it?"

"How can you say such things, and you with an honors degree in agricultural science from Cork?"

"There was no love or affection in this house. We were cowed into silence at table and beaten if we giggled in bed. We were told not to play with the McCormacks or the McCabes because the girls got into trouble and because they called piss 'piss' and shit 'shit.' When I get up in the morning and look in the mirror, I'm still amazed I haven't got two heads."

"The boys are happy, they never say a wrong word to me."

"Why should they, and you wife and mother to them both? They'll never turn to look after another woman while you're alive, and they'll be too old and blind with masturbation to notice one when you're dead."

"Holy St. Anthony and St. Jude preserve us, but they taught you the strange thoughts in Cork."

The following morning the grass was wet, so she went round the road to Uncle Lar's, not across the fields. The lane from the road to his house was a quarter of a mile long and only eight feet wide with a high grassy strip like a backbone in the center and stone-paved ruts on each side. It was a mysterious lane, running darkly between thick hedges of salley trees, fir trees, ash trees, and rowan trees, which Uncle Lar called quicken trees. To add to the mystery it had two sharp bends but it ran dead straight in between. The first stretch was like a tunnel because the trees met overhead. In the second stretch, where the hedges were more open, the sun cast streaks of light and shade on the path, and here she liked to linger and inhale the scent of gorse blossom, pick blackberries, bilberries, or wild strawberries in season, or climb up the gate and look across the moor to the mountain. In August the lane would be cool and shady with a rising hum of flies and bees; in December the hedges would be bare and the colors of the mountain subdued; and in April the green countryside would be scarred with black strips of plowed land. The third stretch of the lane ran downhill to her uncle's house, a two-story building with grey slates and a big red-roofed hayshed at the back and a form on which he stood milk buckets by the door.

The world to which the lane led was as secret as the lane itself. It was a sheltered world where no one ever scolded or looked askance. Uncle Lar never locked the door. If he was in the fields when she came back from school, she would go straight to the kitchen and help herself to a slice of brack from the pantry. She liked having his house to herself because the silence made her linger and notice things they did not have at home. Often she would go upstairs and make his bed, and whenever she heard the purr of his tractor in the yard she would put on the kettle and run out shouting, "Uncle Lar, Uncle Lar, I'm making you a cup of tea!"

During the summer holidays, she followed him into the fields and rode home on top of the trams behind the tractor while the leaves of the trees brushed her face in the lane. In July she would go with him to the bog to "rare" turf, but she would spend the day picking frochans and threading them together on blades of grass for safe keeping. At home in the evening she and Uncle Lar would eat them with sugar from a mug and he would laugh at the red stains on her mouth and fingers.

One windy evening in July she went with him to the Two Triangles to tie trams, and when he had secured them he lay in the lee of one of them and lit his pipe with the collar of his jacket up over his head as a windshield. She still remembered the sense of comfort she got from the flame of the match, the wind making cello music in the electric wires and singing like sea waves in the branches of the trees, rising and falling seemingly without end. As they walked home, twigs were snapping in the hedges. Her legs were cold and her knickers wet because she had sat on damp moss.

She walked the length of the lane, seeking the solace of numbness, fighting against the self-indulgence of tears. Hugh was in the Two Triangles spraying winter barley against brown rust, and Uncle Lar was leaning over the gate with a curl of smoke rising from his Peterson. He put a welcoming arm round her and walked with her to the house, stopping now and again to emphasize a point with his pipe. It was something he had never done before, and she wondered if he were trying to conceal the fact that he was short of breath. He looked older, his neck thinner, and his head more turnip-like, and she longed for the length of a summer day to talk and inhale his dry-sedge smell. It was not a sweet smell, the smell of his skin and clothes; it was a keen, clean smell, and she knew that if she ever met a man with a similar bouquet she would not wait for him to ask her to marry him.

"Uncle Lar, do you ever have a bath?" she asked.

"The last bath I had was in the Pacific over thirty years ago."

"You smell exactly as you smelt when I was a girl. I just thought that it's a very healthy smell."

"Some men need to wash and some don't. Now, Hugh is like me. He's clean by nature. Your father on the other hand always stank like a polecat."

"How is Hugh?" She tried to ask the question with casual unconcern.

"He's a good farmer, good with crops and good with cattle. And he's good company too. When you went to Dublin, I felt lonely, and when he came he made me laugh again. He doesn't say much most days, but he gets things done. When one of the heifers got the bloat, he didn't even mention it, he just mixed some veterinary paraffin oil, molasses, and pleuronic and painted it on the flanks of the others."

"So that they'd lick each other into health?"

"And do the vet out of a check."

They went into the house and she asked him if he'd like a cup of tea. He sat by the window and watched her fill the kettle.

"Do you like the city?"

"I do and I don't. It's like a rabbit warren, a maze of passages too complicated for any one person to get to know. When you arrive first, you're so excited you tell yourself that you won't rest till you know every inch of it, but after two weeks you're so overcome by the sameness of the burrows that you content yourself with two or three well-known runs. At first I thought the city was as mysterious as the country, but now I know I was wrong. The mystery of country lanes, like the mystery of the best-loved nursery rhymes, makes you dream of greater mysteries, whereas the city in its indifference only breeds more indifference."

"When are you coming back to us, then?"

"I haven't yet decided."

"You said you were only leaving for a year."

"I still have till September," she laughed.

He took a sip from his cup and drew a quarter bottle of whiskey from his pocket.

"It warms up the old system." He poured a gurgle of it into his tea. "For nearly fifty years a drink never passed my lips, but now I have a tipple every day. There's no harm in a drink at my age, as a little holiday from life's infirmities. Would you care for a drop in yours?"

"Yes, please."

"You're a rare girl, Patricia. I thought you had come to lecture me, and here you are sharing my whiskey. Another girl would have said no. A girl can easily get into the habit of saying no."

She put a thimbleful of the whiskey in her tea to please him and handed him back the bottle.

"How are you and Desmond getting on?" he asked.

"I haven't seen him since Easter, but I'm going down to Dunbarron this evening."

"Why don't you take him to the village? Hugh and I will be going for a drink, and the four of us'll raise the roof of Dartry's for an hour."

"All right," she said, wondering what Desmond would say to the idea.

"He's a sensible fellow is Deeny, a good forestry man, but would he make a good farmer?"

"I don't know."

"What do you think of Hugh?"

"I don't know much about him."

"He's a Teeling and a sound man, a man you could take with you to cross a river in flood. That's what life's about. You can't fight on all fronts at once. There's so much uncertainty and aggravation that you need to have your own corner to go back to, a place with company you can rely on."

She asked herself if, in spite of his experience of men, he had misjudged Hugh, but she quickly put the question from her mind. Sitting here in the familiar kitchen, she could see only the Uncle Lar who had pampered her as a girl. The raucous renderer of "Waltzing Matilda" was a figment of her mother's mean imagination.

"How can we celebrate your homecoming? You always come to see me, and I never make enough of you."

"You make too much of me, Uncle Lar."

"I know what we'll do. We'll have a big supper after we come back from the pub."

"It will be a bit late," she hesitated. "We won't get back till midnight, and by the time we have supper on the table it'll be two o'clock in the morning."

"We'll do a pot roast, put it in the oven before we leave, and it'll be ready as soon as we come in the door. All the time we're in Dartry's, we'll be thinking of it bubbling in the casserole and the sweet smell of the mutton leaking from the range into every corner of the house."

In the afternoon she drove to Dunbarron to see Desmond. At first she thought he was not himself, but when she told him about the proposed drink in Dartry's with a supper to follow, he laughed and said Lar was more than a soak, he was a brick.

"Pity I can't go to the pub," he said. "I've got to go to a wake in Borris, but I'll be back in time for supper, make no mistake."

She went back to Lar's in the early evening to prepare the supper. He brought her in peas, onions, carrots, parsnips, and a turnip, which she chopped and put in the bottom of his big enamel casserole. Then she placed a leg of mountain mutton on top of the vegetables and put the lot in the oven before they left for the village.

Hugh drove and Lar sat beside her in the back, explaining why wheat was more affected by yellow rust than barley, while she inhaled the pure scent of hawthorn blossom from the hedges. In spite of the dark presence of Hugh, she never felt so happy, so determined to enjoy every minute of the evening. The city and Elsynge were on another planet. She was surrounded by familiar fields and flat roads, straight as railways, running between cutting-like hedges, with the afterglow at the end of the vista and a sliver of a moon like a brightening face in profile against the darker sky behind them.

This was a world she knew so well that she could look at it without being aware of herself in the act of observation. She knew the name of every bush and tree, and of every flower that grew between them, and she knew the intimate workings of the society that loved and worked among them and knew them intimately too. It was the society from which she started and from which she drew the strength that enabled her to master other possibilities, but for her it could be only the beginning, never the middle or the end. She sighed with painless regret. Life had denied her a home, had condemned her to a series of campings, but for this one evening in the company of her uncle she would recover some of the innocence of the girl who made tea for him when she was six and waited for his return from market in the lane.

Dartry's was packed, but after fifteen minutes they managed to get a seat in a corner. It was typical of a Saturday night, the pub full of men who had not had a drink all week rubbing shoulders with men who had little else. At the far end of the bar was an old fiddler whom she recognized, but from where she sat his fiddling seemed like miming—not a note could be heard above the confusion of talk and laughter. As she was the only woman in the bar, she was aware of hungry eyes turning toward her, emboldened by drink and male companionship, ready to light up in laughter at the most prurient joke. Uncle Lar and Hugh were tamping the tobacco in their pipes, and she was pleased to be with them because she knew she could not drink here on her own. Through the smoke that rose between two broad backs, she saw a face of startled dissociation at the door. In dismay she opened her tobacco tin and began rolling a cigarette with nervous fingers, knowing that it was already too late to care.

"Fancy meeting you here!" Bernard smiled down at her.

"Where on earth have you come from?" She made room for him on the wooden bench.

"When I got up this morning and remembered you'd gone, I knew it was time I saw the midlands. I drove down after lunch but I got lost without a map, and no one seemed to have heard of Tallage. All I knew was that you came from near a village of that name, and when I finally got here I was told that there were so many Teelings in the parish that it would take a day to find you. So I did the sensible thing. I put off the search till tomorrow and took a room at the inn."

"You're staying here?"

"In the room above this hippodrome, to be precise."

"Uncle Lar," she said, pulling his sleeve, "this is Bernard Baggotty from Dublin. And this, Bernard, is my cousin Hugh."

"Can I get anyone a drink?" Bernard got to his feet.

"We're all right yet," Hugh said.

"Don't mind us." Lar resumed his conversation with Hugh.

Bernard got himself a pint of stout. She wished he had not come. In the local phrase, she would have gone to the neck in the Nore to ensure that he stayed in Dublin. He looked out of place here, a light-boned feuilletonist picking careful steps among heavy-footed farmers who judged men by their farms. Here his fine words were worthless gew-gaws. Here a stake in literature was nothing compared with a stake in the land.

"You come from a rare part of the country," he told her. "On the way down, all I could see was the road before me

204

and a hedge on each side with the odd bullock scratching his neck on a gatepost. It's a protective landscape, a landscape that would enfold you like a warm womb and shelter you from the bite of the world's winds. You could keep your innocence here for a lifetime and go to the grave like a child."

"You're making the mistake of all journalists. You've just arrived, you haven't finished your first pint, and yet you're summing up the life here as if it were a game of ludo."

"I don't underestimate the difficulties."

"You should refrain from estimating at all. You speak of innocence. The men in this pub have never been farther than Galway for the races or Dublin for the hurling final, but they'd buy and sell you and then complain that they hadn't made a big enough profit."

"Though I think you protest too much, I had a glimpse of what you mean while I was ordering at the bar. There were two men in front of me, and I couldn't understand a word of their conversation. There's a freemasonry of farmers—"

"Journalism again! How can you see life as it is if you surround yourself with a fog of cliché? There's no freemasonry of farmers unless there's a freemasonry of plumbers, carpenters, accountants, and literary journalists. Those men you overheard were talking of nothing more mysterious than brown rust, hoose, and sturdy, but they are things you'll never know anything about."

"I think the country acidifies your wit. If I may say so, you're sweeter in town."

"That's because you talk more intelligently in town."

Lar got up and placed a hand on Bernard's shoulder.

"What are you drinking? Stout?" he asked.

"We're out of sync," Bernard replied. "Now it's my turn to say 'I'm all right'—or was it 'Don't mind me'?"

"I've often said no to a drink myself, but I've never taken no from another man."

"As I said, we're out of sync."

205

"What we need is synchromesh to marry our different speeds of drinking," said Lar. "If we're to be friends, we must drink at meshing speed. It saves all the nuisance of double declutching. Which reminds me, Patricia, are you having a double?"

"Yes, if you're buying, Uncle Lar."

"What was all that about?" Bernard asked when Lar had gone to the counter.

"He's just bought a 145 h.p. tractor with twelve forward and four reverse gears, all in synchromesh. Synchromesh, you see, is on his mind," Hugh laughed.

Lar came back with the drinks and placed a fresh pint of stout beside Bernard's half-full tumbler. Then he sat down beside Hugh to take up the thread of a conversation in which there was much laughter and shaking shoulders. She felt uneasy with Bernard, and envious of her uncle and Hugh because of the fun they seemed to find in everything they said to each other. Bernard was being tiresome, conjecturing on the love lives of the more red-faced farmers and the nature of their relationships with their prize heifers. She listened in silence and told herself that she could not really blame Lar for ignoring him.

"You're kidding yourself, Patricia," Bernard said after a while. "You come down to the country for solace, but there is no solace for you here. It is an alien way of life, but because of the accident of birth you think you are part of it. Let me tell you now, you're a loner, a citizen of no city; you're as much a stranger here as you are in Dublin. I am also a loner, but unlike you I've pulled up the roots of my loneliness and examined them."

"You'd advertise them from every rooftop, dear Bernard, if you knew that anyone would listen."

"My loneliness is not of the flesh but of the spirit. If only I could believe in a spiritual ether in which all minds floated freely, sharing its sustenance as we share the air. But there is no spiritual ether and there is no universal mind. There is only a fairground full of selfish, self-absorbed egos."

"Why do you tell me this?" she asked impatiently.

"Because without you I would not have thought of it. You are the tongue in my bell, the clapper that makes me ring."

"You should make up your mind about me some time. Last week you said I was the breakwater of your bridge, and the week before, the capstone of your cromlech."

"All that is only a periphrastic way of saying that I could not live without you."

She felt relieved when the landlord shouted "Drink up, boys" for the twelfth time and Lar said that this time he meant it. She and Bernard stood outside while Hugh and her uncle went for a pee. The moon hung in the southwestern sky over a tundra of bluish white cloud like a field of thin snow. The field was uneven, full of hollows and hassocks, and the fine snow that barely covered them gleamed beneath the quarter moon. It all looked so real that she longed to walk across it alone, away from Bernard and Hugh and the wild insobriety of the evening.

"When shall I see you tomorrow?" Bernard asked.

"It's a bit awkward. I don't know."

"You're at your most mysterious. I haven't had a straight answer from you all evening. You're not hiding a jealous husband hereabouts by any chance?"

Lar returned and slapped Bernard on the back.

"You're coming to supper with us now," he said.

"Supper?"

"It's waiting for us in the oven at home."

"I've already had my supper," Bernard said.

"No," said Lar. "You've had dinner or maybe tea, but not supper. In my house no one has supper before twelve."

"You should call it breakfast in that case."

"You can call it what you like, but you're eating with us tonight."

"Let him be, he's tired," said Patricia.

"He can rest in the back of the car, and Hugh will drive him back to Tallage when we've eaten."

"Really, I don't think I should," said Bernard.

"It's settled," said Lar. "We must talk, you and me. We haven't had our talk."

They did not talk in the car because Lar and Hugh sang all the way home. Lar started off with:

> Once a jolly swagman camped by a billabong
> Under the shade of a coolibah tree.

Then Hugh sang "The Wild Colonial Boy" and, as they turned off the road into the lane, they both roared:

> So stir the wallaby stew
> Make soup of the kangaroo tail

It was one by the kitchen clock when they got home, so the pot roast, which should have been taken out of the oven at twelve, was what Patricia euphemistically described as "well done."

"We're behind schedule," she said. "It's too late to boil potatoes."

"Nonsense, girl," said Lar. "A supper without potatoes is like a summer without a swallow. I wouldn't sleep heavy enough if I didn't lay down a ballast before turning in."

He put a skillet of potatoes on the hotplate and pulled a woolen sock out of the hob-hole with a bottle of whiskey inside it.

"Now, tell us about yourself." He handed Bernard a full glass.

"I'm a writer . . . and I live in Dublin." Bernard looked as if the effort of dredging up the right description had exhausted him.

"Are you one of those fellows who write for the newspapers and make life sound like one accident after another . . . Farmer Killed by Tractor, Mother of Two Drowned in Well."

"No, I'm a short story writer."

"And what kind of stories do you write?"

"Stories that will make the reader wish for a novel," Bernard laughed.

"You sound like a poet. Are you a poet?"

"No."

"Do you know any poets?"

"Patricia thinks I know at least two."

"What's the difference between a poem and a short story?" Lar took a pull from his glass.

"Why do you want to know?"

"I read a poem at school, but I've never read a short story."

"A poem is neat brandy, but a short story has a dash of soda in it."

"So if you 'reduced' a short story, you'd end up with a poem?"

"If you were a poet."

"You say you write stories. Now, I could tell you a story or two from my time in the Northern Territory, and they're not Territorian tall tales either. When I first went to Australia, I worked with a stock farmer called Red Morgan, and one day his wife vanished and never came back. We scoured the countryside for miles but we never found as much as a footprint, and then nine years later Red Morgan died and left me his farm because he and his wife had no family. One day I was coming home across the paddock when I saw a dog sniffing an old tar barrel. I went over to have a look, and I noticed that where the rust had eaten a hole in the side a bone was sticking out. I opened the barrel and what did I find in it but a human skeleton! Red Morgan had killed his wife and put her body in the barrel and sealed it. Then he left the barrel at the end of the paddock as a homemade mausoleum he could admire every day. I dug a hole and buried the barrel and the bones on the spot, but I never went to the police. What would have been the point? Red Morgan was dead and I had his farm. But I'll go bail that there's many a murderer like him walking round scot-free today."

"You could be right," Bernard said.

"How would you like to write a story about Red Morgan?"

"I'll think about it."

"And while you're thinking about it, tell me this. How did a poet like you come to meet an agriculturalist like our Patricia?"

"We met by coincidence. We happen to live in the same house, Patricia in one flat and me in another."

"The city is a black hole in which the blackest strangers rub shoulders." Lar refilled Bernard's glass and Hugh's.

"The potatoes are done," said Patricia, pleased to be able to change the subject.

"When you've teemed them, we'll all guess the number in the pot," said Lar. "The man who comes up with the right answer will have the pleasure of carving the joint."

"It's a chore, not a pleasure," Bernard said.

"Carver's perks are no chore," said Lar. "The man who carves will be able to keep the best part for himself—what Red Morgan used to call 'the Pope's eye.' "

The porch door opened and Desmond Deeny stood blinking in the light.

"Leave it to a man from Dunbarron to arrive in time for supper," Lar laughed.

Patricia introduced Bernard and Desmond, who shook hands with the seriousness of men determined to spot every straw in the wind.

"I've been trying to see the resemblance between you two, but it isn't for a man to see," said Hugh.

"Why should we resemble each other?" Bernard asked.

"You're both friends of Patricia's, aren't you? You're both potatoes chosen from the same basket."

"Come on, time for the guessing game." Patricia tried to laugh.

Lar guessed first, then Hugh, then Desmond, then Bernard, and finally Patricia. As befitted good judges of

210

potatoes, they were close in their estimates, but to Hugh's obvious annoyance it was Bernard who won. At a quarter to two they sat round the table while Bernard complained that the meat was too overdone to admit of elegant carving. However, the peas, carrots, parsnips, and turnip made up for any shortcomings. They were impregnated with the flavor of the meat, and the steam from them rose sweetly into their flushed faces.

"What's your favorite vegetable?" Lar asked Bernard.

"Spinach, when it's fresh from the garden."

"Have you ever had the poor man's spinach?"

"What's that?"

"Goosefoot. Some people would call it a weed, but you can boil the leaves when they're young and you can make gruel from the seeds."

"You seem to know a lot about it."

"If you're interested, I can show you some. It grows wild behind the cowhouses."

"Why do you tell me all this?" Bernard asked.

"No reason, if you like I'll tell you about coltsfoot."

"You're a good cook, Patricia." Desmond Deeny's comment came like a burst of sunshine during a shower.

"Divil the better in the parish," said Lar.

"Do you always have supper so late—or so early?" Bernard asked.

"We eat when we're hungry," Lar replied.

"A working man needs his tucker," said Hugh, bent over his plate to shorten the journey of the peas on his unsteady fork. His heavy eyes fixed drunkenly on Bernard and a trickle of gravy found its way into the cleft of his chin.

"It isn't good to eat so gargantuan a meal before turning in," Bernard said.

"You're a jackaroo in these parts." Hugh turned to him.

"What's a jackaroo?"

"What we Aussies call a greenhorn, a man who doesn't know his arse from his elbow."

Lar brought down the butt of his fork on the table and, with an energetic wave of the arm, sang:

> *"So stir the wallaby stew*
> *Make soup of the kangaroo tail."*

Suddenly he stopped short and a hush like a black frost fell on the company.

"More vegetables, anyone?" Patricia asked, but there were no takers.

"Are you English?" Hugh turned again to Bernard.

"Yes."

"Are you a poof?"

"No, are you?"

"In Australia we have a theory that all pommies are poofs. Now I'm not saying that you're a poof, but I'd bet a week's wages that you've figured in the dreams of poofs."

"As you Aussies would no doubt say, I'm a man more poofed against than poofing," Bernard said drily.

"I don't think we Aussies would say that at all, would we, Lar?"

"Your tucker's getting cold," Lar said to Hugh.

"There are more potatoes in the skillet," Patricia reminded them.

"I'll get them," said Desmond, who liked conversation he could understand.

"Have you thought about my question?" Lar said to Bernard.

"Which question?"

"I asked you if you'd like to write a story about Red Morgan."

"Why should a Londoner want to write about the Australian outback?"

"Not about the outback, about Red Morgan. After, all you can make him Irish or English if you like. Murder doesn't recognize national boundaries."

"I still don't see why I should write about him."

"Say it was to please an old man who once gave you a

late supper. You see, Red Morgan isn't the only murderer I've known, and strangely he was just an ordinary man. They were all ordinary men, like you or Desmond there, open-faced and quiet without a trace of the mark of Cain."

"You would think a murderer would have cold eyes," Desmond Deeny said.

"Not one bit," said Lar. "Most murders are done on impulse. The murderer strikes in anger maybe, and the next minute he can't understand what came over him. He usually strikes down someone close to him—a wife, a mother, a sister, or a brother—and if left alone he will live the rest of his life like you or me. The moment of madness will never overtake him again."

"Poisoners are different," said Desmond Deeny. "There was a poisoner in Derryowen who had a weak eyelid that kept closing in sharp light. Poisoning, you see, isn't a crime of passion. It's an act of calculation."

"What do you think?" Lar asked Bernard.

"I'll tell you what I think." He pushed back his chair and got to his feet with a clatter. "You all think you're clever. You'd like to know the truth about me, every jot and tittle, but the truth can't be bought like an acre or a bullock. You talk of murder, you talk of Goosefoot. In fact, you've talked about everything except ostriches. Or are you about to tell me that you're going to sell your cattle and buy a flock of ostriches? The midlands are flat, unlike the Wicklow mountains, so mercifully it will be unnecessary to exalt every valley, to make the crooked straight and the rough places plain."

He was standing in the middle of the floor, his hands shaking, his lips distorted, his eyes wild with emotion.

"Sit down, Bernard," Patricia said. "Your supper's getting cold."

"You've got cheek, after misleading me as you have. It was Uncle Lar this and Uncle Lar that—how he touched your breasts in the bedroom and said you were a woman, how he taught you to laugh, to drive a tractor, to milk a cow—but when I come here what do I find? A dry old man with the cunning of the devil. Don't think I don't know that all this has been set up for my benefit—the visit to the pub, the Australian ballads, the late supper—but I'm not so easily played on. You think you know everything. You think she has told you everything, just as I thought she had told me everything. But fools that you are, you know nothing. All you can do is foul the air with hinting, but you won't tempt the hermit crab from his shell. You haven't heard of the hermit crab? He isn't like other crabs because he's born without a shell of his own, so he kills a whelk and eats it and lives in his victim's shell until he outgrows it. Then he kills a bigger whelk with a bigger shell and so on till he's finished his growth. Now, after all that, would you call the hermit crab a murderer?"

"What's come over you, Bernard?" Patricia tried to attract his attention, but he looked over their heads at a daddy longlegs dashing its wings against the windowpane.

"You talk to me about poets and double declutching, about wallaby stew and a homemade mausoleum, but I know your every trick because I'm a literary man and symbolism is my business. I've been goaded before and I haven't budged from my shell, so don't think you'll succeed where your intellectual superiors have failed. The artist is proof against your sallies; it is his vocation to carry the burden of his secret to the grave. Now it's your turn to worry. Now you too can feel the spreading paralysis of innuendo. Now go to bed and sleep on that if you can!"

He made an obscenely dismissive gesture with both hands and swung through the doorway as if he were about to carry off the jamb on his shoulder.

"What did you put in his whiskey?" Hugh asked Lar.

"I've never seen a man so drunk," said Desmond Deeny.

"I've never seen a man so ripe for the madhouse," said Lar.

Patricia switched on the yard light and followed him.

"Where are you going?" she called.

"To Tillage or Tallage or maybe Tullage. I refuse to spend another minute in this bedlam."

"I'll drive you back to Dartry's." She ran beside him, trying to restrain him.

"Look, I know perfectly well where I'm going, and you're the last person I want to take with me. You kept me dangling for six months while you philosophized about your precious pratt, but one fool wasn't enough for you. You needed Hodge as a second string to your bow. You're not a woman, you're a monster, a prick-teasing tomboy infatuated with the invincibility of her virginity. No, don't touch me, you bitch—"

He pushed her into the thorns of the hedge and strode through the gate into the shadows of the sycamores.

"Where did you fish him out of?" Lar asked when she came back.

"He's a writer," she said. "He's always making connections that aren't there. If he didn't, I suppose he'd have nothing to write about."

"You'd be better off steering clear of his type."

"How did he come here?" Desmond asked.

"He lives in a flat next to mine in Dublin, and he followed me down. He's staying at Dartry's and he happened to see us in the pub."

"When are you going back to the city?" Lar asked.

"Tomorrow."

"We can't have everything, Patricia. We all have to choose, and choosing means giving up. I hope you give up the city; it's doing you no good."

"I must be going." Desmond rose from the table. "Soon it will be time for breakfast."

She followed him out into the yard. The light came on in the Land Rover as he opened the door.

"I'm sorry about tonight, Desmond."

"It had to happen some time. When you were home at Easter, I thought you'd changed."

"You don't understand."

"I always understand less than I feel." He smiled as he turned the ignition key.

Now the sky was cloudless. The spent moon like an orange lith hung cold but radiant over Hurley's Grove. She stood under the yard light at the gable and watched his tail-lights vanish at the gate.

The following afternoon she drove back to Dublin, empty, dispirited, and bruised. Bernard had made a nuisance of himself. To stop seeing him would be painful but it was unavoidable. She had lost Desmond Deeny and she was on the verge of losing the affection of Uncle Lar. She could live without Bernard but not without her uncle, so the violence of surgery had to be done. If thine eye offend thee, pluck it out, and cast it from thee. It was a philosophy for the strong, and no one had ever called her weak. With the rigor of implacability in her heart she entered the city and drove down the narrow quays. She could, and would, cast out devils. And if necessary, she'd cast them out through the prince of devils.

14

The door of the flat was unlocked, and she knew immediately that something was wrong. Then she saw the stepladder and his legs suspended through the trapdoor, his ragged jeans too short, his yellow socks in folds about his ankles.

"Oh, no." She slumped against the door.

She could not see his head and shoulders, they were above her in the darkness of the attic. She put her hand up his trouser leg and, touching cold, unyielding flesh, saw a sealed envelope on the table, her name in his crazy italic hand, all strokes and angles in black, uncompromising ink. The first time she read it she barely took in a word. Then she went into the bedroom with a drink and lay on the *grand lit,* her eyes closed against the light, the cold of his leg in her stomach in spite of the warmth of the scotch. After half an hour she read the letter again, slowly and painfully as he himself had written it.

Dear Patricia,
Forgive this final intrusion, but there's no trapdoor on the landing or in my flat.

217

Over the last year or so I've watched the shadows closing in, creeping closer like wet mist over low bogs. The poets are not what they seem. As you now know, they are out to get me. All is grey today. The New Yorker *has returned my story with a printed rejection slip, and telephones keep ringing in my ears. In my need I turned to you. You could have redeemed me, but why you didn't is not for me to say.*

In my end is the defeat of Goosefoot. Now he will never know the truth. He thought I was the murderer. So did you, and the "poets" and your confounded Uncle Lar. But let me tell you a secret. I'm innocent. Don't breathe a word in my defense, however. Keep your counsel, as I did. Laugh at my wounded name. Refuse to report me aright to the unsatisfied. Wounded, my unregenerate bollocks. What a jackass was Hamlet to ask Horatio to absent himself from felicity a while.

I go not in rage but regretfully. Regretful that I failed to fuck you. My love affair with you began at the One Thousand Guineas at Newmarket four years before I met you. There was a twenty-to-one filly called Miss Right whom I desperately wanted to mount, but unfortunately bestiality has never been le vice anglais. *You may raise a smile but I can not. It is all too deadly serious. I saw you in a paddock in a ballroom and knew you were my only chance, at last my twenty-to-one filly in skirts. You know the rest. I hoped against hope and piling evidence, but when your uncle mentioned Goosefoot I knew you had crossed the floor. I blame, not you, but your teachers. If you'd read Eng. Lit., even in Cork, you'd have been able to distinguish between bad doggerel and bad poetry.*

You'll find £11.44 in my hip pocket. Put it on Devil's Bongo in the Derby. He's now forty-to-one. If he comes in, I'll owe you nothing for all the drinks you bought me. A final word, the summation of one man's experience: there's no water in the well at the world's end. I'm telling you because I know you'll think nothing of it. You'll just remind yourself to take a hip flask, as any sensible woman would.

"I have no love left," said the hermit crab, abdicating a shell that never was his own.

Bernard Baggotty

P.S. Mullally's had a heart attack. You'll find him in the Mater Hospital.

For a long time she lay bound on the bed, waiting for the liquidity of tears to release her. She remembered him at Fairyhouse, at Leopardstown, in Phoenix Park, and in Grafton Street on a Saturday morning, and then she tried to see the sprightly dancing Miss Right bearing his weight in the Guineas. She remembered him in The Inkwell before a play, anxious about tickets he had booked a month before. He kept looking in his wallet, forgetting each time the pocket in which he had put them, until the responsibility became so great that he told her to put them in her purse for safe keeping.

A few weeks ago, a knock at the door woke her in the night. She'd pulled on her dressing gown and listened with an intimation of fear to a step on the landing and a hoarse, birdlike cry followed by a sob.

"Who's there?" she called.

"It's me, Bernard," came the reply.

She opened the door and at first she could not see him. He was sitting on the threshold at her feet, hugging his shaking knees, curled up like a fetus in the womb.

"Can I come in?" He got up and caught her hand.

He was wearing puce pajamas and Indian sandals, and he laid his head on her shoulder and pressed her breasts against his chest.

"I've had a nightmare, it was horrible."

"I'll make you a cup of coffee."

"I'll have cocoa if you've got it. Coffee will only keep me awake."

He was shivering like a man who had come in out of a snowstorm with melting sleet on his cheeks. Pretending not to notice, she led him to the chair by the gas fire.

"Do you ever have night thoughts?" He sipped his cocoa. "Thoughts that keep you awake with their jostling."

"No, but now and again I have morning thoughts. I sometimes wake at six and can't get back to sleep because at that hour the simplest problems seem insuperable."

For a long time he said nothing, and she wondered if he were so lost in guilt and fear that he had not heard.

"Morning thoughts are what the fortunate have for morning horrors," he said at last. "Morning horrors are rooted in fear, a pathological reluctance to face the day. Dreading what's in store, you edge your way forward surreptitiously until half-past ten. Gradually, the fear diminishes, and by eleven it's gone. Though I don't rush to the nearest pub at opening time, I find it a comfort to know that you can get a drink. It's like knowing that if it should come to the worst, you have one shot left in the locker."

She had seen so much and understood nothing. After an hour, she realized that she was not going to cry, so she burned the letter on a dinner plate, flushed the ashes down the sink, and called the police.

Detective Inspector Farrelly was the personification of restrained sympathy, as if he had deliberately allowed his rounded shoulders to droop further and his hooded eyes to glaze over.

"You knew the deceased?" he asked, as if he did not know.

"He was a friend."

"Forgive my being personal, but did he have a key to your flat?"

"Not as far as I know. I can only think that he may have had a duplicate from Mr. Mullally."

"Did he have financial worries?"

"He didn't worry about money, he just put it all on the horses."

"Did he have any other worries?"

"He was worried about one of your colleagues, Detective Inspector McMyler."

"McMyler? Tell me about him. What does he look like?"

"He's a tall, thin man with a blue shoulder bag, a corduroy hat, and a strange gooselike walk. He came here once, and after that I saw him in pubs, at Fairyhouse, and between Greystones and Bray on the train."

"You say Mr. Baggotty was worried about him?"

"Yes."

"Why was he worried?"

"He thought the police were keeping an eye on him."

"Detective Inspector McMyler, as you call him, is not a policeman."

"You mean to say Mr. Baggotty has not been under surveillance?"

"Why should he be?"

"He told me that he was resigned to living under suspicion until you caught the man who murdered his wife."

"Do you know where the man who calls himself McMyler lives?"

"No, he just turns up unexpectedly in pubs and at the races and then disappears perhaps for weeks."

"If you see him again, be careful. Don't try to follow him but ring this number right away. It's absolutely essential that we get in touch with him. Mrs. Baggotty was murdered and the case is still unsolved."

"If McMyler is not what he seems, where are the real police?" she asked.

"The real police have been busy, but the best detection, like perfect murder, doesn't advertise. At first we suspected Baggotty but it soon became apparent that he was more confused than guilty. Since then the hunt has not relaxed, believe me. It's just gone to a different neck of the woods. Mrs. Baggotty was the second woman to be mur-

221

dered in the last year after receiving anonymous telephone calls. We think that both murders were committed by the same man."

"What were the phone calls about?"

"We don't know. Both women died before they could be questioned."

"I've received anonymous phone calls."

"Were they obscene?"

"They were more crazy than dirty."

"You'd better tell me about them." Farrelly pulled out a notebook.

She told him as much as she could remember, and with spasmodic thrusts of the jaw he took down the gist of her words.

"We're dealing with no ordinary criminal," he said at length. "This one's a literary crackpot as well."

"Do you think McMyler could be the murderer?"

"I don't know, but it looks as if he's up to nothing good. I'll make inquiries in The Inkwell. The landlord may be able to give us a lead."

A week later she gave a certain amount of evidence at the inquest and listened to the ludicrously commonplace verdict—suicide while the balance of the mind was disturbed. When she got home, she looked incredulously round the flat, half expecting to find herself in an asylum. The green emulsion, the musty curtains, the smell of cooking fat, the bric-à-brac that passed for furniture, all forced themselves on her attention with the indignity of an obscene gesture. Tomorrow she would go to school and try to avoid the headmaster, while at the back of her mind the image of an empty house would burn red like a boil in tender flesh. In the evening she would sit in a dark cinema because she might have to talk to another human being if she went to a pub. She wished to be alone in the empty city without tears or laughter, to tell herself of withdrawal and an ebbing tide. Numb and cold, though the evening was mild, she looked out of the bedroom window. The first blackbirds had left with their young, and another two were busy with straws on the lawn. She wondered if they were building again from scratch, or if they had occupied the vacated nest in the ivy hedge. Two magpies swooped geometrically in black and white across the garden. A clock struck seven and she realized that she had not moved for an hour.

The next morning was bright with an enlivening breeze that lifted Mrs. Elsynge's dusty gown but not the weighty skirt beneath it. Patricia, who was watching from the lab window, turned away as she saw Elsynge himself hurry from the house, white socks flashing under too-short trousers.

"A telephone call for you, Miss Teeling," he said from the glaring doorway. "I'll keep an eye on things while you take it."

The telephone was in the hallway of the house, on a rosewood table beneath a cracked mirror. She turned to make sure the staff room door was closed, certain that the voice would be that of McMyler.

"Patricia?" It was her mother's voice, unmistakable in its animal hoarseness.

"Yes, Mother. What's wrong?"

"It's Lar. He ate two smoked mackerel for supper last night and they lay on his heart, poor man."

"Is he all right?"

"He was dead in bed when Hugh called him this morning."

"I don't believe it."

"It's the drink that did it. Himself and Hugh came back from Dartry's as full as ticks and, as if that wasn't enough, they ate a dirty big supper on top of it. Who ever heard of any Christian eating two smoked mackerel for supper? Tom Lydon was coming home from a wake and he heard the two of them singing their heads off as he passed the house at two o'clock in the morning."

"No one can say he left quietly."

"When are you coming home?"

"This afternoon. I'll be down by four."

"Don't delay and don't forget to buy a couple of bracks in Naas."

She looked in the mirror as she put down the phone. The downward crack cut her face in two, making the familiar strange, making it unbearable as the ache of vacancy within her. Elsynge came out of the lab when he saw her.

"I'm afraid I'll be away for a few days. My uncle died unexpectedly this morning."

"An uncle is hardly a parent, Miss Teeling. This is most regrettable. The exams are only days away, and you've had two days off last week already. These absences could not have come at a more inconvenient time."

"They may be inconvenient but they're unavoidable. My uncle was more than a father to me. Wild horses and the Minister for Education himself wouldn't keep me from his wake and funeral."

"Too bad, Miss Teeling, too bad."

"I'll leave at lunchtime, and I'll be back on Thursday morning."

Her uncle was in a coffin on the bed upstairs, not in a brown shroud but in his best navy-blue suit. His thick-jointed fingers were locked together like stubborn roots, his bloodless lips pressed tightly against his teeth, and his shoes more polished then she'd ever seen them on a Sunday. He seemed to have shrunk since she last saw him, yet his body filled his suit. It was not really his body, she told herself. It was a shell that did not belong to him, as the shell of the hermit crab belongs to another. She bent over him and kissed his cheek, firm as set plaster and slightly sweet-smelling like October apples in seasoned hay. She did not truly know what she was doing. She made tea and handed round slices of the barmbracks she had bought in Naas. She spoke to women she knew but vaguely and watched grave men making short work of six bottles of whiskey in a while of an evening. Her mother was in charge of the food and Hugh was looking after the drink. Her father was sitting by the kitchen door with a glass that was always empty in his hand, and Desmond Deeny was talking to Patsy by the fire. Everyone looked different, as Uncle Lar looked different, but only she could see it. For the neighbors it was a night out, time for two or three decorous observations about the dead before reverting to the eternal verities of crops and cattle, but for her it was the end of a road she had not kept in good repair. Here the grief was bearable because it was surrounded by affection, but in the empty city she would see herself as she was, as Lar must have seen her in his last days.

Desmond left the fireside and sat beside her.

"I know what you must feel," he said.

"I haven't wept, not yet."

"He was himself even in his instructions for his funeral."

"Did he leave instructions?"

"Hugh found a sealed envelope on his dressing table. He will be the first man from the parish to be buried in his Sunday suit and shoes. He asked for his wallet as well with a ten-pound note inside it."

"I didn't know that."

"It's true. I was here when they laid him out. Your mother said that paper money would go bad, so she put some loose change in his trousers pocket as well."

She left the kitchen to be alone. The lane was full of parked vehicles and the sky was a lake of stars, inconstant lights drowned in waters far away. She remembered another night as she came home from October devotions with Uncle Lar, a night with a full moon that looked oddly worn.

"The moon looks old tonight." She took his offered hand.

"Why do you think that?" he asked.

"It looks like a worn coin. The rim is not altogether round and the face is rusted away."

"But the moon is a coin," he laughed. And he told her the most delightful story about an Irish giant and an English giant who tossed a gold sovereign to settle a dispute about who should own the Isle of Man. The English giant won the toss but the Irish giant was so angry that he flicked the coin with such force that it never came down again.

Retracing her steps to the house, she paused by the hayshed where Hugh had parked the 145 h.p. tractor. From the other side of the wall two thick voices crackled and sputtered.

"But will she get it? I wouldn't bet on it."

"If she gets it, she'll be the best catch in the parish."

"It'll come in handy for young Deeny."

"Don't forget the Australian. Lar was a great one for the family name."

"He did little enough himself to preserve it."

She walked quickly away as if to escape a bad smell. In the kitchen she sat beside Patsy, who was looking into the eye of the range.

"I still can't believe it happened," he said. "Without knowing it, I expected him to live as long as myself."

"He will too. He'll live as long as we live."

"The doctor said he probably choked on his vomit in his sleep."

"I prefer Mam's verdict. It's gentler. He ate two mackerel for supper and they lay on his heart, poor man."

She went upstairs and sat by the coffin in the bedroom. Wax from a blessed candle dripped into a sconce. A shadow moved as a draft caught the flame. The sea-murmur of conversation came up through the floorboards. A waft of fields and hedges stirred in the heavy curtains, sweetening the already cloying air. She got up and looked down at the death mask that had replaced the once familiar face. His favorite sayings came back to her—"All present and correct." "Good morning! You stink of Pears soap." "A lisping lass is sweet to kiss." And of someone who'd just died, "All he needs now is a bit of parsley." She had talked to him for hours and hours but never once about religion and politics, the so-called serious subjects she discussed with Bernard. Yet she knew Uncle Lar in a way she could never have known Bernard. He was rounded and solid where Bernard was formless and soft. He was a man who had grown out of the earth like a tree, a man with a presence that lived in other men, a man who was more aware of the world than of himself. It was sad to reflect that though he had been a model of good husbandry and genial sobriety for most of his life, he had ended his days in an indignity of drink and self-delusion. She had seen it happen and had done nothing to stop it, because to try would have been to deny not only the manhood to which she responded but the love for him that moved in the marrow of her bones. Something fierce had moved in the marrow of *his* bones, the desire to mold her into a rare and special person who would take his place in the world as a man and still remain a woman. Though in his youth he had sown his wild oats in every hedge and ditch between Slieve Bloom and the Comeraghs, he had probably never given his love to any woman except herself. He was the kind of man who recognized the existence of women only in relation to other men, and that perhaps gave him a kind of tunnel vision which was at once the strength that bore him through a lonely life and the weakness that finally defeated him.

A widow who once had an eye on him came into the room and knelt beside the coffin, though she must have known that Lar's religion was one of untroubled reductionism. He went to Mass on Sundays, but not a minute too early, and received Communion once a year, but never before Trinity Sunday. Between times he said that priests were like politicians, too simple-minded to merit the attention of an intelligent man. Patricia knelt beside the widow and waited for a prayer to enter her heart. When all that came was a well-worn Our Father and Hail Mary, she got up quietly and returned to the kitchen.

After the funeral the family went back to her uncle's and sat round the table in the parlor. The infirm solicitor adjusted his papers and spectacles and read the simple will. The entire estate went to Hugh except for a gift of ten thousand pounds for Patricia. When her mother heard the news, she snorted in dismay and stomped out of the room. Her father and brothers left next, and Patricia offered to make tea while Hugh talked to the solicitor. It was wrong, she felt, to blame Hugh. She did not like him, but it was her uncle's will and Hugh was his chosen beneficiary. She sat by the range in the kitchen while he saw the solicitor to his car.

"So it's finally over." He poured himself a glass of whiskey when he came back. "Would you like a drop to strengthen your tea?"

"I don't think so."

"The old boy wouldn't have said no."

"He said no for most of his life."

"But he still had enough life left in him to let rip at the end."

"You must be pleased about the will," she said.

"He told me a few weeks ago but I thought it better to sing dumb till I'd heard from the solicitor."

"It's a good farm."

"It should fetch a fair penny."

"You're not going to sell, are you?"

"As soon as I've tied up the loose ends. With the money I should be able to buy a place of my own in Australia."

"That's not what Uncle Lar intended. He left you the land because you're a Teeling, because he wanted you to preserve the name."

"You heard the will. There were no strings attached."

"He thought there was no need for strings."

"I couldn't live in this place without him. Who is there to 'stir the wallaby stew'? And what is there to do but get drunk every night and try to sober up in time for work in the morning?"

"Uncle Lar lived here for over thirty years."

"And what did he achieve?"

"You know the answer to that."

"He was a lonely man with no family of his own. When you went to Dublin, he didn't know where to turn."

"I was four years in Cork and he didn't complain."

"Dublin was different. He wanted you to go to university, to learn the science of farming, but he couldn't understand why you turned your back on him to teach young gurriers."

"He never said that to me."

"He must have been doting at the end. He hinted more than once that I should marry you."

He flung back his cuboid head and laughed at the sheer absurdity of it.

"Why don't you stay for a year or two and give the place a chance. When you get to know more people, you'll think different."

She did not want him to go. She couldn't bear the thought of a stranger in Uncle Lar's, the house and farm lost to her forever.

"I've been here over six months, not bad for a man who came for a fortnight."

"I suppose you stayed long enough for your purpose." She rose to go.

"You're like Lar," he laughed, "you have no sense of the impossible."

She walked round the yard, touching objects with her forefinger as if the very touch could turn time on its head, as if it could inoculate her against loss and pain. She touched the moss-motled gate pier, the remnants of past plows and harrows, old tractor wheels and batteries, a car radiator and a drum of diesel oil. She paused by the frame of his old bicycle, sunk in a sense of past seasons and lost days, of quiet lives flowing smoothly to the grave. She entered the shed for the scent of turf and fled from the clock for the new electric fence, which ticked hoarsely and flashed amber like a jaundiced eye. How could Uncle Lar have allowed such a monster to pollute the perfect silence of the shed where she had watched him mend punctures as a girl? And she realized something that had never been plain before. What gave her uncle's house its magic was its silence. Whenever she came to see him, she came alone. And when she played, she played alone, away from her two brothers and the other children of the neighborhood. It was a world that she herself had created, and because she had created it alone, it was inviolable—or so she had thought.

From the gate she looked across the moor to Slieve Bloom, gently rolling, low as sand dunes, with scooped-out hollows that harbored shadows in spite of the height of the afternoon sun. All was peace before her, mysterious blues mixing with greens and here and there a stretch of brown broken by the vaguely geometrical patterns of the forestry plantations. The mountain at least had changed little. It was still the quilt of many patches that Uncle Lar used to show her as if he were pointing out the kingdoms of the earth which would one day be hers for the taking.

Ignoring the road, she took a short-cut across the fields, along weed-choked headlands beside stands of still-green wheat and barley. She opened the gate with the big syca-more for a pier, and the poison of the last three weeks broke in her breast, flowing like sour vinegar through her veins. Her body shook uncontrollably, a low branch caught her hair, tears scorched her cheeks, a pet calf followed her, and she walked haltingly over the poached ground, uncaring and unseeing, only aware that she had been holding herself rigid against the brunt of life and that now she was thin liquid rushing like a river in a thaw. When she came to the last gate, she paused as if to listen to the storm within her. Her tears had stopped but her breasts heaved painfully. It was not her fault, nor was it Uncle Lar's. It was the wicked perversity of life which made those who love most truly wound most deeply.

"You can well cry now," her mother said as she came in the door. "I'll bet you're satisfied now, my girl. You wouldn't take my advice and stay. You had to go gallivanting up to Dublin town and turn your back on a house and farm any sensible young woman would go to the neck in the Nore to own."

"How can you talk of land, Mother, and Uncle Lar only buried this morning."

"If you couldn't think of yourself, you might have thought of Patsy. Where am I to find the money to set him up in his own farm?"

She went to the bedroom to pack her things.

"Where are you going now?" her mother asked.

"Back to Dublin. Believe it or not, there's more peace there than here."

"So that's the thanks I get after all my praying and worrying."

"Land, land, land," said Patsy, "when all we need at the end is six feet by two and a half."

"It isn't much," said Patricia. "It isn't even two square yards."

"The great thing," said Patsy, "is that we can all afford it, even with land going three thousand pounds an acre."

15

The city was a bowl of fine dust that tickled her throat and nostrils. The mornings were warm with still air between the desks harboring pockets of cloacal odours. The Leaving and Inter Cert classes sighed over their revision and Elsynge lectured the staff on the iniquity of tipping.

"Tipping encourages laziness. It deludes pupils into thinking that they need only revise six or seven questions. Those of you who have ever glanced at the racing pages must know that the straight tip is an invitation to lose one's shirt."

It was almost the end of term and Elsynge knew it, knew that both staff and pupils were dying to see the back of him for two months, knew that for the nonce he was a wasp without a sting.

The evenings were empty and still. After school she came back to the flat unable to face cooking a proper dinner. Some evenings she had a bowl of soup and scrambled egg on toast, and other evenings French bread and cheese with a glass of ale from the fridge. Mr. Mullally was still in hospital. Living in the silent house was like camping in a derelict cathedral. She had lost direction, she lay becalmed without desire for change or movement. To go back to the country was out of the question, and to remain in the city was living death. She had stopped going to the cinema and theater; she could no longer lose herself in a film or play. And whenever she went for a drink it was only to be reminded of Bernard and the futility of human relationships. It was as if her first life had ended and she was awaiting a metamorphosis that refused to happen.

At last the school year was over. After the goodbyes she returned to the flat and sat by the window above the garden. The two blackbirds were hopping from the fence to the lawn and back again, cleaning each other's beaks and fossicking for worms among the clover. They were by no means as efficient as the first pair, neither as practical nor as systematic. They did not keep watch for each other or swoop from the bottom of the garden into the nest in one beautiful, looping curve. Lacking confidence in their aerobatics, they came up the fence in short hops and entered the nest from a post only six feet away. As she remembered the ease and expertise of the first pair, she suddenly found herself weeping into the curtain. Her tears came from a well of inconsolable loneliness and she knew that she must go out and find another human being to talk to.

She put five pounds in her purse and took a bus to O'Connell Street. She had a drink in a pub in Lower Abbey Street but no one looked her way. She crossed O'Connell Bridge and turned left along the quays past cranes and moored boats, stacked timber and heaps of coal with the river at full tide thick-skinned and opaque. An old man on a bollard pissed along the length of his walking stick. A black-and-red Norwegian boat with rusty tackle trailed two frayed hawsers. She paused by a decaying lock leaking polluted water. She crossed the footbridge over the canal and caught her breath. McMyler had risen from a wooden bench and with his back toward her was heading for a row of working-class cottages which made her think of crammed rooms, steamy kitchens, and heaps of damp clothes waiting to be ironed. Was this where he lived, surrounded by dereliction, breathing the heavy menstrual smell of the river mingled with the smell of coal and rotting seaweed? She followed him down a narrow street, keeping well behind, quickening her pace only when he turned off abruptly to the left, but when she came to the place all she could see was an empty cul-de-sac. She stopped and looked round, and there he was coming up behind her.

"A surprise, Miss Teeling." He raised his corduroy hat, his smile faintly playful, his eyes bright with geniality.

"Oh, good evening, Mr. McMyler."

"What a coincidence! I was thinking of you only this morning. As I got out of bed, I said to myself, I must have a word with Miss Teeling . . . but the world and the devil, though regrettably not the flesh, are too much with us . . . thoughts accumulate like junk in a loft . . . and now it's time to share them."

As she looked into his open face, she almost blushed to realize that there was no wrong in him. It was the face of detached reflection, not of sexual aberration and the spilling of blood. He touched her on the sleeve, and curiously he communicated, not detachment, but loneliness and withdrawal, all the wisdom of which urban man is capable, yet denies. He was a kindred spirit as Bernard was a kindred spirit, wrongly accused. "Don't breathe a word in my defense, however. Keep your counsel, as I did. Laugh at my wounded name." How ironic that he and Bernard had never become friends.

"I live in the next street," he smiled. "Do come in and take a glass of malmsey and a biscuit before you resume your walk."

The evening light smiled back on his handsome face, and his laugh, one of innocent complicity, of past enjoyments shared unconsciously, smoothed the last wrinkle of doubt in her mind.

"A glass of malmsey would be lovely," she said, and he

234

led her round the corner into a street with no cars and with no curtains in the windows of the houses.

"I have the road to myself. It's up for redevelopment. All my erstwhile neighbors have fled."

He led her through a gateway without a gate to a door with flaking paint into a hallway that smelled of mice. The stair carpet was threadbare with unpolished rods, and the smell on the landing reminded her of an incontinent child whose sister read philosophy in Cork. As he fiddled with his key ring, she found herself wishing that she had not come.

"Do you live alone?" she asked.

"Quite alone. When my sister died four years ago, I withdrew to the first floor and no one has disturbed me since. I choose to live upstairs because I like being above the street."

He led her into a comfortably furnished room, one wall of which was lined with paperbacks and another with book club editions of the classics flashing gold tooling on a material that sought desperately to look like leather. Against another wall was a sideboard with a record player and speakers, and under the window was an old chaise longue that made her think of the word "hurly-burly" and then made her wonder why she had thought of it. For the first time since she left the street she breathed freely, as if she had suddenly come in sight of the sea. However, the smell of the room was more reminiscent of a garden than the sea, suggesting fallen petals and crushed grass. She noticed a pomander on the mantelpiece and she wondered how many more were concealed behind the books. She picked up a biography of Havelock Ellis while he inspected a bottle from the sideboard like a man who had inspected it many times before.

"Do you read a lot?" she asked as he handed her a glass of malmsey.

"I read poetry in the evenings and the *Upanishads* after midnight."

235

"When do you listen to music?"

"Only on Sunday mornings. I play Handel and Corelli when the sun is out and Bach when it rains. I'm fond of music but it's too heady a luxury to indulge in lightly."

"Why do you read the *Upanishads* rather than the Bible?"

"Because Western man has defiled the Bible. He has quoted it too often in support of more iniquitous acts than any forbidden by the Ten Commandments. The *Upanishads* remain pure because they are beyond the perception of the impure. Unlike the Bible, they can never be defiled. To me they are manna I must eat every day. I look forward to them more than I look forward to dinner."

He was sitting at the table with his corduroy hat at his elbow. He half turned and brushed the rim with his fingertips, then moved the hat to the other side of his glass like a grand master moving a knight at chess.

"Do you read poetry?" he asked.

"Very rarely. I'm a scientist."

"What a pity! A conversation about poetry is only less pleasurable than poetry itself. Poetry is a pure white cloud painted on a windowpane. You look at the window and you think you're looking at a sky in summer, but when you open the casement you see that outside all is blackest night. The knack is to enjoy the painted clouds and keep the window tightly shut."

"Bernard Baggotty was fond of poetry."

"Bernard Baggotty was a capitalist. He saw words as debenture stock and commas as—"

"You know he's dead?"

"Why should we speak of him?"

"Did you know his wife?" she probed.

"No," he said, leaving her in no doubt about his determination not to talk about her either. He put his hand under his hat and drew out the red notebook he had shown her once before.

236

"The wisdom of the Vedanta transcribed in my own fair hand. I wish you to have it as a vade-mecum."

"I mustn't. I really must be going."

"But you've only come!"

"Term ended today. I'm tired. I feel like an early night."

"Then it is time to show you the Temple of Daphne."

He opened a door she had not noticed and stood aside to let her pass. As she entered, the walls seemed to crowd round her with a stifled scream, all four of them covered with blown-up photographs of herself, some in color and some in black and white, some showing her legs, some her throat, some her eyes, but most of them her face, serious and introspective, as if preoccupied with the manifold shames of the earth. She stepped back with a shudder as the key turned in the lock behind her.

"Why have you locked the door?"

"So that we won't be disturbed. I wish to tell you things . . . things you've never known before."

"But there is no one else in the house."

"There are vandals. One can never be too careful."

"How did you get all these?"

"I took them with my camera. They are nowhere near as good as they ought to be, but that is not your fault."

She looked up at the ceiling above his bed and saw herself at Fairyhouse on Easter Monday, a wisp of hair blowing across her mouth, her left hand raised in a gesture of expostulation. Then she noticed something among the photos that had until that moment escaped her, a long, thin sword hanging by the hilt from the picture rail above the mantelpiece. She could have sworn that she'd seen it before, had seen it all and had not marveled. She sank weakly onto the bed, realizing that what she remembered was a dream. She saw Mrs. Baggotty with a bread knife through her heart and she put her hands to her mouth and clenched her teeth to stem her sudden nausea.

"No need to worry, Patricia. I may call you Patricia, I hope."

He sat on the bed beside her with his hand on her bottom, and she felt her body go rigid as she calculated her chances of escape. Slowly, she told herself that she must remain cool, wait for him to put a foot wrong, pretend to do his bidding from choice, not coercion.

"I know it must come as a shock," he told her with a convincing show of sympathy.

"I had no idea . . ." she said feebly.

"How could you know? You thought I was Detective Inspector McMyler, keeping an eye on Baggotty, whereas my only wish was to be near to you."

"Why didn't you tell me? If only I'd known . . ."

"It wouldn't have been the same. The excitement of the game, you see, is sweeter than the moment of victory. I loathed Baggotty. I wanted to have you for myself, but because of my nature I had to go the long way round—"

"You have me now." She tried to smile at him.

"Do you like my photographs?"

"They're very professional. I had no idea I looked so soulful," she laughed convincingly.

"They were taken with a telescopic lens in all conditions and weathers, the best on dry days with a freshening breeze. You're at your most spiritual with the wind in your hair and your lips parted, as if you were calling 'Away, come away.' The first time I saw you, I told myself you were a daughter of the gods, divinely tall and most divinely fair."

"When was that?"

"In Grafton Street shopping on a Saturday morning. I followed you into The Inkwell and ordered a pint of stout the same as you. Then I saw you take out a square tobacco tin and roll a cigarette in brown paper, and I wished I were the smoke in your mouth and nose. But I didn't fall in love with you till I discovered that you kept your loose change with your matches, paper, and tobacco in the tin. It seemed so economical, as if all you required from life could be contained in a two-ounce tobacco tin. 'There,' I said, 'is a girl a man could please.' When you rose to go, I sucked the froth from the bottom of your glass and followed you home, got to know where you lived, got to know of your involvement with that Fescennine Flâneur, Bernard Baggotty, Esquare. Really, I could have told you there and then that he was only an attendant lord, one that will do to swell a progress, start a scene or two, in short, not your leg of mutton at all, at all."

"It's a pity you never spoke plainly. You wasted so much time . . ."

"But now we can be friends."

"We *are* friends." She smiled.

"I've always had a weakness for tall women. I have a lovely Picasso print of two women running by the sea, but you're lovelier than any woman Picasso ever drew. The proportion of leg and back is perfection itself. If only you could see yourself with skirts asway—no, skirts aswirl—like a stately ship of Tarsus, bound for th' isles of Javan or Gadire . . ."

"So it was you who made all those literary telephone calls," she laughed.

"I hope you liked them. I spent hours rehearsing before that mirror trying to get the rhythms right."

"They were delivered with unparalleled aplomb. Oh, I'm so tired. I really should be going," she yawned.

"Before you leave, I would like to take a picture of you as La Morphise."

She weighed his gentle smile and wondered if he were stronger than she.

"You haven't heard of La Morphise? Before I met you, she was my ideal of Irish womanhood."

"She doesn't sound Irish to me."

"Her real name was Marie Louise O'Morphi, daughter of a humble Irish cobbler who emigrated to France, but she rose or lay down to become one of Louis XV's most influential mistresses. More satisfying for me, though, she became a model for Boucher, who immortalized her in some of his best paintings."

He took a biography of Boucher from a shelf and showed her a picture of a woman lying naked on her belly on a bed.

"I want to take a photograph of you in that position."

"Whatever for?"

"Because I think it will put the Boucher in the shade."

He pulled his shoulder bag from beneath the bed and drew from it an expensive-looking camera and a string of accessories.

"Is that what you keep in your bag?"

"I always carry my tackle. A creative photographer knows not the minute nor the hour."

"I'm too tired to pose now, but I'll try to look my best for you tomorrow."

He eyed her broodingly, and she told herself that the charge of unleashed violence she sensed in the air might be real. With a laugh that concealed fear, she stretched herself on the bed in the position of La Morphise.

"That's no good. You'll have to take off your clothes."

"But I'm a prissy schoolmistress, not a model."

"Remember, the school year is over. You're now on holiday."

"I'll strip to my underwear. I'll leave on my bra and knickers."

"No, that would be kinky. Boucher rightly painted La Morphise *in puris naturalibus*."

"I'll bet you'll think the less of me if I strip. You'll never look my way again."

"On the contrary, I'll think you a healthy, uncomplicated young woman who isn't encrusted with the legacy of puritanism the Cromwellian soldiery left this side of the Shannon."

"I'm a virgin"—she played her last card—"I've never stripped for a man before."

"I have a sixth sense for virgins. I can sniff them out like a cocker spaniel flushing woodcock. As soon as I clapped eyes on you, I knew you hadn't been polluted, which is why I've named this bedroom the Temple of Daphne. I know all about you, so don't be shy. You'll be stripping for the camera, not for me."

"Will you turn your back while I undress?"

"If you insist, but I shall think you the more conventional for it."

"I don't want to be thought conventional."

She turned her back to him and unbuttoned her coat-dress with all the fingers she could muster. She knew that he was standing by the fireplace studying the droop of her bottom, the straight sword hanging like an inverted note of exclamation above his head. He was quite mad, his reality not terrestrial but interlunar, and she had to pretend that nothing was amiss, that this was the kind of thing that happened to science teachers every day. She lay on the bed and closed her eyes.

"I don't wish to be recognized, so I'll turn my head away."

"In a picture like this the nates, not the face, are the mirror of the soul."

She lay on her belly with her legs apart, one on the bed and the other hanging over the edge, her face buried in the pillow while she counted the flashes up to six. Then without warning he began caressing her back, neck, and shoulders, his hands quick and seeking, running lightly along her spine, up and down like the fingers of a pianist on a keyboard. They paused and pressed hard on her kidneys, found her shoulders again, and after a wicked glissando hammered out the First Mephisto Waltz on her buttocks.

"Have you ever looked searchingly at any of Rubens's women?" His voice was dry as withered sedge, a voice for late October.

"Not as searchingly as you, I'm sure."

"He paints a little dimple at the top of the rear cleft which I find very affecting. I mention it because I'm much taken with yours."

"But Rubens's women are fat."

"You're not fat, I know. You're beautifully muscular. When we get to know each other better, perhaps we could try a fall."

"What a good idea."

"He's a very rumpacious painter, is Peter Paul Rubens." His nimble fingers glanced off the soft flesh inside her thighs in a *con brio* passage of self-conscious virtuosity. Lightly, like a sea breeze, he brushed her pubic hair, and she found herself borne upward like a kite over a cliff, then tugged sideways by a warm eddy of desire. She must have lost consciousness for a moment, because the next thing she was aware of was the weight of his naked body on hers, a hot cathode between her thighs, his basil-breath like a fog in her ear. She tried to rise like a camel beneath him.

"No, don't move. I'm not going to take your virginity. All I wish for is sexual ease, not convulsion, a gentle expiration on the brink of the fiery fosse. Other men may kill the thing they love but I shall nourish it with my last breath."

The strength had left her legs. He was pressing into her flesh like a die that would emboss every inch of her, but her flesh lost its form, then it flowed like thin liquid, which she longed for him to cleave unflinchingly as the breakwater of a bridge cleaves a river in spate.

"Your virginity is your most precious possession," he whispered, "and the man who takes it is a thief, though he may write a Ph.D. thesis to prove otherwise. Do not think of it as a wasting asset or an obstructive membrane. It is a spiritual condition which can be compared only to the morning of a June day before the rain clouds forgather from the sea. It is all too typical of decadent societies to seek to recover it after it's been irrecoverably lost. Virgin restoration was commonplace in Victorian London. It's still commonplace in Japan. But how, I ask, can you restore a spiritual condition by stitching into place a square of sheep gut? Never forget that your inner temple is a place of worship that no man must enter, that no man is worthy to enter. The man who enters must pay the full price of his knowledge. He must pay with his life."

As he spoke, the cathode slid along the lips of her vagina with a gentle stroking motion. She wanted him to take her. She raised her bottom against him, but the liquid warmth between her buttocks told her that he had meant what he said, that easeful expiration without the hassle of penetration was indeed what he desired.

"That was good," he whispered soothingly, his weight now the greater for being dead.

"You once told me that the Vedanta made a distinction between the pleasing and the good. Was it really good or was it just pleasing?"

"It was both. With a woman like you, the Vedic distinction is quite irrelevant."

"I didn't feel a thing." She tried to keep the conversation going in the hope that he might let her go.

"Very satisfactory." He handed her a paper handkerchief from under the pillow.

"Where are my knickers?"

"I've put them in my bag with the camera for safe keeping. Please don't misunderstand me. I don't propose to use them to wipe the lens. I shall keep them as a souvenir of our first evening together."

"Luckily, I always carry a spare pair in my bag."

Still on fire, she dressed slowly, aware that she must not appear to hurry.

"I dreamt about you last night." He stepped into his trousers. "We were both camping in a hickory wood in Minnesota and you collected sticks and made a fire to cook our evening meal. That night we slept together under a tree and I kept waking up all the time because of the smell of hickory smoke from your knickers. I decided that it would be ungracious to tell you, but I laughed to myself when you gave me hickory-smoked ham for breakfast."

"When will you expect me tomorrow evening?" she asked.

"At eight. No, come at seven. We'll have an extra glass of malmsey and longer prelims."

He unlocked the door for her and accompanied her down the stairs. In the hallway he took her right hand and planted a kiss in the center of the palm. Then she was in the dark street, walking slowly but deliberately because she knew that he was still watching her. When she turned the corner, she began running, uncertain of the way in her haste but hoping that she was going in the direction of Ballsbridge.

It was almost seven o'clock when she got home. The hallway was in darkness because the bulb had fused last week. She groped for the stair banisters, and as she ascended she saw a chink of light beneath the door of Bernard's flat. On the landing she heard talk and laughter, and in the background the sound of lute music. Who can it be? she asked herself. Mr. Mullally was still in hospital and no one else had a key. She knocked and waited for the door to open.

"Patricia, come in. Come in and join the party," said Tom-Tom O'Malley with a drunken slurring of both vowels and consonants.

"How did you get in here?"

"We were invited round for drinks by mine English host."

"When did he invite you?"

"A few weeks ago," said De Barra. "He wrote to us c/o The Inkwell and sent us the key of the flat with the letter."

"I don't believe you," she shuddered.

"Here's the letter," said Tom-Tom. "See for yourself."

She unfolded the crumpled sheet and recognized Bernard's eccentric hand:

Dear Rosencrantz and Guildenstern,
I was reading The Oxford Book of Contemporary Verse *the other day and found to my horror that it contained more prose than poetry. It made your bad doggerel look like a mere peccadillo. So, come back, come back. All is forgiven. In an hour or so I'm off on a long journey to one of the few sovereign states without immigration controls. I plan to come back to discomfit my enemies, but lest I should be detained I am leaving a 35.2 fl. oz. bottle of whiskey for you in a plastic bucket under the sink. I know how disappointed you will be at my departure, but I hope it will not deter you in your ambition to become Ireland's first ostrich farmers. You have my unstinted admiration. Every poet, I think, should own an ostrich and those who aspire to be poets should eat nothing but ostrich legs. The ostrich, incidentally, is a much-maligned bird, more maligned than the rhea or the moa (R.I.P.). It has a stride as long as Finn McCool's and a running speed in excess of Caoilte's. But have a care. Never stand behind it because its fart is more lethal than its kick, especially after a meal of goosefoot, which it believes to be fit only for swine. And as we all know, there are a lot of them about. I enclose the key of my flat and street door, so have the good grace to drink to me, not with Celtic abandon, but with Anglo-Saxon restraint. In other words, leave a hair of the dog in the bottle for the morning.*

> *Your sport is now ended.*
> *In haste,*
> *Hamlet*

The first thing she thought of was that he had invited them round to poison them.

"Have you eaten anything from the fridge?" she asked.

"The fridge is bare," said De Barra.

"Was it a full bottle of whiskey?" she asked.

"A full liter bottle," said Tom-Tom.

"With the seal unbroken?"

"Yes."

"Where is it now?"

"Drunk. There's only a thimbleful left, ochone."

She picked up the bottle and sniffed it, but all it smelled of was whiskey.

"Only a gentleman, a scholar, and a poet could have thought of it," said Tom-Tom.

"He's dead," she said. "He hanged himself soon after he wrote to you."

"Ah, go 'way," said De Barra.

"He invited us to wake him, then," said Tom-Tom.

"A gentleman, a scholar, and a poet," said De Barra.

"But above all a gentleman," Tom-Tom emphasized.

"Good night," she said, but they were both too drunk to hear.

When she entered her flat, she looked round uneasily, but everything was as she had left it. She lay on the *grand lit* and closed her eyes, conscious only of a dry, featureless plain. After ten minutes she got up and made sure the door was locked. She did not feel safe. She felt that she had been invaded by an alien life that threatened her not so much physically as psychologically, threatened to expel her from the center of her personality and make her live on the periphery of the dark.

She made herself a cup of strong coffee and drank it quickly because of a sudden she felt the need for haste. She wrote a check for Mr. Mullally and put it in an envelope with her keys. She wrote a note to Detective Inspector Farrelly, giving him McMyler's address and telling him about the photos. When at last she ventured from the room, the landing was in darkness, the poets already gone. She walked to the end of the road and put both envelopes unstamped in the nearest pillar box. Finally, she packed her suitcase, filled a pillowslip with odds and ends and stowed them with her other belongings in the boot of the car.

It was one o'clock when she left, and she drove south past Bray, past Wicklow, keeping an eye on the mirror to see if she were being followed, trying to put from her mind the horror of the evening. She would not be giving evidence against him. She was going to Rosslare, whence she would take the morning ferry to Fishguard. After that she would drive to London and, she hoped, life-enabling anonymity. She had been polluted and defiled, smeared with the frass of other lives, and nothing but a fresh start would cleanse her. She was leaving with ten thousand pounds and no ties, and no one knew where she was going. That was important. She could have caught a ferry from Dublin or Dun Laoghaire, but it would have been risky. She was less likely to stumble against someone she knew in Rosslare.

"Taking me for a ride, Miss Teeling?" The voice flared in the dark like a match singeing hairs on her neck. McMyler was sitting behind her. The car swerved and lost speed.

"No, don't stop. You drive beautifully—almost like a man. I've never had such a ride. Deceptively smooth or smoothly deceptive, I cannot say."

Cold metal pricked her between the shoulder blades. She tried to think of a pretext for driving south in the small hours of the morning. She tried to say something but her mind was blank.

"Where are you taking me?"

"How did you get here?" Her question made her heave with fear.

"You didn't expect a stowaway. Have I upset your plans?"

"No."

"Where are we heading for?"

"Rosslare. I'm going to meet a friend off the boat."

"Is that why you've brought a suitcase?"

"It's not my own."

"You drank my malmsey and promised to come back for more."

"So I shall."

247

"You mock me, Miss Teeling, and so did Gladys Baggotty."

"I've never mocked you."

"Like her, you trifled with my proclivities."

"How did she trifle with them?" She tried to deflect the conversation from herself.

"If you must know, she put the crotch of Mr. Baggotty's underpants in an omelette and laughed as I cut it open."

"A practical joke."

"Her last, Miss Teeling. Now slow down and take the first turning on the left."

It was a narrow lane running like Uncle Lar's between two high hedges. Hopefully, she looked in the mirror but the road behind was bare. She drove slowly over loose gravel, and as they approached a large tree that looked like a sycamore he told her to stop. She eased forward to draw level with a gate but he cursed her for a stupid woman and made her reverse.

"You're very particular," she told him.

"I'm a perfectionist in a world of bodgers."

"You've lost your sense of humor. When you take yourself seriously, you're like any other man." She tried to keep him talking.

"You once said I was witty. But wit is only gleaming spindrift in the wind. What matters is the sea below, heaving like the belly of a slut in labor. There's a sea inside me, enough to float an armada, but now it's heavy without spindrift, without even the whitening curl of a wave. And who's to blame? Who was the wind that whipped me, that blew my spindrift in a shower against the sun?"

"I'll blow it again."

"You'll trick me again!"

"I've never tried to trick you."

The conversation was compulsively serious, untypical of the McMyler she had known. Unavailingly, she raided her imagination for an image that would make him laugh.

"Have you prayed tonight, Miss Teeling?"

248

"I told you once before I'm not religious."

"If you bethink yourself of any crime unreconciled as yet to heaven and grace, solicit for it straight."

"You're out of your mind." She couldn't restrain herself.

"Because I frequent the classics?"

"No."

"Because I summarize the *Upanishads*? You laughed at them, didn't you?"

"I didn't laugh. On the contrary, I respect them as the flowering of a culture I have yet to know."

"Brahman is not mocked."

"I'm not mocking, only praising."

"You refused to read them."

"I lack the religious sense."

"If you loved me, you'd have read them."

"I didn't love you but I wished for you."

"How?"

"I wished for you to touch my knee."

"And I did."

"Then I wished for more."

"Whore. All women, even the wise virgins, are whores."

His hand shook in agitation. She felt the edge of tempered steel through her dress.

"Women are made and unmade by men." She tried to placate his misogyny.

"You made light of the *Upanishads*." He spoke as if he had not heard. "And you didn't listen when I defined for you the concept of Pure Consciousness."

"I listened as best I could."

"*Where there is consciousness of the Self, individuality is no more*. Annotate that, Miss Teeling. And remember, apt quotation will enhance the value of your answer."

"I'm a simple scientist, educated to first-degree standard only." She tried to flatter him with humility. "I have no aptitude for philosophy."

"In that event, give me one good reason why you should live." He did not try to conceal his contempt.

249

"I'm not even twenty-one."

"No, don't look round."

"I've spent the best part of my life among books. I haven't yet begun to live."

"Yet you've lived long enough to make all the wrong choices. Life is but the making of choices, and the best of life is but the making of the best choices. You have not made the best of life, Miss Teeling."

Her knees trembled but she told herself to be calm. It was not the end. She had escaped from his house, and now she would escape from the car. Somehow or other she must get out into the fields and the dark. She would keep him in conversation, then in midsentence she would open the door and tumble head first into the lane. The Mini had only two doors. He'd have to climb through to the front. It would give her the necessary start.

"I know you don't trust me, so I'll make a bargain with you," she said. "I'm willing to be your prisoner till you get to know me. You can take me back and lock me up in the Temple of Daphne and have me to yourself for as long as you like."

"You treat me like a child, Miss Teeling, but I have long ago put away childish things. That is something no woman has been intelligent enough to see. They take me for a schoolboy, good for a laugh and jape, but for seven blissful months I thought you knew better. All I beg for is one woman to save the women of Dublin. Just one to atone for the scores who have sinned against me."

Suddenly she dived but McMyler lunged. Her high, short cry woke four rooks in the dark sycamore. Quietly, they changed position on the branch as if to ease their weary feet, then resumed their corvine slumber over the flow of viscous silence in the lane.

The man who called himself McMyler drove north to Dublin in the red Mini alone. It was a lovely morning, dry and austere, with a wasting moon in the south and a ragged finger of black cloud in the north. At first he drove slowly but when the sun came up on the right he immediately accelerated. It was an orange sun, enlarged by a summer haze, and it seemed to run behind the trees, keeping pace with the car as if it would not be shaken off.

Two days later he was arrested by Detective Inspector Farrelly in Ringsend and charged with the murder of Gladys Baggotty. Within a week of his arrest, the mutilated body of Patricia Teeling was discovered by a farmer under a heap of brushwood in a field not far from Arklow. Farrelly traveled south, poked at the brushwood, and slowly walked the length of the lane. Then he traveled north to Ringsend and lay on McMyler's bed looking up at the ceiling as if he were in the Sistine Chapel. He was a wise and thoughtful man who listened more readily than he spoke, but that evening he confided to his wife that he was worried about the psychiatrists' report and McMyler's refusal to utter anything "except well-phrased inanities." An acquittal on the ground of diminished responsibility would, he told her, be a thoroughly unsatisfactory conclusion.